OUT
OF THE
WILD

OUT
OF THE
WILD

Mike Tomkies

JONATHAN CAPE
THIRTY-TWO BEDFORD SQUARE LONDON

First published 1985
Text and photographs copyright © Mike Tomkies 1985
Jonathan Cape Ltd, 32 Bedford Square, London WC1B 3EL

British Library Cataloguing in Publication Data
Tomkies, Mike
Out of the wild.
1. Animals – Biography
I. Title
591.9411   QL791
ISBN 0-224-02317-9

Typeset by Computape (Pickering) Ltd, N. Yorkshire
Printed in Great Britain by
Ebenezer Baylis & Son Limited
The Trinity Press, Worcester, and London

Contents

In memory of Geoffrey Kinns

PART ONE

1 · Close Encounters with the Wild

I stared into the fierce face of the wild animal I had allowed to take over my bedroom, my feelings of excitement tinged by more than a little fear. The pine marten, one of our rarest mammals and certainly our rarest carnivore, made little high-pitched whirring growls and every so often paused to launch short bluff attacks towards where I sat quietly in a chair ten feet away. He was just trying to show me how tough he was, and that I had better not attempt anything so foolish as to pick him up. A few hours later, after feeding him all he could eat, I let him go again. Now, four years later, having established his hunting territory round my home, the marten has become almost as tame as a little dog, and I regularly feed him bread and raspberry jam. Very gently, his dark eyes fixed upon mine, he will even remove a morsel from my hand with front teeth that are capable of inflicting serious injury. The delicacy he shows in this reminds me of the time I carried an injured badger into the cottage in order to treat its wounds. In an instant its head whirled round and the powerful jaws took a strong and painful hold of my gloved fingers. The bite was only a quarter as hard as it could have been, however. It was as if the badger was informing me in clear mustelid language that if I actually hurt it I would lose part of my hand.

When you look after wild animals that need your help, you can expect such moments as these; moments of drama, humour, sublime pleasure, of exultation even, when the tenuous bond between man and animal is strangely enhanced.

For the past twelve of my nineteen years in wild and remote places, I have lived at Wildernesse, an old stone cottage set between two small woods below a deep cleft in the mountains of the north-west Highlands of Scotland. There is no road, electricity, gas, telephone, TV or postal delivery. My nearest neighbour lives over six miles away, and the only access is by boat up a long and often stormy loch.

In one sense it is a lonely place of course. Isolation from daily contact with other people has sometimes turned loneliness to moments of despair, especially when I have been tired after trekking many miles of empty mountains on foot, or have had to struggle with publishers at long distance over my wildlife books, from which I make a fairly meagre living. How often, though, have such flagging spirits been quickly lifted by the antics and, yes, the friendship of wild creatures that have needed my care in one way or another. There were, for instance, four unforgettable little foxes, including a vixen, who made a spectacularly successful return to the wild. I particularly remember the owls which lived in the kitchen − trusting Wallie with his smashed-in face, Holly with her broken wing held out like a barn door, how they met in the wild and came calling at the kitchen window for the beautiful young Crowdy. I recall feeding the hungry male buzzard in winter and the days of watching his parents at their nest. Then there was the badger with her awful neck injuries, which also lived in the kitchen, so placid and self-contained, before returning to her wild domain and finding a mate.

All these creatures possessed individual personalities, each quite different from the others. All of them − including the pine marten − belonged to species which have been persecuted by humans, and in various ways all had come out of the wild and under my care.

When giving such care it is essential to comprehend the creature's instincts, to behave in a way that will allay its fears and suspicions, cater to its dominant senses, and always to forgive its apparent lack of understanding. For wild animals are not underlings or inferior species. All too often we look at them through

10

the arrogant screen of our own complicated and artificial lives, and so we see them falsely. We patronise them for their so-called lower existence, their ignorance, their unreasoning 'savagery', their inconvenient interference with humanity's headlong rush to gain its own comfort and pleasure at whatever cost to nature. Nothing could be more of a barrier to the sort of trust I was shown by creatures of the wild than attitudes such as these.

For thousands of years human beings have struggled against the wilds, to make life better only for themselves, regardless of which plants and animals survived and which would be wiped out. Meanwhile the human population has grown to 4·76 billion and is still increasing in the areas least capable of supporting it. Over half humanity is either starving or seriously under-nourished, while we in the West go on producing from our semi-wrecked landscape excess crops and foodstuffs which our marketing procedures make it difficult for us to get to those who starve. Our last wild places, forests, lakes, rivers, natural habitats and eco-systems are in need not just of conservation but of enhancement, for in them lie infallible recycling plants that neutralise our wastes, filter our water, regulate climate, produce oxygen and provide spiritual inspiration.

The human race is not the sole arbiter of life on earth. If our neglect continues, be sure that nature will exert an immense power to redress the balance. Mammals, birds, fish and insects exist in a far older and more perfect world than any we have been able to create for ourselves. These creatures live by instincts and senses we are fast losing or have never developed. They recognise natural rhythms to which we are no longer attuned, voices we cannot hear. They fulfil their roles as intended while we devote massive energy to attempts at escape. For all our learning, inventive brilliance and individual genius, humanity on the whole has shown far less real survival instinct than a herd of red deer.

Most of the creatures in this book have passed out of my life now, or at least from daily or regular contact. Some have remained so trusting that I can still approach them closely in the wild. None of them can I claim as my own. Certainly, in return for that trust, I loved them, and found it painful when the time came to set them free. It has been a hard and valuable lesson to learn – that love often consists of knowing when to let go. Yet there is nothing so rewarding as to remain in communication with creatures incapable of human tongue or emotions long after parting with them.

To relieve the pangs that isolation and parting inevitably bring, there is nothing so effective as to sling a pack on my back and trek high up into the hills to observe again the rare species that still abound in the Scottish Highlands, one of the last great wilderness areas left in Western Europe.

One June day, as I was trying to get down to some writing at my desk, the sun beamed so strongly through my study window that I could not concentrate and had to give up. I packed my camera gear, a few sandwiches, a bottle of fruit juice, boated down the loch and then hiked up a steep mountain to a hide which I had set up overlooking a golden eagle eyrie. The hide was so erected that I could get into its rear flap out of sight of the eyrie. After sliding in cautiously and setting up the camera, I saw the mother eagle on the nest, still completely unaware of my presence.

The period that followed was the most enthralling I had ever spent watching eagles. During the twenty-one hours I stayed there, she left the side of her downy-white chick for only half an hour. At one time the male flew in and began tramping about impatiently, as if wanting her to go away for a flight with him in the bright breezy summer air. Not until he had flown off four times to return with leafy sprays, which the two worked round the eaglet to screen it from the wind, did she consent to his wishes and go with him.

Shortly after dawn I slipped quietly out of the hide, first crept and then tramped down the hill in a wide arc so that I would not be seen at any time from the nest, and boated home to snatch a brief hour or two of sleep before going to check a buzzards' nest in an oak wood some miles away, near which I also had a hide.

As the boat neared my home bay, a large bear-like head appeared, framed between the logs of my garden archway. Moobli, the gentle giant of an Alsatian, who for eight years had helped me track and find wildlife, had come down from his bed in the woodshed to welcome me home, whining with relief that I was not to stay away another night. I fussed and petted him, gave him some food, then crashed into bed for a brief but deep sleep, for it had been impossible to snatch any in the cold uncomfortable eagle hide.

After waking, I gulped down some breakfast, and set off again in the boat for the buzzards' nest. This time I took Moobli. He would not be able to trek up to the hide with me but just to ride in the boat again, to be in my truck when I got back, made him happy.

Later, as we drove along beside a winding silvery sea loch, I kept the camera by my side and also a sharp look-out for the odd otter that might be swimming among the shoreside kelp. Suddenly I saw what looked like large black conical-shaped bottles floating in a peaceful lagoon. The only trouble was these 'bottles' appeared to have whiskers!

A quick look through the binoculars told me they were the heads of common seals, which are no longer 'common' in fact, and that there were three pairs in the sea there. Each pair stayed close together. They appeared to be mating.

I pulled into a lay-by behind some trees and was just creeping back with the camera, when I heard a brief swish of wings above. A cuckoo had landed in an ash tree over my head. Click – for my closest shot of a cuckoo, always a hard bird to photograph. I scrambled cautiously down through the trees to the beach and lifted the camera.

One pair of seals was close to shore, gambolling and rolling round each other, surfacing now and again, and clutching each other blissfully with their short front flippers. Sometimes they rose two feet out of the water, biting each other's noses, nibbling each other's eyes lovingly, as I clicked away. They revolved and turned, huffing with pleasure. As their rear flippers entwined together they looked like two pairs of large gloved hands, twirling with extremely sinuous and delicate movements. How wonderful it must be to make love in this way, borne up by warm cherishing seas, in a quiet watery paradise. I looked away to see the other two pairs were courting and mating in exactly the same way. The nearest pair saw me then, but in their ecstasy seemed undisturbed by my presence.

The wind had almost died down as I drove on to the

beautiful oak wood where forestry keeper Peter Madden and I
had built a large moss-covered hide overlooking the buzzards'
nest. Within minutes I was hiking up another steep mountain,
but only to about 500 feet. Again the rough terrain was such that
I could slide into the hide without being seen, after the usual
precaution of making sure neither of the adult birds was flying
nearby at the time. There were two chicks in the nest.

Buzzards are really just small eagles which hunt the lower hills
and open glades in woodlands. In some ways they can be more
rewarding to watch at the nest than eagles for they come in
far more frequently than does the mighty king of birds.

I did not have long to wait. Soon the mother buzzard soared
easily through the trees and landed on the nest of big twigs
which lay in a fork of the thick oak. She had no food in her
talons. As she looked round the nest, tramping about slowly,
her face seemed to show disappointment that her mate had not
left any prey either.

About half an hour later I heard distant '*kee*' calls which came
closer and closer. The smaller male landed on the far edge of the
nest with a frog in his talons. As he stood there with it, the
mother buzzard did not move but just glared at him. He seemed
to wilt slightly before the fierce look in her dark brown eyes,
then he quickly turned and flew away, leaving the dead frog on
the nest twigs.

The mother looked down fondly at the two downy-grey
chicks, which were clamouring to be fed. Their faint '*phee-oo*'
cheeps could hardly be heard from the hide. Then she walked
carefully round the edge of the nest on her long yellow legs,
clamped her talons on to the frog and with strong upward heaves
of her beak ripped snippets of flesh, tendering them gently to the
stronger nearest chick. Oddly, she made no effort to feed the
other chick, which did not seem to be able to get round its nest
mate.

More rewarding hours followed, during which the female
flew off to meet the loudly calling male and came back with a
woodmouse he had caught and clearly given to her. This time
the smaller chick did get a few morsels as she happened to land
on its side of the nest, before the bigger one pushed it out of
the way.

Tired after the hard night in the eagle hide and the brief snatched sleep, I felt myself beginning to doze. After taking nearly a whole roll of film, I backed out of the hide and hiked back down to the truck and Moobli.

As we later pulled up above the anchored boat, Moobli lifted his great head and gave a little whine, his huge black muzzle scenting something strongly beyond the open window. I climbed out carefully, and heard two loud '*boff! boff!*' barks. There, only forty yards away and lit by the sinking sun on a grassy ridge in a superb green dell, a perfect sylvan setting for him, stood a jaunty little roebuck in his bright auburn summer coat. He was giving vent to his displeasure and alarm.

I looked away, slowly took the camera from its pack and I was darned if he didn't just wait there while I clicked off four good photos. Then he bounded away like a giant hare, his dog-like barks growing fainter and fainter as he vanished upwards between the trees.

Later, as we boated home, the dying orb of the sun danced a dazzling radiant path across the sparkling waters and, despite my tiredness, I knew that in the last few hours I had reaped fine fruits for my small labours.

As we landed Moobli leaped out gleefully with a loud splosh, looking forward to his evening meal. I hauled the boat out of the water on to its wooden runway. Then with camera pack and bags of supplies, I set off in Moobli's wake up the path near our little west wood. Suddenly, high on the hill beyond the conifer trees, I heard two sharp barks '*raowl raowl*', not as deep and far more musical than the barks of the roebuck. I knew the sound well by now, dropped my load and dashed through the trees, hoping to get a glimpse that would confirm my belief.

I came out on to a rocky ridge and looked through the binoculars. Yes, there she was – Aspen, the first young fox I had kept at Wildernesse and who now, surprisingly, was using the same area as the big wild dog fox which held the immediate territory. The last light of the sun lit up her dark fur, as auburn, lustrous and distinctive as ever, her white tail tip flashing as she slipped furtively through the long grasses and clumps of bracken.

Once she stopped again, looked down at us and gave another

muffled '*raowl*' bark, an alarm call, the sort a vixen will make to warn her mate or cubs of danger. It was muted now, as if she had recognised us and was just letting us know we had been spotted.

Inside the cottage, as I cooked food for myself and Moobli in euphoric mood, I recalled all our days of trying to study wild foxes, and our adventurous times with Aspen and with all the other little foxes I had looked after through the years.

2 · Tracking Foxes

During my first four years in the Highlands, I saw only two foxes in daylight, though occasionally I glimpsed them in my headlights at night. The first came within yards of my remote croft on the sea island of Shona. I was lying down to rest after some hard work building with logs when I was woken by frantic bleating cries. I got up and saw a large browny-red fox, which seemed to be playing with a small lamb. While the lamb bleated helplessly, the fox shot beneath it, forced it up and off its legs, jumped over its head and pushed it down with black-tipped paws – enjoying itself like a cat with a big white mouse. Whether it would have killed the lamb I do not know, for I moved quickly and the fox raced away. The second appeared when I was trying to locate a fox for the local shepherd, who claimed that a marauder was wantonly killing his lambs, not even taking the tails or ears for the cubs to play with, as foxes usually do. I had just rounded a small knoll when I heard a spitting snarl, rather like a cough, saw a flurry of reddish-brown, then the blackened hairs at the tip of a thick brush, as a big fox shot back into a fissure in a huge rock pile. It turned out to be one of the fox's many daylight resting places rather than a regular den.

A great deal is said and written about the intelligence of foxes and their immense cunning. From the beginning I had wanted to get on close terms with foxes in the Scottish wilds, to study their

17

hunting and feeding habits and their territorial behaviour. Over the years I was to experience examples of undoubted cunning, especially when a fox was extricating itself from a tight corner. Yet I was also to find that some foxes can be unaccountably stupid, sometimes exposing themselves to dangerous situations when there was little chance of tasty reward.

On August 4 in my first year at Wildernesse, when Moobli was but a pup of nine months, I took him for a trek to the far end of the long woods which clothed the steep slopes above the loch three miles from home. We were heading back through silver-trunked birch groves above the precipitous rockfaces and the lower woods of small oaks and hazels, when we came upon what was clearly a fox family's playground.

In a soft grassy plateau between the bracken and rocks lay the old skeleton of a hind red deer. Whitened bones lay scattered everywhere, and between them were the scuff marks and prints of a big fox. The front two pads of the four toes (bigger than a dog's) and sometimes the two front claws were showing in the dust, together with many more smaller prints which had been made by cubs. Some smaller bones had been bitten in half, while bigger ones lay so far apart it seemed they had been used as playthings, the cubs carrying them about and dropping them again at random. A huge rock with an overhang protected the east, a fallen birch sheltered the north, while another to the south-west shielded the area from the prevailing winds. A good spot for a fox playground, and it must have seemed like a last refuge to the weak hind who had died in it and whose flesh must have given the foxes much-needed food the previous winter. I approached the place upwind on two occasions after that but never caught the foxes there, nor could we locate a regular den.

On September 1 we set off to climb the highest mountain on the far side of the loch, a short dash of under 3,000 feet to its peak. Although we were briefly enveloped in mist on the summit, we were rewarded not only by the sight of a small flock of ptarmigan, whirring away on snow-white wings and snorting like little pigs at our intrusion into their alpine world, but by finding a fresh fox scat on a grass tuft at 2,300 feet. A little further on I found a freshly dug fox earth in an unusual sandy bank, complete with fresh tracks. It was interesting that a fox would live and hunt at such a height, far above the few boating tourists or fishermen who might picnic or camp on the shores or lower slopes.

At that time I was rearing two wildcat kittens, Cleo and Patra, which a friend had found hissing and spitting in a deep ditch. At three months old, they were running free and using our old woodshed as headquarters. When we arrived back, I hastened to see whether my little spitfires were safe. Only Patra was in the shed, high up on the firewood logs and looking really scared. Of Cleo there was no sign.

Suddenly Moobli gave a low muted growl and charged off to the north end of the west wood. Every few bounds he leaped high, all four feet clear of the ground like a massive springbok, so he could see over the bracken. My nose caught the pungent sweet ammoniac scent of fox. I had heard stories of urban foxes killing cats but, knowing the repulsing powers of a cat in trouble, hardly believed them, except it be a big mature fox against a small or young cat. Moobli was making loud baying sounds deeper than any bloodhound's. I had never heard him do this before. While I did not want him scaring away *any* wild creature, I was glad he had on this occasion, for it seemed clear a fox had come close, probably investigating the scent of the young wildcats, and that we had arrived home just in time.

We finally found Cleo crouching under a big tree stump and successfully rounded her back to the shed, where I blocked their entrance hole for the night. I felt sure after that experience the fox would not come back for a long time, at least until the wildcats were big enough to protect themselves.

No further fox traces appeared until late September when we were trekking the lochside woods a mile east of our home. There we located two old hind carcasses, sixty yards apart. Whereas the first was short of bones, the second had too many. There were thirteen large leg bones, including four thigh bones, and again the ground around had all been stamped down into bare mud, with a few fox tracks showing. Here seemed proof that foxes play around with bones, and that they had carried many from the first skeleton to the second, before using its site as a playground.

Near the end of the year we made a trek in small snow blizzards and hail showers to a peak overlooking the great glen below Guardian mountain. So powerful were the gales up on the tops I felt as if I were about to take flight myself. Once we had to shelter behind a rocky overhang from the blitz of the hail. We saw only two ravens and four hind herds in the distance, but at 1,500 feet Moobli nosed out a huge fresh fox dropping, almost big enough for a large dog. So even in such harsh weather a fox would still hunt at this height.

By now I had acquired from London Zoo a large and ferocious wildcat I called Sylvesturr, which I hoped eventually to breed with one of the females. In January he escaped from his enclosure and was free for eight days in cold rainy weather. I had a deuce of a job live-trapping him back. When I did he was suffering from pneumonia and I had to nurse him in a heated room in the cottage. The only good thing about this sad episode was that his scent and presence in our woods would almost certainly keep any big marauding fox away from the youngsters, giving them time to grow bigger.

It was clear, however, that foxes *had* been keeping watch on the area. The very day after Sylvesturr's return I found in the west wood the carcasses of a freshly dead hind and her calf which had been opened up. The entire stomach of the hind had been rolled away, along with some entrails, as if the fox or foxes had wanted to ensure their contents did not taint the meat. This meal must have sufficed for a few days, for although all the wildcats were penned in new enclosures on February 5, no more fox traces appeared. Then, six days later, I found a dead deer calf between the walls of an old ruin in the open bay east of the wood across the burn. Moobli was better at tracking now and he scented several fox trails and scats left on high heather tufts near but not in the ruin. Maybe its walls made the foxes fear a trap.

It was on February 23 that I saw the first Wildernesse fox in daylight. We were returning from a foot-blistering twelve-mile trek along the shore to the west, endlessly plodding up and down through the bogs, deep tussocks, over cliffs and rocky shore, trying to keep to brief deer paths as twiggy scrub willow and bog myrtle bushes scratched at our legs. We had seen little but a few singing wrens and a buzzard turning on two mobbing hooded crows. Suddenly Moobli got a strong scent and began to hurry ahead. I hissed him back, hoping to see what he was now after.

To my surprise, a huge browny-red fox swerved up from the shore, where it had been taking a drink, and with its long dark brush following like a wedge-shaped banner, dashed into the bracken caves beside a fallen birch.

Camera now ready, we reached the tree, but not a second glimpse did we get. The fox had sidled along the far side of the trunk, out of sight, and up the deep gorge of a burn, de-scenting its feet in many rocky pools so Moobli could not track it. It was interesting that it had been on the shore directly below the first fox playground we had found – further proof of a family in that area. On the trek we had found two more dead hinds and a couple of old sheep carcasses, all flesh long since gone. As always in the harshest season, grazing herbage at its worst, the weak, sick and older animals died yet had helped to keep alive scavengers like crows, ravens, buzzards, foxes and even eagles. Some fox scats were filled with the blue-black wing-cases of beetles plus a good deal of sheep wool, showing that even when foxes cannot eat ewe *flesh*, wool still got into their droppings, from rooting under the old carcasses for grubs and beetles.

By early March it was clear foxes were paying our woods regular calls. One dropping had two tiny vole claws in it. At first, as Moobli scented out urination points, I believed the theory that the foxes were marking the outposts of their territory. It soon became clear they scent-marked mossy rocks and tufts well inside their boundaries too, leaving 'fox newspapers' to inform others of their status, size, sex and doubtless their mating inclinations too. Amid snowstorms on March 10 we trekked to the peak of Guardian mountain, nearly 2,200 feet high, and again found new fox scats at over 1,500 feet. Many along the edge of the burn gorge above the cottage seemed to indicate the burn as the eastern boundary of the first fox family.

Tracking the west wood next day, we found that a deer calf which had died five days earlier had been well chewed from the anus round the rear haunches and on the upper foreleg. The tongue had also gone, clearly a fox delicacy. Then we found a robin's feathers on a moss-covered rock. Possibly the fox had caught it on a low roosting perch and had carried it to the rock as a dining place. Later remains, also on mossy rocks, showed that foxes like such high spots, at least four inches above the ground, not only for scent posts but for eating. While dining at a slight height above the ground, they could keep a constant lookout for signs of danger.

Three days of blinding snow blizzards ended on April 9, and the clouds rolled away. The sun blazed down with its first real heat of the year as we enjoyed our best day of snow-tracking so far. We followed the deep slots of a small herd of hinds and calves until, rounding a rocky buttress, we came upon them wrinkling their velvety noses at us half a mile above the west wood. While returning home, Moobli got a strong scent on the loch shore. He padded along like a wolf, giving an odd '*huff*' grunt now and again, a sign he was on a fox trail. It was then I first discovered that a fox will avoid snow if it can. The trail followed the shore, crossed the burn and then went all along the pebbly beach of the large east bay where the snow had not settled due to the relative warmth of the lapping water. The fox had probably been scenting for carrion on the north wind. Once it had mounted a mossy rock to lay a fresh wet scat on its top. The dropping appeared to be all mud until I examined it through a magnifying glass and discovered that it was full of the tiny chetae of earthworms. The fox had been subsisting on a diet of worms whose flesh had been digested, leaving the mud in the worms' digestive tracts to pass out in the dropping.

Only once, where the snow had reached all the way to a treeless portion of the burn's eastern bank, did we find fox prints in the snow itself. They were heading upwards and in a dead straight line, not staggered like those of a small dog or other mammals, as if the fox had walked on stilts, or had only two legs. I wondered how the fox kept its balance. Once across this short area of unavoidable snow, the scent headed towards the burn itself, then petered out. I was sure the fox had paddled on upstream, before emerging with de-scented feet, but though we tracked the banks a further 200 yards, Moobli could not pick up the trail again. The deer-calf carcass between the suspicious walls of the old ruin was still untouched.

In other snow blizzards over the years, I have sometimes removed the haunches of newly dead deer for Moobli and the wildcats to eat. While tracks showed that foxes later inspected the bloody carcasses, even scraping at one or the other of the extended forefeet of the deer, they never actually ate the carrion until at least four days had elapsed. This also applied to deer I had not touched. So strong is the fox's suspicious cunning that, even when hungry, it prefers to make sure all is safe first, or that there is no trap.

High above us, in a clump of birches below a sheer rockface, two hooded crows watched a few hinds and calves wending upwards, dragging tired feet through the snow. One of the calves looked puny and sick, hardly able to walk. Perhaps the fox was up there watching it too from some safe cranny in the rocks. In harsh times animals have no choice, and must batten on to weakness when they can.

On April 21, long after the snow had gone, we had another fine tracking day, even locating a poor barn owl, rare for the area, that had been killed by a wildcat. Coming back through the eastern woods, I found the remains of one of the hoodies under an ash tree near an open marshy area. Its wing feathers had all been neatly clipped off as if cut by a knife – not the work of a wildcat, which rips and rakes them out. I envisaged the probable scene.

The crow had been enjoying an early dawn breakfast, crouching among the little tents made by the grasses and broken bracken stalks. It had heard a slight noise as the fox stalked it, or maybe the fox had given a little bark, which had made it crouch down. The fox had scented the pocket of air thus dispelled from beneath the bird, knew exactly where it was before actually seeing it, and had pounced. Certainly Moobli was getting fox scent, cocking his leg on tufts, which he now only did for fox. It was an unusual find but it seemed the most cunning of birds had been outsmarted by the most cunning of Highland animals.

As spring bloomed into summer there was far less fox activity in the lochside woodlands. Insects and beetles abounded, voles and mice were highly active and breeding, as were the mountain birds, and the foxes now lived in and hunted the higher hills. I was trekking with Moobli up a big river valley three miles north-east of home on August 16 when we found a small fox dropping on a rock which had been almost completely covered by the biggest fox scat I had ever seen – a full six inches long, with blue beetle wing-cases in it. It seemed the big fox had overlaid the other as if to demonstrate who was boss in the area. I imagined the smaller fox coming back, seeing the big scat and deciding to get out of the territory rather fast. Three days later we found a scat containing beetles, woodmouse bones, frog bones and vegetation remnants just above the west wood, the first there since winter. On August 27 we found that the foreleg knee joint of a hind carcass lying 500 yards up from the shore had been carried to near the waterline, probably by a fox on his way to drink after his feast. Next to the knee joint was a medium-sized scat.

All at once foxes ceased to visit the area round our home. I was sure it was because I had released Cleo and her two kittens at the end of July and, finally, old Sylvesturr in early September. No fox alive would tangle with such a 16 lb bundle of ferocity armed with ten long scimitars, especially one that would charge a huge Alsatian like Moobli up to the fencing wire of his pen. Even on long stag treks we found no traces of foxes. Maybe they were lying low from the noise of the official stag stalkers' guns.

Through early winter the foxes also stayed away. Snow tracking in late January showed that Sylvesturr, who had set up home in the long woods one and a half miles away, was still coming back about once a week to take food I set out. Cleo and the big male kitten Freddy, however, were staying round the cottage area and eating my food in the open pens at night. But on February 1 fox tracks from a well-chewed deer-calf carcass near the east wood burn showed that a fox had carried an 8-inch by 5-inch piece of skin and hair a quarter mile up the steep hill to the north-west, before leaving it. A week later there was a fresh scat near the hind carcass above the east bay. Again, a bone had been carried for fifty yards, then dropped.

These strange carryings happened again four days later. A strip of skin with plenty of flesh left on it was carried from the east burn carcass to the middle of the west wood, and another to the centre of the east wood. It was not done by the wildcats, for Moobli was getting plenty of fox scent.

On a supply trip on February 13 I was told that the local pack of foot foxhounds, a hunt subsidised by the Government to 'control' foxes because of their alleged depredations on young lambs in early spring, were the next day setting out from the farm nearest to Wildernesse. Although the farm was six miles away, I always dreaded the possibility that the hounds would pursue a fox into our small wooded area where, because we had never offered any threat, it might seek sanctuary. If that were to happen, and Moobli tried to defend his territory, the hounds might gang up on him, or even go for the wildcats. To defend Moobli, or the cats, I in turn might be induced to perform some dastardly deeds with the axe. At the time my feelings about hunting by hounds were vague, but basically I was against it. When questioned I had let my feelings be known.

I spent the day of the hunt power-sawing fallen logs and stacking firewood in the shed. Luckily, I saw no signs of the hounds. Later I was told a vixen had been killed just over two miles to the west. It could have been the mate of the big fox whose tracks I had found at the first woodland 'playground'. There was no way of knowing for sure.

On a trek eastward next morning we found a deer-calf carcass which had been pulled to bits by foxes, with much urine on a mossy rock nearby. A mile beyond the woods were the remains of a hind. Again foxes had carried pieces many yards. The skull was fifty yards to the north, the bottom jaw three yards to the east, and the four legs were scattered ten yards east of the jaws. All the legs had been bitten off at the knee joint, the foxes cleverly cutting through the tendons with their teeth rather than having to chew through thick bone. A calf carcass forty yards further east had all been eaten and was just a bundle of skin and bones. Not far away was a tragic scene. An old ewe sheep had been caught up in brambles near the bed of a burn where it had drowned and been washed downstream in a spate during recent rainstorms. A horrific death. Foxes had been at her too. No wonder the foxes came near us less often when there was plenty of carrion further away, clear of the wandering wildcats.

As if to prove me wrong, a calf that had died just above the west wood had its stomach and intestines neatly rolled out intact. Nothing more happened for nearly a month. Then, on March 14, I found the fifteenth deer fatality of the winter – a calf that had died while trying to shelter under a rock some 200 yards above the cottage. Foxes had rolled out the entrails and dragged the carcass downhill by repeated tugs at the meat. All that was left was a bundle of skin and bones, with two rear thigh bones detached. A fresh hind carcass lay near an upper fork of our burn. On a trek up the long river valley to the east, Moobli scented out the first dead stag. A hole had been opened up just behind the ribs, typical golden eagle's work.

Concerned at the number of dead deer I was finding in our own woods besides those discovered on longer treks, I alerted the Red Deer Commission and was assured that, providing prime adult deer were not the victims, high mortality among so fecund a species was normal every few years. They also confirmed my view that because red deer seek shelter when sick, our own small conifer woods would naturally become a main mortuary for the deer stocks in the area. In fact the count went up to thirty-two dead deer that harsh wet winter. What was the deers' loss also proved the gain of every carrion-eating species, from eagles downwards.

On April 7 I went to see an old retired keeper who lived twelve miles to the south. John kindly told me of an eyrie I did not know, then gave me the benefit of some of his own fox experiences. He believed foxes could 'talk' to each other. Once, using stalking skills evolved over a lifetime in the Highlands, he had followed a fox and his vixen for nearly a mile.

'Every so often the dog came to an area of softer earth and began digging a new den. Just a yard or two, then the vixen looked impatient. The fox trotted off and started digging another – and the same thing happened. In all he began digging five dens until the vixen was satisfied. She went in, examined it, then came out again. From then on she was the boss of that den. I've often seen a vixen near a den, or up to a hundred yards away, walking up and down impatiently, waiting for the dog fox to arrive with some food. When he does they sort of caress and kiss each other, make high-pitched noises as if talking.'

I told the keeper of my unsuccessful attempts to wait with a camera downwind of a fox playground or a deer carcass. John laughed.

'You'd have to be very lucky to get an unsuspicious fox. Usually when approaching a carcass, or even their den with cubs in it, foxes walk round in a large circle, testing the wind.

They soon know you're there, won't go near until you've long been gone. And if a fox scents or sees humans nearby, it will wait to warn its mate too.'

Highland foxes are heavily persecuted – by sheep farmers, crofters and keepers – for their alleged preying on lambs, poultry and game birds. Terriers, usually Highlands or Jack Russells, are taken to occupied dens in spring to kill cubs. Thus pressure on adult foxes to kill stock is eased. The vixen often bolts to waiting guns. Snaring is another method, though it was banned in Forestry Commission plantations in 1980 after a public outcry when a roe doe was found in a snare. Night shooting with lights is practised, often conducted from a van or when the fox comes to a known carcass or offal bait. Local Government-subsidised foxhound packs began to operate after the open gin trap was banned in Scotland in April 1973. Although illegal, poisoned baits are still set out for foxes.

Long before the open gin was banned, John favoured what many feel to be the more humane drowning trap, which some farmers are still trying to get legalised. Here the baited gin is tied to a large stone and set just beyond a jetty on an islet, natural if possible, in a hill pool. The fox, not liking to get its feet wet without need, makes for the jetty to jump on to the islet. When it is caught the fox jumps and the weight of the trap pulls the fox under water where it swiftly drowns. This trap is said to be selective for foxes, but statistics gathered by the National Farmers' Union of Scotland before the gin was banned show that seven keepers caught in the drowning trap 997 foxes, several hooded crows, three wildcats, two otters, one badger, one buzzard and one mallard. John disclosed his sad experience of finding a drowned golden eagle in a gin.

'I was very unhappy about that. I have nothing against eagles and it was a magnificent bird, over six and a half feet across the wings. I tried to get it stuffed but couldn't find anyone to do it. In the end I just buried it.' He thought for a moment, then added, 'I don't personally *like* killing foxes either. But a keeper wouldn't last long in these communities if he was against controlling foxes.'

It was a view I was to hear many times, including some weeks later from my farming neighbour, who said he always hated killing cubs as they were 'so beautiful'. He reckoned some 80 per cent of Highland foxes in the Lochaber region took lambs, as opposed to only 10 per cent down south, and that measures *had* to be taken to control their numbers. I was unaware at the time that he had become Vice-Chairman of the local Hunt. Indeed, it was not until later in the year that I discovered one of my best friends, a farmer from England who had a 400-acre holding thirty miles away, had become one of the Hunt's district chairmen. Since he had once expressed doubts as to the efficacy of hunting with hounds, I asked him why he had taken the job.

'I was *blagged* into it,' he said with a laugh. 'I was a relative newcomer, no one else wanted the task, so I was sort of coerced into taking it on!'

Towards the end of May I went to check a tawny owls' nest in a huge old snag, which had earlier contained three eggs. The nest hole contained only an addled, half-empty egg and many wax-sheathed feathers of two fledglings. All had been neatly severed. As a fit fox can scale a fourteen-foot wall and this nest hole was a mere eight feet from the ground, it seemed certainly a fox's work. Sad though it was for the owls, at least it was evidence of a fox family still in that area.

On June 5 wildcat Cleo, who had returned to the pens three weeks earlier after mating with old Sylvesturr in the wilds, gave birth to four kits. Naturally I wanted to ensure she raised them all successfully, particularly the weak runt of the litter, a kit which I called Liane. From my desk on June 11 I heard a loud dog-like yiping near the house, and I dashed outside. Moobli was sniffing at a rather ugly, extremely skinny foxhound bitch, which was yiping with fear, her tail kept down tight between her legs. As I came round the porch logs, she reared up on to my bird table, snaffled a chunk of bread, then as Moobli gave a growl of apparent disapproval, ran away through the east wood with it, still giving little yipes as Moobli chased her away. She was clearly very hungry, so I called him back and told him off – until I realised he was only doing his job, to guard the area.

It was then I remembered the wildcat kittens. The last thing I wanted was a strange hungry hound round the place just now. If she investigated the pens she would certainly upset Cleo, might even cause her to kill one or two of her kittens. That night I left the back and front doors open, knowing Moobli would sound the alarm if she returned, or chase her off again.

Where had she come from? It was not the hunting season. Sometimes, to save costs, I knew that some of the hounds were boarded out with sympathetic farmers during the off-season. Maybe this bitch had not liked her new home. Next day she came back and left a large dollop by the cottage. She snapped defensively at Moobli, who was playing around her, too gentle to hurt a bitch. She refused to come to me, so I threw her one of his giant sterilised meat sausages. She snatched it up and I commanded Moobli to see her off, which he finally did – running by her side with little growls, not biting at her but firmly escorting her through the west wood. This time she carried on going, no doubt back to where she belonged.

Busy now with the wildcats and on eagle photography and treks over a large area of the rough terrain, there were no more incidents with foxes until July 24. That day I went outside quietly to photograph a large flying buzzard and saw Cleo standing high in the pens, ears back, her banded tail fluffed as thick as a flue-brush, growling loudly. Facing her, just outside the pens, glaring in with large orange eyes, was a fox. It was visibly wilting before the ferocious wildcat stare. My only thought was to get the fox out of there and teach it a lesson it would not forget. I crept back to the door and let Moobli out.

'Go on, boy. See him off!' I said.

Moobli dashed off like a charging cougar. By the time I got round the cottage both had disappeared, and I heard his deep baying near the burn in the east wood. I stumbled through the bracken as fast as I could, hampered by the long-lensed camera. I reached the burn in time to see Moobli floundering out of the far side of a pool, the fox a mere foot in front, and Moobli's jaws actually clamp on to the very tip of the fox's brush. But as Moobli struggled to get his footing out of the pool, the fox tore itself free, made a great leap of about ten feet on to a slab of rock, hooked its forepaws over the top, and disappeared into the thick herbage. Moobli wanted to go downstream where he could cross. Knowing the fox would be a long way off before he could reach the other side and start tracking by scent, I called him off.

I felt certain the fox had come round after scenting the kits, hoping to pick one of them off. Surely it wouldn't come back after that experience. Two things about the incident impressed me. One was Cleo's brave defence of her kits – she had showed no fear whatever of the fox – and also Moobli's speed. Two days later I proved to be not only wrong about the fox but even more amazed by Moobli's speed.

I was coming back from picking blackcurrants near the beach when Moobli suddenly dropped the stick he had been carrying and dashed of. Silently and fast, he vanished round the corner of the cottage. Thinking he must be chasing a deer out, I was angry and whistled him back. There was no response. Then I heard his deep bark, again from the burn. I dropped the bowl of fruit and this time unhampered by the camera made slightly better speed. Moobli had cornered a fox, maybe the same one, in another deep pool, this time in midstream and ringed by boulders. The fox was snapping, rearing at him, but his huge flashing teeth and dodging speed kept it there. I scrambled nearer over the rocks. Bedraggled and soaked like a skinned cat, it rolled in the water, in terror, something feminine in its submission, making odd '*bick oorr, bick oorr*' sounds in its throat.

As I dashed into the pool the fox snarled with open mouth, a desperate look on its face. I grabbed the end of its thick tail and hauled it out, then carried it snapping like that back to the pens, making sure its feet did not touch the ground so it could spring up and bite at my legs. I reached a twelve-foot pen which had now been separated from the main one containing Cleo's family, lifted its gate and gently swung the fox inside.

It ran, limping on one of its rear legs, to the far end, then crouched down in the bracken that had grown through the bottom meshes. I put in a good den box filled with hay and a bowl of water, praised Moobli and rewarded him with a tasty titbit in the cottage, then went back to the pen with some meat.

3 · A Lost Hound

It was the expression on the fox's face when I went back with the meat that I will never forget. As I had carried her from the burn I had seen that she was a vixen, and now she lay with her chin resting on the water bowl from which she had taken a few drinks. Her eyes were deep orange, with elliptical pupils like a cat's, and they seemed to hold an indescribable sadness as they followed all my actions without a single movement of her head. Reflected there were all the centuries of human persecution against her kind. Distrust and resignation as to her fate were there too, for she must have thought she was going to be killed.

They were intelligent eyes, and as I dropped the meat in a yard from her and she looked first at it then back to me, a sort of wonder dawned in them, as if she perceived I was not going to kill her but was actually trying to help her. I sat down talking to her quietly. She got up once, limped round the pen and made three rather weak pokes through the fencing with her long muzzle, then returned to lie down and rest her head on the bowl again and look at me with a quizzical gaze.

Her bright orange-red fur was drying now in the sun and as it was the first time I had been so close to a wild fox since I was a boy, I looked at her closely. Her paws were tipped with black fur, as were the backs of her ears, one of which had a small tear and was bleeding slightly. It could not have been a wound

31

inflicted by Moobli's massive teeth. Her black nose, small, sensitive, dog-like, was flanked by white chops and the white spread over her bottom jaw and along her cheeks, except where it was interrupted by dusky patches that travelled to the inside corners of her eyes.

Her rear left leg was weak but was not broken and I could see no other signs of any wound. I felt sure she was one of the foxes which had paid us regular winter calls in the last three years, possibly a new mate of the big fox after the vixen had been killed by the hounds in what appeared to be the west edge of that fox's home range.

At that time I was attempting to tame the wildcat Liane inside the cottage, an intricate and difficult task since the rare fierce Scottish wildcat had long been held to be both intractable and untameable. Cleo and the other kits were due to be released in a few weeks' time in a rabbit-filled area nine miles away. As I hoped Liane would stay around the home woods after that, I didn't want to try and tame the fox as well. I decided to feed the vixen up and release her some distance away when she recovered. By 9 pm she had eaten the meat and drunk most of the water. I renewed both.

Next day the vixen did not look well and spent most of the time sleeping in the den box. She had left one large muddy scat, indicating she had been eating only worms before we had caught her. Apart from providing new meat, which she didn't touch, I left her alone.

In the morning I was saddened to find her dead in the den box. When I examined the body I was surprised to see maggots falling from a wound on the inside of the rear left haunch, the leg on which she had been limping. The flesh inside was dark green and looked gangrenous; she had finally died of blood poisoning from a wound I had been unable to see. When I looked closer I saw twin puncture marks just over an inch apart, and realised the likely cause. We had recently found one of old Sylvesturr's twisted tapering scats in the west wood. He had probably come to investigate his mate Cleo and her kits, and the vixen had been in the wrong place at the wrong time. She measured 3 feet from nose to tip of tail and had clearly lost weight in the days after the battle, for she weighed only 6 lbs. As I buried the body, I

opposite: The garden at Wildernesse in spring.

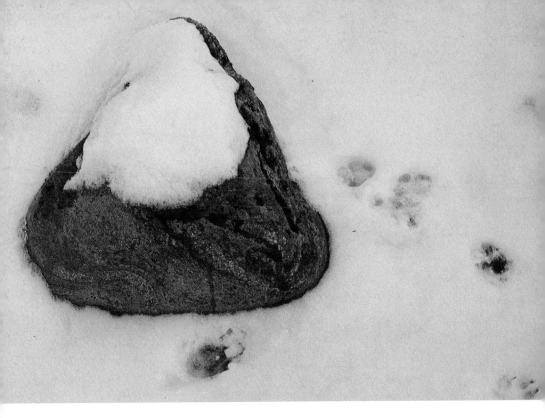

above: Tracking wild foxes in the snow. Here the fox took a side step to the left to leave its scent on a rock.

below: A deer carcass torn apart by foxes in winter.

above: A vixen which had been cornered by Moobli in the burn.

below: A litter of fox cubs killed by terriers and dug out by crofters after the adults had been allegedly preying on poultry. (Photo by Geoffrey Kinns)

above: Aspen, the first of the wild vixens I looked after. All these young foxes had been caught by the foot in gin-traps.

below: When she realised Moobli was harmless, Aspen assumed the predator role and went on the attack. Gentle Moobli remained tolerant.

reflected that at least I had further proof that a mature wildcat can see off a fox.

On July 30 I rowed with Moobli to the best beach a mile away to the west to fill some sacks with gravel. We then climbed up the steep hillside for nearly half a mile to check a badgers' sett. We found it empty, but as we rested on a flat rock above it, I saw some bracken moving oddly way below. Up with the fieldglass. There was a huge fox, a dog-fox judging by its bulk and the width of its head, stealing along in a patch of tussocks, looking down and forwards, his ears pricked as if he was listening as much as looking. Suddenly he reared up into the air, both front paws extended, and pounced down like a cat. He did it three times, after prowling a few yards each time. On the first two pounces I think he only got moths or grasshoppers but on the third he caught either a mouse or frog – I could not see clearly at that distance – for he shook it hard, then chewed it up quickly.

He headed north-west, skirted a large grey boulder, over an open patch and into some bracken. He had a great white tip to his tail which showed like a flag, even above the bracken. He turned west up a small dry burn gully, leaped on to an old ruined stone wall which was overgrown with grasses, prowled along it, leaped down again, clearly scenting something for he sneaked through some more tussocks, and made another cat-like pounce.

Then he headed west again towards the long woodlands above the loch. He must have come across our earlier scent trail in the slight north-west wind, for he suddenly performed an almost complete somersault backwards, then ran, skulking low in fright, to a large area of thick bracken and vanished. Hoping to find a den he might have in there, I put Moobli on his lead and hurried down to track him. The Alsatian got the scent immediately and started to haul me along eagerly. Then the fox darted out of the bracken on the same route he had gone in, cunningly doubling back on his old trail and so confusing the dog, and dashed away into the woods.

It was the first time I had enjoyed a prolonged view of a fox hunting its normal summer prey in seven years in the Highlands and, because I had only come to bag some gravel, I had no camera with me. My curses fortunately went unheard. I doubted he was more than two years old – a *young* fox in his prime, the sun shining on a superb coat. He was clearly not the big old-looking fox I had seen taking a drink two years earlier, for that fox had a dark brush with no white tip. Yet he was clearly now in that fox's territory. Had he taken over from the other, who might now be dead?

A few days later, coming back from a supply trip, I stopped off to bag some cementing sand from a huge badgers' sett on the shore four and a half miles from home. My farmer neighbour had told me of some sand holes made by foxes about fifty yards up in the woods from the sett, and that it was in that area the Hunt usually managed to kill a fox every year. As we boated in I saw a large bank of sand shining golden just where he had described it. We climbed up but found no trace of foxes. Badgers had taken over that bank too, and had dug two big holes, throwing out about a ton of sand. As I filled bags with some of it my shovel hit something hard. It was the skull of a huge fox, with just one canine tooth left, nearly an inch long. Certainly the skull of an old fox. It was a clue, that was all. Maybe it had been injured by hounds and had died in one of its old earths. Now badgers had taken over and thrown the skull out.

As we burbled home in the sinking sun, I caught another glimpse of the big young fox near the long woods. He was bounding along with a sort of joyous air. When he heard the engine, he stopped, looked down at us with curiosity, then bounded up and over a ridge. Some instinct told me we would be seeing a lot more of this fox, so I gave him a name there and then. I don't know why, but I called him Cedric.

One day in early August I took Liane out in the late afternoon to the front pasture. I was trying to train her to run back to the house or the woodshed when she was scared. Suddenly Moobli gave a brief '*whuff*', took a few steps, then looked back at me for orders. I did not want a fox coming close at the wildcat's tender age, and said, 'See it off!'

He shot into the tall bracken on the north hill. I could see that something was rustling through it a few yards ahead of him. Whatever it was and Moobli then vanished into the dip over the brow of the hill. There was silence. A minute later I heard two high yipes above the west wood, then Moobli came back grinning from ear to ear. 'I saw him off, boss,' his expression said.

If it was a fox, even Cedric, it did not come back. As usual in summer the foxes were living and hunting higher in the hills. Apart from finding fox scats and signs in the hills on autumn stag treks, I had no more close fox experiences until I saw some big tracks near the little west wood burn on November 11. For some reason I woke up two days later in the middle of the night, fully alert. Bright moonlight flooded through the window. I got up and looked out — just in time to see a shadowy figure crossing the front pasture from west to east. It was a huge fox, undoubtedly Cedric. I reckoned he weighed at least 15 lbs. He stopped once, a paw upraised, sniffing the north wind, then carried on. I did not let Moobli out for I was no longer afraid for Liane. She was almost full grown now and was quartered in the woodshed. She was exceptionally fast on her feet, and could detonate the usual wildcat's devastating frontal display well enough to set any fox back on its heels while she escaped through the ground hole in the shed. She sometimes did it when Moobli got too boisterous. A fox of such size could certainly not follow, even if it tried, and with carrion about it had no such need anyway.

When some meat scraps disappeared from the middle of the west wood next day, I put some more in and round the old live cage trap but wedged its falling door open. If the fox took the meat I would try and trap him, take a few close photos, and let him go again. But when we found Liane near the trap next day I abandoned the idea. Apparently she had scented the meat from 200 yards away.

Five days later Moobli barked and ran down to the log gateway. There was a black and white bitch foxhound before him, yiping submissively, tail between her legs again. She walked to the end of the boat bay and stared at the water as if about to plunge in. I did not want a foxhound about the place, especially if it was part of a hunt. I called Moobli back to let her go on but as she turned she stumbled, her rear left leg weak. Half an hour later I found her in the east wood, looking thin and pathetic. I carried out one of Moobli's meat sausages and kept calling her until finally she came, whining in her throat. She looked old and had strange scabs on her back. She grabbed the meat like a wolf, her teeth just missing my fingers.

Afterwards she hung about the cottage, the last thing I wanted, for Liane's sake, never mind Cedric. Finally I chased her off, but found her again later, sitting among the ash trees on shore, looking this way and that, as if at the end of her tether, not knowing where to go next. Then she set off to the east. I felt troubled about her later, and also annoyed at whoever was responsible for the poor creature's state. I took Moobli to look for her all over the east bay area, but she had gone.

Early next morning the bitch was back, inside the porch. Moobli chased her off and she lay on her back near the shore, her legs in the air and squeaking with submission, though he did not attempt to bite or hurt her. When we returned, she also came. She looked very bedraggled, and whined to show she was friendly.

'All right, old girl,' I said as I stroked her gently.

I put her on a long leash in the spruce glade and cooked two of the big sausages. With these and a tin of dog meat and several handfuls of meal, I filled two large dishes and took them to the hound. She craned forward and ate as if she hadn't had anything for a week. Slurping, burping, she gulped like a vacuum cleaner, as if the food were being sucked down her throat.

She spent the next two hours whining, squeaking and barking so that I found it impossible to work on my book. Eventually I sighed, put on my rain gear and boated her the six miles to the farmer's house. They would know how to get her back to the Hunt kennels. I was greeted with:

'Oh, you've got it, have you? It didn't come back from a Hunt three days ago and we were wondering where it had gone.'

I pointed out the bitch's poor condition, and that it was limping. How could it have got into that condition in just three days? They told me the hounds were starved for three days before a Hunt to make them fit. So I had been right; it hadn't eaten for a week. The bitch was put into an outhouse and I was invited in for coffee.

I told the farmer that when I had hunted cougars with hounds in Canada (to radio-collar them for a study, not to kill them) the hounds had been starved just the one day before. Three days without food would simply make foxhounds go cadging round crofts instead of chasing after foxes. I mentioned the four occa-

36

sions on which I had seen foxhounds rear up and filch food from my bird tables.

But I did not want to quarrel with the farmer and his wife for I had some respect for them. He ran one of the best farms in the area, grazed sheep and cows over 5,000 acres, and had recently secured grazing rights over an adjacent area of similar size. He let holiday caravans, hired out fishing boats and was also a stalwart of the local Community Council. He was a highly intelligent man, who examined farming and conservation matters deeply from his own point of view. Over the years we had enjoyed discussing the merits and otherwise of heather-burning and of ploughing and draining land. In his view, making land more fertile was beneficial to many forms of wildlife as well as the farm stock. Besides, I parked my truck on his tenanted land, half a mile from the public pier, and for this privilege I paid a small annual rental. It was not a large sum, but more than the yearly rates for my cottage. I did not want to be in conflict with local people, certainly not with him.

Although he laughed at the idea of hounds feeding from my bird table, he pointed out that there must be many foxes in my area, for when sheep were gathered from that end of the estate there were never any lambs with them. I replied truthfully that, apart from the hardest weeks in winter, when a few sheep came down from the snowy tops along with deer, I seldom saw a sheep within a mile of the cottage. According to him, farmers did not want to eradicate foxes, but just to keep numbers down. Too many on the Hill means more lambs killed in the competition for food. What he didn't like were unrealistic conservationists who wanted to protect the 'lovely fox' and even regarded sheep as unnatural to the Highlands.

I was not against sheep, I said, agreeing with him that their grazing and dung helped more grasses to grow, and that in hard weather sheep carrion provided food for rare birds as well as carnivorous animals like foxes. The farmer reckoned that in the critical three weeks at lambing time in our region of Lochaber as much as 70 per cent of fox food was lamb meat. In his estimation an average fox family killed about eight lambs each season. He had once found the remains of forty-five lambs round one fox den.

In fact, studies made by the Animal Breeding Research Organisation in Edinburgh show that some 17 per cent of lambs on Scottish hills die within twenty-four hours of birth, mainly due to the poor ewe nutrition in winter. The figure goes as high as 40 per cent in the harshest sheep areas. Thus, when lamb remnants are found near fox earths, it is not easy to discern which have been killed by the foxes and which have been picked up already dead. In any case, foxes eat many voles, which are hosts to a tick that transmits 'louping ill' to sheep. Foxes also eat many rabbits, which compete with sheep for grass, and clear up carrion which harbour thousands of pest flies.

As we parted amicably, I told him that I had fed the foxhound some 3 lbs of good food.

'You should charge the Hunt for that, and also your petrol up and down the loch!' the farmer's wife said.

I decided not to do so. I didn't want to be paid for helping that poor hound. I found out later that the bitch had been rather lucky. Some hounds when chasing foxes had been known to fall to their deaths in chasms, or been killed in snares, and a few had died from eating illegally poisoned baits put out for foxes. When I reached home I found the petrol in my boat tank alarmingly low. I would have to row some of the way out on my next supply trip.

A week later, the farmer invited me in for a warming cup of coffee before I faced the Force Eight westerlies on the loch. He told me the Hunt had been on his land that week but had got no foxes. Then two lads from Devon had come on holiday, experts at 'squeaking' out foxes, and had got four, two of them near the area where I had found the big fox skull. None of them had been particularly large. So it seemed Cedric lived to hunt another day.

'It was amazing to see the foxes work their way towards the squeaking from the top of the hill,' he said. 'They came within twenty yards, and the lads shot them in the head. They could sell the pelts for £10 or £12 each, which paid their holiday costs.' He said they came because they liked hunting foxes and because the Anti-Blood Sports supporters were strong in their area of Devon.

I put my lips to the back of my hand and made the squeaking a Sussex gamekeeper had taught me in boyhood. It is supposed to sound like a rabbit in distress. The farmer seemed surprised I knew the technique. I told him it didn't work with foxes out my way, where there were no rabbits.

In early December the snow storms began their first real onslaught, and huge lead-heavy flakes fell straight down like little plates. Across the loch the hunched brooding shape of the highest mountain and its courtier hills had whitened like sugar cakes. As yet the earth and its beaten herbage retained a vestige of autumn warmth, but the snow fell doggedly, whispering over the grasses, into the curled dead leaves, as if knowing it would overcome. I was woken at 4 am on December 10 by loud '*kahf kahf*' barks. In moonlight I saw a big fox padding over the frosty surface of the front pasture towards the east. Later we found not only its tracks but also those of a badger.

After three days of snow a bright sun gleamed on the landscape. As I set off with Moobli for some snow tracking, little waterfalls tinkled between melting icicles in the burn. We plodded upwards to the north-east. I kept to the piston-deep tracks of red deer for they know the lie of the land, and thus avoided falling into a deep drift. At 1,500 feet we found fox tracks starting from a small cliff overhang. It had been running uphill sideways, putting most of its weight on the inside feet like a skier. Now it had slowed to a walk, the tracks in the usual straight line as if it had hopped along on one leg. They led to an oval depression where snow had melted from the grass of a deer calf's bed. The fox, out night hunting, must have scented the calf and gone to investigate, hoping for a carcass and food. It had been unlucky for there was no sign of a struggle and the calf's tracks showed it had bolted downhill. No harm done there, for the calf had been moved on to where herbage was easier to find.

We climbed higher. In the deep drifts the fox had tried to bound along, its brush clipping the snow deeply at each jump. We neared a tall cliff. Suddenly there was a sharp '*raowl*' bark and there, for a second, was the fox. It was a broad-headed male but not as big as Cedric, and he had been resting beneath an overhang. He glared at us in astonishment, then shot along the foot of the cliff and bounded up a small cornice as I struggled to fit the telephoto lens. He stopped briefly at the top to look back;

I saw the dark orange glare of his eyes in the sun, then he was gone. My camera clicked on empty space.

Just par for the course with wild foxes, I thought ruefully, but it was interesting that this fox, with no white tip to his tail, was probably on, or just overlapping, the eastern edge of Cedric's range. A few days later I searched the eastern woods but still could not find a den, although we did see eight woodcocks, the highest number ever in a single day, exploding like brown rockets all round us.

On December 16 Moobli went outside at dusk and gave his 'fox' whuff barks. I saw something moving on the north-west hill, then heard a fox bark faintly back. Two days later a fox barked from the ridges just above the west wood when I went out with a light and Moobli to try and track Liane, who had not come for her food. She had gone into the wood herself, and we just caught a glimpse of her haring back to the shed. I hoped Cedric was not taking too close an interest in her.

Just before Christmas I started to break in a new pair of boots on a hard snow trek to the north-west, where I hoped to find Cedric's tracks. We came upon them half a mile from the cottage, going downhill in hard crusted snow. The fox had hopped down, two foot by two foot, like a hare, his left foot always slightly in front. His rear feet sometimes fitted into the front tracks, sometimes halfway between. He was certainly big, his front tracks a good two inches long. On crusty snow, which had a light covering of fresh, the prints could look old because each time the animal pulled its foot out, new snow fell into the track. This obscured it slightly, making it appear old.

When we got back Moobli picked up a scent in the east wood. We found where Cedric had been scraping for worms, grubs or beetles under fallen logs and branches. I had the feeling he came round so often out of a genuine sense of curiosity, quite apart from the fact that our woods held better foods than the open Hill.

I spent New Year's Eve, as always, out in the freezing woods in a tent, cooking supper on a campfire, renewing my vows to keep writing about and working for the last wild places, and feeling a little smug as I had not had a single drink. Moobli slept in the tent flap all night; not a sound did he make. Cedric did not come anywhere near to keep us company.

4 · *Escaping the Hunt*

As I was driving back to my boat from a supply trip in early February, I was surprised to see an acquaintance of mine, who had started working part-time for the neighbouring farmer, shouting up into the hills and brandishing his stick. Before him, tail between its legs, ran a sheepdog.

'It belongs to the farm in the next glen,' he explained. 'We can't have stray sheepdogs running around here. They chase the vulnerable hogs!' (Hogs are year-old castrated lambs being fattened up for the market.)

He was the first sheep-worker I had known to admit that sheepdogs on the loose were often a danger to sheep. But it had been rather a day for admissions. While shopping earlier, I had heard a crofter who had lived in the region all his life express the view that but for Government subsidies – each breeding hill ewe attracted a grant of £4.50 per year at the time* – many

---

* In 1984 this subsidy, known as the Hill Livestock Compensatory Allowance, was £6.25 per year for each pure-bred breeding ewe, and £4.25 for cross-breds. In 1980 an additional new compensation scheme began, under the sheep regime of the EEC. This scheme supports the lamb market and farmers who sell lambs for less than the projected market price can apply for compensation to make up the shortfall. In 1983–4 £126.9 million was paid to British hill sheep farmers under the new scheme, compared with £54 million before.

small-scale operators would not bother to keep sheep at all.

I had been told that the Hunt would be out on the near-by hills on February 12, but not a hound did I hear or see. However, a big fox, probably Cedric, had been chewing at the carcass of a stag which had drowned after being chased into the loch by poachers on the far side. Moobli tracked fox scent for 300 yards, round in a half-circle, then lost it amid the frozen rocks of a large gully.

Six days later we found a dead young roe buck on the shore and dragged it into a bracken bed near the west wood for scavengers. A stag-calf carcass which had lain for five days in the bay past the eastern burn had been visited by a smaller fox. Its tracks and scent trails came from the east, so it seemed there were still two lots of foxes in the locations we had already found.

At this time I had to go south to deliver the manuscript of a book and its photos to my publisher. When I returned a few days later the roe-deer carcass had almost all gone. Huge piles of fox scats showed that Cedric had dined well, had known we were away and therefore feasted at leisure. Liane was fine in the woodshed, but had sheep ticks in her neck. I soon found the cause. Four sheep had moved in and were eating the regenerating seedlings in the woods. They had knocked down several of the little cages round new young trees I had planted, for their wool was entangled in the mesh. There was no point in complaining to the farmer for he could not possibly fence off 5,000 acres, but we soon herded the sheep out.

I also found that during our absence Liane had made herself a new den in thick bracken inside the open wildcat pen. It was a snug hole from which she could see out at all times, as if she were playing safe while having daytime snoozes. Coming back from a trek a few days later, I discovered the reason for this. We found many big and medium-sized fox scats on mossy rocks near the burn just above our northern fence. It seemed a *pair* of foxes had visited often while we were away. Moobli scented out a big hind carcass that had been rolled downhill, eaten out and was just a wrap-tangle of skin and bones. Despite Cedric's size, this was surely the work of at least two foxes, and it helped explain Liane's behaviour. While she could repel a single fox if it showed aggression, she would be far more wary about tackling a pair of them. Did this mean ferocious old Sylvesturr was no longer around? He and Liane together could certainly have driven them off.

Just then I heard a short bark. I looked up to see a huge fox with a white-tipped tail, undoubtedly Cedric, sneaking through the heather on the highest ridge above us. I lifted the camera and got two photos in poor light before he vanished, giving another bark, probably to warn his mate when over the far side.

In late March Liane came into her first oestrus and began spending many hours in the woods, just returning briefly to the woodshed for her food before haring away into the darkness again. I hoped this meant she was meeting Sylvesturr, or another wildcat tom. It certainly seemed to indicate that the foxes were no longer near.

On a supply trip soon afterwards I found a ewe sheep entangled in a bramble bush not far from the farm. I freed her, getting my hands gashed as she leaped about, then went back to tell the farmer as he might want to cut the bush down. I was cordially invited in for a snack. As we talked I casually mentioned that I would like a fox cub to keep and to study. He had no objections to that – as long as I did not rear it to maturity and let it go! Could he get me one, perhaps, when at dens with terriers?

'Afraid not,' he replied. 'If I carried a live cub the terriers would be at me all the way home!'

It was during an exhausting eagle trek on March 27 that we found a first-class fox den. It lay between large boulders on a steep rounded buttress a full 1,300 feet above the small lochan that nestled below the south-western slopes of Guardian mountain, a good four miles from home. It was too far away to be a den of Cedric's, and was only found by accident through coming upon it from above, for a broad ledge in front of the boulders prevented the site being seen from below. There were many scats round it, with bits of wool from sheep carrion and feathers of small birds, together with a few that looked as if they had come from ptarmigan. The earth of the ledge was all scuffed up. We waited a good while downwind but no foxes came out to pose for the camera.

In early April Moobli nosed out a newly-dead deer calf amid small trees thirty yards below the kitchen window. Boating home in howling gales four days later from an overnight eagle trek, I was forced to shelter behind a small sand spit in order to bail out, and there found a fox den. There were large scats on the grassy bank above the shore. Though over two miles from home it was clearly one of Cedric's, for it was below the first fox playground we had found. It had recently been vacated, probably because the gales had sent spray lashing into it.

On April 28 we made a long eagle trek up the wide river valley to the east and found a fox den on the rising eastern slopes, three miles from the loch shore. It had been freshly dug out under a big rock, with earth scuffed everywhere. We then found a dead deer calf which, from Moobli's behaviour, had been torn about by foxes. So we now knew of four resident fox families in an area of nine miles by four, though we did not know how many foxes were in each. Often we found smaller fox scats overlaid by larger ones. From those in Cedric's territory, which I reckoned extended from the far end of the long woods three miles west of us to roughly half a mile beyond our eastern burn, I deduced that he was quite tolerant of vixens (probably from his own family) but was not tolerant of other males. Slightly larger scats than those of the vixens were covered with his own droppings, and twice he even overlaid Moobli's giant dollops.

By May 8 I knew for sure that there was another fox on Cedric's ground, and probably a vixen feeding cubs too. I was boating up the loch to check some rockfaces to the west, Moobli running along the shore for exercise, when a large ewe appeared over a ridge and stood stamping her feet at him. He had been well trained to ignore sheep and circled well away from her before starting to scent towards the long woods.

Suddenly a browny-black fox leaped up the far bank of a deep burn and shot away between the trees. Moobli instinctively started after it, but I knew he had little chance of catching a fox with a 200-yard start and, not wanting him lost for hours, called him back. As I pulled the boat in to the shore, a lamb picked itself up from the bracken beyond the ridge and tottered down into the water. I rowed after it and snatched it out. It was bleeding from the throat where the fox had attacked and its trachea was exposed. The ewe had run away. Without treatment the lamb wouldn't survive, so I took it quickly home.

The lamb, which I called Clarrie, put up a tremendous fight for life over the next few weeks. As she recovered she kept toddling up the slopes to graze. Every so often I would spot her blazing white uniform and go to fetch her down again. I did not want her to risk another encounter with the fox. She soon became part of the family. Moobli loved her, and in the end even Liane accepted her after a nervous start.

No fox came near again until May 26 when Moobli gave his fox bark after scenting it in the west wood. I just caught a glimpse of it heading up over the tussocky slopes. Again it was not Cedric, but probably his vixen.

By mid-June I was working with eagles again and could not look after Carrie every hour of the day. She spent some nights out on the slopes. As usual in summer, the foxes were hunting higher. At any rate she remained unmolested.

In connection with my eagle work I went to visit a leading Government conservationist, and we also talked about fox-hunting. He offered the opinion, shared by some of his colleagues, that all fox-killing should stop for a fixed period of a few years, and farmers could be given compensation for any lamb actually killed in this period.

'Fox numbers would probably explode at first, then mange and disease, shortage of winter food supply, would bring them down again,' he said. 'By putting terriers into dens, killing the very young and the less fit old, you are virtually ensuring healthy, vital, virile breeding stock! As for hound hunting – how many dogs are you using, feeding, training, transporting? How many men are involved, their time, the loss of other productive work? How much disturbance of other wildlife occurs through hound hunting in the spring nesting season? All round it must be uneconomic.'

On my way home I called on a friend, a keeper called Greg Hunter, who had helped me find eagles on his estate many miles from my home and with whom I had been on several fine wildlife treks. Greg was one of the most efficient fox-killers in the region, not so much with the hounds, though he had few objections to them, but as a lone operator with snares, terriers at the den, and shooting at night by the lights of his van. I put the views I had heard to him as well as my own. He pooh-poohed

45

them goodnaturedly. 'First, the Government would not pay compensation for lambs killed by foxes as it would be very hard to *prove* that a fox caused death. Secondly, if hunting helps to ensure a virile breeding stock, what is the complaint? We are doing the foxes a favour!'

Greg went on to say he didn't think much of some of the young local shots as they were too untrained. He had taken three of them to put terriers down a den on the land of one of his neighbouring farmers.

'Two big almost full-grown cubs came out, and everyone just stood looking as one climbed up a ledge and over the top! I had to run from way beyond them over the ridge and shoot it with my shotgun. I told them to go home, then had a three-hour wait for the vixen as I knew she would come back. Then I heard a stonechat scolding and there she was, looking at me through the grasses. She ran off and I fired three times with the rifle, the vixen turning away from each shot as it struck the ground near her. Then at 400 yards she stopped and looked back. It was as if she knew the accurate range of the rifle, that I couldn't hit her at that distance.'

I had arranged to drive across America and Canada in August that year, to meet some distinguished biologists who had written to me after my Canadian wildlife book was published,* and also to revisit some old friends and haunts. My acquaintance who worked part-time for the farmer agreed to boat down the loch to Wildernesse to feed Liane while I was away. He also took little Clarrie to join five other orphan lambs on the farm itself. Moobli stayed with friends in Sussex.

When I got back on September 21 I was disappointed to learn that Clarrie had died at the farm, apparently from eating over-rich foods. Looking after her had been a lot of work for nothing, I thought. The fox might just as well have had her. Liane too was missing. Apart from a fox dropping filled with blackberries below the west wood, and a few small prints in the mud near the shed, Moobli could find no scents at all. Fortunately Liane returned three days later.

On October 2, on a trek to photograph rutting stags, I found

* *Alone in the Wilderness*

46

not only that the fox den on the buttress above the lochan near Guardian mountain was still occupied, but evidence that Cedric was still alive. I was dead beat and sweating as we swung round in a wide arc back towards our home loch when, near the first fox playground, Moobli found one of his eating places. It was on a large flat rock, sheltered by a recess which turned it into a shallow cave, at the top of the birch groves. Scuffed earth and two huge scats revealed he had grown even bigger in the past year. His scent was all pervading; he had been there recently.

On a stag trek in late October we located another fox den between rocks near the burn of the long wood, a mile nearer home. It had a rotting lamb skull and a sheep jawbone in it. But there were no big scats to show it was Cedric's.

Through November, as the weather worsened, tracking evidence increased. A big fox began to visit our woods from the east, once leaving two droppings at a crossroads in its trails, probably signs to a vixen.

In mid-month the old wildcat den up to the north-west seemed to be newly occupied and Liane had begun to eat twice her normal food in the shed. Was she sharing it with another wildcat, perhaps old Sylvesturr? I kept watch for two nights but did not see one. Then a big fox began paying us regular visits from the north-west. It was becoming clearer that wildcats and foxes can use the same area yet avoid each other.

On a long snow-trek on November 27 we found Cedric's tracks heading north-west, and right beside them the smaller tracks of a vixen. Now we *knew* he had a mate. We tracked them for nearly a mile, to the new den above the long wood burn. In that wood we found a big dead hind, after being alerted by ravens calling in the trees above it. Sylvesturr's main den was now re-occupied, evidence that the old cuss could still be alive.

The fox visits were more frequent through December and January as more deer had died in the open. A hind carcass which had fallen into a deep natural hole remained untouched, as if the foxes distrusted the 'walls' round it and liked to see all round them when eating. The old carcass of a ewe which had died in the spring half a mile to the west, was now just shreds of wool left on the hill. All the bones had been taken by foxes, probably for the marrows. We found that the skull and some major bones had been stuffed into a deep rock crevice many yards away, as if to hide them from bird predators who rely on sight. This was my first hint that foxes will hide food in a cache.

It was on February 10 that I had my one and only personal brush with the local Hunt. I had boated out to have a rare pub drink with a friend. Several young men, all of whom went out with the foxhounds or supported the Hunt, seemed to converge on the place. There was one I did not know – the huntsman himself. My friend introduced us.

'Ah yes. I've heard of you,' he said. 'We're hunting your estate, and the next door one, next week. We'll be bringing the hounds down to your place.'

I bridled at this. They knew I did not like fox-hunting and of course I could not stop them doing it. I said that I had a young wildcat running loose, and a fine gentle dog, and I did NOT want the Hunt over my own particular piece of land. The huntsman maintained airily that once the hounds were loose it was not possible to control where they went after a fox. If a fox sought sanctuary on my own land, I assured him, then it would get it. And if the hounds ganged up on Liane or Moobli, I had a rather sharp axe with which I might loosen hounds' heads from shoulders.

The moment passed, we all had a lot of drinks, and I recall we all ended up arm wrestling on the tarmac outside, on the coldest night in the area for thirty years. Somehow the talk got round to how right it was to kill foxes, there were a few remarks, and I got really angry at the threat to bring hounds right to my remote home.

Returning from a supply trip five days later I saw outside the farmhouse a large square truck from which exuded a strong smell. It was full of foxhounds. Standing beside it were the farmer and the huntsman. They were old friends. I wondered if the story of our argument had been told. But friendly greetings were exchanged and I tried to defuse the possible situation by saying it had been a rather mad night and I couldn't recall all that was said!

'Ah well,' said the huntsman. 'At least none of us disgraced ourselves!' I must say I liked him for that.

The very next day I was writing at my desk when I was startled by the muted baying of foxhounds. I dashed out to see five of the hounds working their way along the high ridges from the west, their noses glued to the ground like vacuum cleaners. Nearer and nearer they came as I scanned the terrain. There was not a human in sight. I rushed into the cottage for the axe. If they did come down and attack Liane or Moobli I would be forced to use it. I got outside again, just in time to see a huge fox get up from a heathery ledge. It was Cedric, and he was almost as big as the hounds.

Seeming casual, not showing any signs of panic or haste, he loped along, merely thirty yards ahead of the hounds, his great white-tipped brush streaming behind him like a banner. Then he headed upwards. I dashed up too, cursing my human slowness, and was in time to see him reach the edge of the burn's deep gorge. Without a pause he made a gigantic leap and sailed into space, all four feet extended like a flying lemur. Surely he would be dashed to death. Out and out he soared, then down and down. He landed on a steep flat rock a full thirty-five feet on the far side, paused a moment as if winded, then bounded upwards and shot away between the leafless trees.

The hounds could not make the leap, one almost fell over into the chasm, and then they had to waste time running higher as if looking for a place to cross. I lost them for a minute, then saw that three of them were heading up to the peaks to the north-west, as if on a different scent. Were the other two on to him? If they were, I felt sure they would not catch Cedric. I kept watch for a while but saw no more sign of the hounds, or humans, and went back to my work. Well, I had asked for it in a way. And yet no humans could have made those hounds come so close; they had been on a genuine scent only.

In late afternoon I was throwing sticks in the front pasture to exercise Moobli when he started scenting towards the east wood. A strong acrid scent hit my nostrils too. Then out of the wood came an old bitch foxhound, huge pink teats swaying beneath her. She had been eating from the hind carcass in the deep hole, and pulled it out of its natural position. Moobli only barked once. She ran up to him, whining submissively, then reared up on to the bird table and stole the bread. I had no wish to chastise her; being hungry was not her fault. I gave her a sausage and followed her down to the west wood, fearing she might find and go for Liane. Like any good dog, Moobli would not hurt a bitch, but when she snapped at him near the gate he gave her a brief working over, as if to send her on her way to the west. At dusk another much younger bitch also came from the east wood but ran off from Moobli, tail between her legs.

I doubted that I would be seeing anything of Cedric for a while, even if the hounds had not killed or injured him. Certainly, I had heard no 'riot' noise as when a kill is made. What had impressed me most was his cunning. He had known exactly where he was going when he led the hounds to the gorge.

Four days later I had strong evidence Cedric *was* still alive. He had been at the hind carcass in the hole, had eaten much of the neck meat, and had left his huge visiting card on a mossy rock nearby. Being chased by the hounds had apparently not made him leave the area. Later I was at my truck when the part-time farm worker came by. He told me the Hunt had worked the two estates for the whole week and had accounted for four foxes. One vixen had been caught above the long wood to the west. I was fairly sure then that Cedric had lost his new mate. Four of the hounds had also been lost for days. I said that hunting in these hard hills and gorges seemed as tough on the hounds as it was on foxes. He agreed. On the previous Hunt he himself had found a hound dead from starvation, its foot caught in a fox snare.

After he left and I was carrying the supplies down to the boat Moobli and I got a strong whiff of fox. Around a huge sand hole on shore below some pine-tree roots there were many prints of a large fox. From Moobli's behaviour I reckoned it was still in there. It had probably been driven into the hole after escaping the hounds. I stamped out all the tracks.

For two days Cedric did not visit the hind carcass. Its flesh was decaying and perhaps was now too rotten, even for a fox. Then we found a dying stag calf in the wood. I removed its haunches and dragged it to the cottage, to be hauled up into the hills later for the local eagles. To see if I could actually get Cedric into it, I carried the big live cage trap over to the hind carcass, tied in fresh bait meat and wedged the trapdoor to prevent it falling. I wore gloves simmered in pine-needle juice.

The next day I found that Cedric had entered it, for his scent was strong, but cunningly he had turned the nylon line holding the meat round a bar so that he could chew at it without exerting any pressure on the line. Well, I could outsmart him by shortening the line. I realised then that I had no real wish to catch and imprison him, even for close-up photos, for once I let him go again he would take off and probably never come back. What I really wanted were natural photos, taken in the wild.

Where was he living? We checked the labyrinth dens to the north-west. He had been there recently. There were two big scats on the outer rocks, but to judge from Moobli's scenting actions he was not in them now. On long treks we found the buttress den above the lochan four miles to the north-west was now unused; so was the sandy hole den where I had pulled in my boat, and also the den above the long wood burn. This was further evidence that the vixen had been killed. On March 3 I found the big fox had shifted from the refuge sand cave below my truck and had moved into last year's badger holes half a mile away, fifty yards above the main badger sett on shore which was still occupied. Sandy earth had been freshly dug out of one of them and Moobli got strong fox scent. As this was near where the Devon fox squeakers had operated with the farmer, that fox was living dangerously.

Next day the calf carcass I had hauled up for eagles had been opened up. Moobli scented about, cocking his leg as usual for fox, then headed west. I decided not to urge him, just to let him go. He zigzagged through the heather and tussocks, turned east, then north, finally west again, leading me slowly but surely towards the highest north-west rockface, which had a huge old rowan tree growing before it. He sniffed about, climbed the almost sheer grassy shelves near the face, then stopped, sniffing and whining slightly. I climbed up the main boulders, looked over their tops, below Moobli. There in front of me was Cedric's new den: a flat-ledge rock covered in wood rush and a V-shaped fissure in the cliff. The moss at the entrance was all worn down. Bits of deer skin and hair lay about and the fissure was as dry as a bone. To reach this den Cedric had to climb up where Moobli had then jump five feet down on to the wood rush and turn right into the fissure. A perfect den, quite invisible from below the face. We had found the nearest of Cedric's main homes at last.

And way to the east of the face Moobli scented out one of Cedric's main caches – a hind's skull and many bones stuffed into a crevice, the grasses all worn down round it.

For many days I kept watch with the camera but not a glimpse of the big fox did I get. One night I went out with a powerful torch, to see orangey-red light reflected from a pair of eyes near the calf carcass. A fox's eyeshine is normally light green but as I had found with deer and Moobli if the light came at an angle, from the side or below, the colour changed to this orange-red. Certainly there were no white stripes of a badger to be seen in the beam.

On a trek to the east we found a medium fox scat laid over one of Moobli's old droppings, and a larger scat not far from it. The fox den at the end of the river valley was now unused. Well, in spite of the hounds there still seemed to be three lots of foxes in the nine by four miles I was studying for them. On April 2 we found the fox from above the badger sett to the west had been at a hind carcass almost a mile up in the hills above it.

A few days later I called on Greg Hunter, but he was not at home. On his lawn were a dead fox and a dead hooded crow tied together. When he returned he had a forestry ranger from the south with him. He said it was sometimes necessary to *show* the locals he was doing his vermin killing job. They had shot three hoodies from a van.

'When you pull up normally, hoodies fly off,' said the ranger. 'But when there's two of you and one drives while the other shoots from the van, they haven't worked that one out yet!' He said hoodies sometimes ganged up on weak sick lambs, and also pulled the tongues from ewes that had rolled on to their backs. I had heard this before but in eight years in the Highlands had never seen either occur.

Although the hooded crow is common in the Highlands, it is not found south of Loch Lomond. Worldwide, it is a relatively rare bird.

We had one of our good-natured, lambasting arguments about hunting. I said that although I had done it for years as a youth, I now disliked killing for sport and getting pleasure from it. Some lads who liked it seemed to have inferiority complexes too, needed to prove something as men. To some there was nothing so ego-restoring as assuming the attributes of God, taking or ending a life, being master of what lives and what dies. Killing for sport was really a schoolboy pastime, I persisted too vehemently, often pursued by folk who at heart were spiritually bereft. But killing for intelligent control, for conservation of a species that was outgrowing its range, was a job for men of real understanding, who did it with genuine regret, who really knew their herd populations, men of love in fact. And killing for necessary food was all right, and in accord with natural laws.

They smiled, partly agreed, then added the point that keen hunters *did* know populations and, because they liked shooting, made *sure* that numbers remained high. That was the whole concept of keepering, after all, and without it indiscriminate killing by poachers and amateurs of all kinds would increase. They had a point. On my way home I met the farm worker, who told me that the Hunt had lost two more hounds around Loch Morar recently, both to illegal poisons set out on the Hill.

At a wildlife slide show I gave in early May to a factor, who had given me permission to look on his estate for eagles, and two of my hide helpers and some locals, I maintained that farmers, conservationists, keepers, fishermen, crofters and stalkers and tourists all looked at the Highlands from narrow individual points of view. The best conservationist was one who saw the whole as a plan. Farmers were often criticised for destroying wildlife habitats, yet on my own neighbour's newly-ploughed fields, now fertile manured land, I had seen more gulls, redwings, fieldfares, curlews, oyster catchers and other birds than on the poor acid soil and natural herbage of the surrounding terrain, by far the most of which was left undisturbed anyway. Someone remarked that he was not a supporter of fox-hunting for the hounds harried more foxes than they caught, and disturbed other nesting wildlife at the same time. In the old days keepers held their jobs longer, he went on, often for a lifetime, knew where all the fox families were, kept them under control regularly with traps and terriers at the dens. There were far more people *and* wildlife in the Highlands in those days too – grouse, hares, eagles, wildcats, pine martens, foxes, buzzards – as the estate game lists conclusively prove.

Suddenly I had the first inkling that sporadic irregular hunting also broke up the dominant resident fox groups which, through territorial behaviour (the weak do not survive), also exerted control on their *own* numbers. Under sporadic hunting, surplus foxes from unhunted areas moved into the hunting grounds, where they tended to attack more sheep due to a lack of knowledge of the best places to find wild prey. I decided to work harder over the years to secure evidence that would shine more light on these theories.

In mid-May I telephoned Richard Balharry, then the Nature Conservancy Council's Chief Warden for north-west Scotland, who made me an offer I could not refuse.

'Do you want a young fox?' he asked. 'I'm starting a small study project on foxes. I have already got a vixen and I want to find a male. I can let you have the vixen cub, a beautiful animal. The only trouble is she has an injured paw after being caught in a trap, though it's healed over nicely now. Would you like her?'

PART TWO

5 · *First of the Trapped Vixens*

I boated up the loch with Moobli and a newly-scrubbed den box, and drove to the Balharry home. Dick had been called to Shetland, but his wife Adeline gave me a cup of tea and a snack. Then their son David took me to the enclosure to collect the fox.

'Her name is Aspen, and she is very shy,' David told me.

It was true. While the larger vixen, about a month older and paler in colour, frisked about and watched us with bright orange eyes, Aspen crept timidly, furtively, into a hiding place between two logs.

David took hold of her thick brush and rear legs, gently hauled her out and handed her to me. As I put my left hand under her chest and my right over her shoulders, I could feel her heart thudding with fear. She struggled a little but made no attempt to bite. She was a lovely chubby little creature with thick lustrous dark-auburn fur, and she had a big white tip on her tail. Across the top of her right front paw was a livid white scar where the trap had got her. It had healed now and all the claws were there. We put her carefully into the den box with some food, then set the box on the front seat of my truck. Her eyes, brown at this stage, switched about watching all my movements, showing whites at their edges. When Moobli put his head over the seat to sniff close, she snapped at him and he withdrew quickly. When I put my hand near, for her to sniff, she snapped at that too. She would not be easy to tame.

We camped out overnight, for just a few hours' sleep, then boated her home. Quickly I made a makeshift pen in a corner of the kitchen and put her in it. All my movements had to be slow or she spat like a cat and dashed about. When I put the den box in she darted inside and stayed there.

Next morning I was worried because she had not touched any of the meats or milk. It took nearly an hour to slide one hand behind her and coax and ease her out. Once she made a symbolic bite at my fingers but I felt no teeth, just a soft snap as from a duck's beak. I lifted her out, set her on my lap and spent a long time talking soothingly to her, telling her she was safe, constantly stroking her fur. I noticed that her thick black whiskers were longer than any cat's. Gently I examined her injured paw. It was swollen into a club shape and some of the toe bones had congealed rather than healed properly, for they did not have the same capability of movement as those in the other front foot. As her elfin face, topped by its two huge stiff ears, stared into mine I thought that if those who put down snares and traps could see her at that moment they might have second thoughts.

I held milk out to her in a green saucer. She sniffed, black pointed nose trembling, then to my delight began to lap it up, until she had drunk a quarter of a lamb's bottleful. I put her back in the run. She sniffed about, picked up a piece of bread, dropped it again, sniffed at the meat, then to my relief began taking pieces of meat over to the wall to eat, furtive in every movement. I hoped then she would be all right.

My plan was to leave her in the kitchen for a few days, so that she could get used to Moobli and myself, then to take her for walks round the 'territory' on a collar and lead. I wanted her to run free around the cottage like a dog, but if she ran away the hounds would almost certainly get her if they returned this way. In due course she could have as her main home one of the old wildcat pens which Liane seldom used now.

Over the next few days I attempted to tame Aspen. Once she scrambled up the chimney and stayed on a ledge. As I tried to lift her down she bit my hand but not hard enough to pierce the skin. I soothed her, wiped her clean and by constant stroking, talking gently, caressing her, *showing* human love to her in the way I had tamed the wildcat Liane as a kitten, attempted to gain her trust. I wanted her to feel that love. When she was hungry or thirsty, I held food or milk out to her so that she had to come forward to take them, had to come close of her own free will.

She liked being held upside down on my lap and having her tummy tickled. Her eyes would half close and twinkle then, and she made frothy bubbles in her mouth. If I sat down with legs straight out, she would come forward furtively and nibble my boots, her eyes never leaving my face. She watched a rolling ball with interest, touched it with her nose but never picked it up like a dog. When I held out rolled-up newspaper, she sniffed it, then seized it in her teeth and began to pull. She came to like, and expect, a tug-of-war every day. Once she vanished behind the far slab leg of my kitchen table, then shyly peeped out to see if I was still there. Slowly I slid behind the other leg and peeped out at her in exactly the same way. When I slid back, she peeped out again, wanting to know where I had gone. When I emerged, she dodged behind her slab again. This became a regular game of hide and seek.

On the fifth day I put a broad leather collar and long lead on her and took her outside. Immediately she bounced about like a hare, pulling with exceptional strength for an animal her size, and tried to burrow through and between grasses, rushes and brambles. While it was fine exercise, making her strong, it was arousing her wild instincts too early and I kept her in the kitchen a few more days.

Sometimes, if she had fed well, she would eat nothing the next day. This must happen in the wild, especially if the parents do not find food. Once, when I found a mouse Liane had caught, I tied nylon line round its neck and jerked it about but Aspen would not chase it. When I removed the line, however, she ate it fast. Soon she took to burrowing. She dug her way under the hearth, tearing away sticks and logs with surprising strength. Then it was difficult to get her out, even by tugging her collar, as her large head kept getting stuck, but she remained passive as I cleaned her up. I did not wash her with water, for fear she might catch cold, but blew out the dust and ashes, while combing the fur. She burrowed under papers, and the cardboard covering a gap under my old cooker, tearing away with both front feet like a furious boxer, looking round every now and again to see if I, danger, was still there. She picked up wads of paper in her mouth and shook them like a little dog.

When I next took Aspen out, she again ran to the end of the long rope and bounded up and down like a little kangaroo, pausing to look at me now and then. Afterwards she sat down with open mouth panting, showing her long pink tongue. I noticed she yawned a lot when puzzled or unsure what to do. I sat down and kept still a long time. Slowly she crept forward, keeping low in the grass, sniffed at my boots, then jerked her head back as if she had been stung. After that she kept sitting down, but not at the end of the tether, and gradually I hauled in the slack until she was only two feet away. Moving slowly, I lifted her on to my lap, stroked her soft head where it lay draped over one knee, and then let go of her. She stayed there for a while, not realising she was free. When she did, she bounded away again. She still felt scared sometimes when I picked her up; her ears went back, though not as far as a wildcat's, and she opened her mouth, but she made no sound, nor did she bite. I also noticed that she did not like mutton. She would just give it a nip or two before dropping it. She greedily ate minced beef or ox hearts but not lamb flank, the cheapest cut of all. Here was a fox that actually disliked sheep meat! She only ate it if there was nothing else. Sometimes she covered meat up with hay, pushing it over with her nose, as if keeping a food cache. She had little body odour; nor did her droppings smell strongly. Usually she urinated on a sawdust pile provided for the purpose. She was easier to house-train than any of the wildcats were as kittens.

One evening I brought her into my study-bedroom. She was immediately curious about the new surroundings, looking at the desk, the bed, the things on the bed, the ceiling, always with sly glances back at me. If she headed for dark places a slight tug on the line made her sit down with a flump. Next evening I took in Moobli too, telling him not to hurt her, for they would have to become friends if she was to run free about the place one day. Good as gold he sat down, but when his head went near, to sniff her, her ears went back, she glared and made a weak '*bic*' spit at him, snapping her jaws. Moobli whined with a hurt look on his face and withdrew his head again. Once she jumped on to the bed and stretched upwards, seeming all long legs, and when she craned her neck over its edge, her tail straight out behind, her body elongated so she looked like a beautiful long slim arrow. I put her on my desk. When I stopped stroking her she crept over the desk top and jumped into a box of soft files. She found it a natural cup and lay looking at me for over an hour as I typed, her head resting on its rim. Every time I looked up it was to see her sleepy eyes gazing into mine. She would now take meat from my hand, approaching gingerly to snap it up, then backing up to eat it a few feet away.

The next time I brought Aspen into the study she charged about, scraped the firewood logs over the floor and dug up the carpet. She even tried to burrow through the concrete floor, her rear legs wide apart through which to throw the earth – if there had been any. This time, when I brought Moobli in, her reaction was different. She stretched her neck curiously, wandered towards him, ready to flee at a split second's notice. When he extended his nose to greet her's she opened her mouth like a great long beak and tried to nip his lip. Knowing I wanted him to accept her, Moobli just moved his head out of the way. Later, when he was lying near the bed and she was under it, she sneaked up to him and sniffed the whole length of his body. It was then she seemed to decide that he was not just a big fox but a *dog*, and all her wild instincts came up. She actually went to attack the giant, barked at his swiftly withdrawn head, then tried to nip his feet and jaw, but Moobli drew his feet in and dodged her easily.

It was interesting to see that once she found he was passive, instead of thinking of him as a kind and harmless animal, she went on the attack, assaulting weakness, taking the predator's role. The fact that he could have ended her life with one swift chop apparently escaped her mind once she felt sure he would not assault her. She soon tired of that game, however, and lay with her head on her paws, which were turned outwards, looking first at Moobli and then back at me, as if trying to work out why two such traditional enemies were being so friendly.

I was now sure that Moobli would not hurt her and began to leave her outside on a rope tied to the bird table, so that she could run fifteen yards in any direction. She was still scared of

Moobli, yet was also intensely fascinated by him, and nearly always went up to him first. He began to play with her, running up and down as she snapped at him, boxing her gently with his paws and easily dodging her bites, which seemed to be made without serious intent to inflict injury.

One day, as I worked at my desk, and Moobli lay dozing on his mat in the open porch, I discovered that while the dog had accepted the fox, Liane the wildcat certainly had not. Usually she spent her days sleeping in her haybox in the shed or basking in the sunshine atop her old den in the pens. If she saw the fox out at all during the day, I presumed she would give it a wide berth, or just ignore it. As I glanced out of the window to see Aspen digging out a shallow hole in which to lie, I heard a strange rumbling noise.

There, below the window, was Liane, her black-banded tail fluffed up to some three inches thick, her eyes like black billiard balls, the hairs along her back bristling. She was growling loud enough for me to hear her through the closed window. As I sat motionless in my chair, the wildcat stalked towards the fox with an odd stiff-legged sideways gait, ears back and mouth open showing her fangs, and from about forty yards away leaped into the attack so fast that she appeared as just a blur.

She bowled the fox right over. Clutching it round the body with her front claws, Liane bit hard into the neck and in a flash was away again. Oddly enough, the young fox seemed little put out by the assault, as if it had been merely a rougher version of what big cubs do to each other in the course of play. The fox picked itself up and started to walk towards Liane, sniffing, as if trying to catch the scent of this strange new creature. The wildcat, however, was clearly not playing, and was preparing herself for another attack. Afraid the fox would lose an eye, I opened the window fast and frightened Liane off with a loud hiss. She stopped briefly to look at me with surprise just as Moobli ran out of the porch to see what was going on. My hisses and the sudden appearance of the dog were enough to scare Liane back to the shed.

I rushed out. Luckily Aspen was unhurt, with not so much as a scratch on her. The incident seemed also to make her tamer, for she just hunched down passively when I went to pick her up.

Clearly wildcats regard foxes as enemies. What surprised me was that Liane had come round from the shed deliberately to launch the attack when there was no real necessity. The fox had shown no indication of attacking her. Perhaps the wildcat did not like a fox being on 'her' territory. Certainly she had shown no fear of it, even though it weighed 7 lbs, and was roughly the same weight and size as herself. From then on I kept a close watch for the wildcat whenever the fox was out on her lead. I was sure the wildcat would soon learn that the fox was not to be assaulted, and would come to accept her as part of the family.

Somehow the incident made Aspen more trusting towards Moobli, as if she felt he had protected her. When both were outside again the next day, I was delighted to see that when he approached her, sniffing, she just extended her pointed muzzle upwards like a needle, and when he went even closer, far from snapping, she bowed her head and kept her brush down while he drooled all over her! After that she often ran towards him and let him lick her, as if he were her father. She also took to running between his legs while he was walking as if playfully to trip him up. Even so, she needed constant watching. Three times on one day I saw her line taut and twitching and each time I went out I found she had leaped over the porch logs and was dangling on the inner side by her neck, but not as yet choking. For the first time I realised what very strong thick necks foxes have for their size. Also that this fox, at least, was slow to learn.

As she seemed to want a run I undid her line at the post. Immediately she dashed off to the east and into the tangle of a rhododendron bush, where the line got caught up again. When Moobli crashed through the bush trying to find her, she spat loud '*bicks*' at him, as wild and obdurate as if she had never seen him before. Yet when I picked her up she immediately calmed down again, after one attempt to bite. Within minutes of retying her line to the post, a common gull from the colony on the nearest islet flew over and twice dived down to mob her with loud cries. It clearly recognised the fox as an enemy, even though the islet was a quarter-mile away. Aspen seemed perplexed, as if unable to see the gull and so work out where the shrieks were coming from. Again she ran to Moobli as if for protection, lowering her head submissively so he could nuzzle

61

and lick her. This seemed good progress in the process of taming her.

This process ended abruptly the very next day, June 14. I looked up from my desk to see that Aspen had gone, taking with her the long line which had somehow come undone at the post. At first I was not worried, sure the line would soon become caught up in the herbage. For three hours I searched with Moobli but could not find her. Well, she should be all right for one night at least, I thought. She had eaten well that morning.

We searched the eastern bay area next day and all the woods beyond it for over half a mile. Moobli picked up scent and ran about but seemed unable to find a conclusive trail. While he had tolerated her well when I was present, maybe he was also a little jealous and did not want to find her. I shut Liane in the pens and set food out in both woods.

By the following morning none of the food had been taken and another search yielded nothing. I suffered agonising mental images of Aspen caught up somewhere by her collar and line and starving, or even strangling to death. I had failed her.

On June 19, sure she would now be dead, I took Moobli to hunt the hill to the north and down to the shore westwards. He suddenly ran off into the west wood and eventually I found him with his head low down in a nearly dry burn bed. He seemed a long time taking a drink. I went over. There was Aspen's line and collar – empty! The line had snagged up in a deep tunnel of pine roots carved out by the burn and had come out again. The ground round the collar was scuffed up where she had struggled to get free. Somehow the collar pin had been forced through the far side of the buckle. It would have taken great strength to do that, but I felt enormous relief that she was free of the dangerous line and collar.

Moobli tracked her scent across the bottom of the wood and to a great tangle of gnarled mossy boulders under which my first brood of wildcats had made a den two years before. From his behaviour it seemed likely that Aspen was in there now. There were many frogs about and three young flew out from a wren's nest above the rocks. Not many for a wren; maybe Aspen had taken one or two of them earlier. I carried the live cage trap down, set it and laid a trail of meat scraps from the rocks to the trap. The food I had set out earlier by this time was gone.

It was then that we found a huge fox scat, far too large to be Aspen's, on a flat mossy rock not far from the den. It was clearly one of Cedric's. It then occurred to me he must have scented Aspen, heard her struggles, and had actually helped her escape. Certainly the forcing of the collar pin to the wrong side of the buckle would have been beyond Aspen's strength alone. I was almost certain Cedric no longer had a mate, and Aspen was a lovely young vixen. It was a long time, however, before I gained clear evidence for the wild hope that now sprang into my mind.

I wanted to catch Aspen just to check she was not injured, but over the next few days the meat in the trap remained untouched. Later the meat was taken but the trap failed to work. I removed it. I had a strong feeling that Aspen *was* being looked after by Cedric. I then had another reason for not trapping her back.

I rang Dick Balharry to give him the news. He told me he had now been appointed Chief Warden of north-east Scotland and so had to move. He had bought an old mill in the country outside Aberdeen, which required a good deal of renovation, and therefore had no more time for his fox project. He had three foxes left. Would I like these too?

On July 1 I drove over again to Newtonmore. These three foxes were much wilder than Aspen had been, and David showed great bravery in catching them and handing them to me to put into den boxes. Two were small vixens, red-brown but not as dark as Aspen, one of which had a white tail tip. They shot about the enclosure like monkeys but did not bite when picked up. The other was much bigger, also a vixen and of a light sandy colour, what is known in hunting parlance as a 'burnt fox'. David told me she was tamer than the other two, but she bit him three times nevertheless, probably nervous after seeing the other two put into their box.

'I lose confidence when I get bitten a few times,' David gasped as he handed her to me.

'So do I!' I replied.

I got one hand on her neck and held her long muzzle closed with the other as I transferred her to a box on her own. Like

Aspen, all three had been caught in traps by one foot and had the same livid scars. They had been kept alive by men who respected Dick for his fox project. Dick said they were not the kind of men to take such cubs home, and put them in a pen with a young terrier so as to train it to kill foxes that way. But a few such men still existed. We agreed it does no good for the conservationist to be militant or hostile but to be diplomatic and help change the old ideas by writings, giving talks, setting an example, influencing the young, and by precise research and presenting the evidence truly. I did not tarry long, however, for I wanted to get the foxes to their new home before dark.

I boated up my home loch and put the two smaller vixens into the wildcat pens with some food, and installed the big sandy one in Aspen's old pen in the kitchen. She looked all around, noting her new surroundings with intelligence. Then she lay deep in the hay quietly watching my movements as I cooked supper. She did not eat anything until I had gone to bed.

What to call them? I had a big vixen, a medium-sized vixen and a little vixen. The names then suggested themselves from these initials – BV, MV and LV – and naturally became Bevy, the big sandy one; Emvy, the medium one with a white flash to her tail; and Elvy, the smallest.

After hearing low growls below my study window, I looked out to see wildcat Liane glaring at Aspen. Liane stalked slowly towards the young fox and, to my surprise, launched into the attack, clearly not wanting the fox on her territory. Aspen was not hurt or upset, but later went sniffing towards Liane as if she was just a boisterous playmate.

Bevy, the largest and most dominant of the young vixens, was tame towards me, but hated Moobli. Every time he came near she tried to attack him. He fended her off easily and never retaliated.

The foxes often had playful mock battles, making high yickering squeaks, like big mice. Elvy would haul Emvy closer by tugging her lead.

above: Sometimes a dominant vixen clambered backwards up a subordinate vixen to anoint its head with scent. Here, the scent drops are exuding from Elvy's rear glands, anointing Emvy.

below: After her escape Aspen occasionally returned to visit the other foxes. Here she lies doggo in the grasses, believing we cannot see her as we pass by.

6 · My Little Foxes

Right from the start the foxes revealed quite different characters. When I went in next morning Bevy greeted me with deep '*urm urm*' noises in her throat, then snapped '*keck*' when I went closer, her ears down like a cat. For several minutes I tried to soothe her, but when my hand went near to pick her up, she slashed at it with her teeth. In the end I covered her with a sack, got a collar and line on her, then tied her outside as I had Aspen. She ran this way and that, soon learned the length of the line after tugging furiously at it with her teeth, and walked about on tiptoe on her two rear legs trying to peer over the herbage. She scrabbled furiously at the ground as if trying to burrow but made very little impression on it. Within two hours she calmed down.

By talking to her (she seemed to like the word sounds) I could stroke her neck easily and even pick her up without her making any attempt to bite. When she saw Moobli again, however, she gave a hiss like a small sheep, a sound that appeared to be made through the nose. She also made a sharp '*raowl*' sound, which I had learned from Aspen was an instinctive call of warning.

As soon as she made this latter bark the smallest vixen, Elvy, came to the front of the pens and yapped back at her like a little dog. Elvy soon proved to be the most outgoing of the three, constantly running about the pens, tugging at the fencing, sniffing the air. Emvy was far more furtive, and lay sullenly in

65

the grasses watching my every movement. Each time I approached the pen both foxes darted behind the rocks of the den, constantly keeping them between me and themselves, with just their eyes and long ears showing. To my surprise they did not use the actual den but hauled all the dry bracken I had stuffed between its top and an aluminium roof to keep the den warm, and slept there. It was as if they wanted to see all round them at all times.

When I went into the pens to catch Elvy, she kept bouncing high into the air, giving high-pitched '*raaark raaark*' squawks as she evaded my clutch. When eventually I caught her, she immediately went passive. She never tried to bite me. I set her out on a collar too. She straight away dashed to the full extent of the line and was switched round by the collar on her neck. Again I realised how strong foxes' necks were, for she did this every time I suddenly appeared, never seeming to learn what would happen, and yet never seeming bothered by the sudden arrest to her flight. Although she ran with a pronounced limp, she could still pull like a little bulldozer. She immediately accepted Moobli; in fact she ran *to* him when I came out.

Bevy was different. She hated Moobli on sight and never learned to tolerate him. As soon as he nosed near out of friendly interest, or just went past yards away, she would arch her back like a cat, put her ears back and give the low '*urm*' moan of protest. Often she launched herself straight at him, snapping at his muzzle and feet. This would never do; a proper order had to be established between them. I was sure that Moobli knew I wanted the foxes, that he would not hurt a much smaller animal, especially a female, so I decided to let them work it out. Time and again Bevy threw herself at him, but he just boxed her off with his paws. He jerked his head away with reflexes Muhammed Ali would have envied, fended her off with shoulder bunts, so that she bounded off him, or pinned her down temporarily with a giant paw. To him it was all a huge joke, but she was in deadly earnest. It was amazing to see her courage and stamina. She picked herself up again and again, hurling herself at him, refusing to give up or submit to any establishment of a 'pecking order', although at 7½ lbs she was barely a fifteenth of his weight. In the end I ordered him away, before she dropped from sheer exhaustion.

If Bevy was tired she gave no sign of it. As soon as we went indoors she tried to stop Elvy eating a piece of meat, then kept trying to mount her as if she were a male fox, often backwards! After a short rest, she decided she wanted to play with Elvy, but because the smaller fox was on a longer lead could not reach her. To resolve this, she grabbed Elvy's rope in her teeth and hauled her nearer, and repeated this several times! Elvy weighed just 5 lbs, and Emvy just over 5½ lbs.

When I went to catch Emvy, she again behaved slightly differently from the others. She crouched down and opened her jaws wide like a beak, but neither bit nor made a sound. If I picked her up, however, she fought with amazing strength with her *feet*, always getting the claws of one of her rear feet in the palm of the hand that held her neck. They hurt too. And her orange eyes bulged like those of a giant woodmouse. I carried her out and set her on a third collar and line with the others.

I spent hours through July watching the little foxes together. If Moobli and I were both in the cottage, and they saw me at my desk by the window, they came to know we would not go outside again for a long while and behaved naturally. They ran about like dancers round a maypole, sometimes entangling and even plaiting their three lines together. I would have to go out again and untangle them. When I did this both Elvy and Emvy ran to the ends of their lines, but Bevy always stopped short, sat down and looked back.

They played like kittens, boxing each other with forepaws and making loud high yickerings, gnawing each other's muzzles, ambushing and jumping on each other from shallow holes they dug, apparently for the coolness the earth gave their bellies. Bevy constantly mounted Elvy, climbing on to her back, but never making the mating movements of a male. And Elvy kept clambering on top of Emvy, who never tried to do it back to her. I noticed particularly that Bevy never mounted Emvy. It was clearly a way of showing superiority – Bevy could dominate Elvy and Elvy could dominate Emvy. Often Elvy climbed backwards up Emvy, clinging on to her like a monkey, so that the slightly larger vixen appeared to have sprouted a hat, a hat composed of Elvy's rude backside and a thick uptilted brush! Not once did I see Emvy object to this, yet Elvy sometimes yickered and mewed in protest at Bevy if the sandy vixen mounted her too often. Although Emvy was slightly bigger and even stronger than Elvy, she was more shy and introverted.

It was some time before I fully understood this mounting behaviour. One day I saw some whitish drops spilling on to Emvy's head from the anal scent glands under Elvy's tail. The dominant foxes were anointing the one directly below them in order with the scent. It is well known that badgers do this so that they can confirm by smell which badger belongs to the family; I had not known that foxes do it too. I went out, picked up Emvy and sniffed her head. The smell was sweet, sickly, rather like burnt bog myrtle, the typical fox smell.

The dominant vixen theory was further confirmed when I put all three into the pens. After a while Bevy went into the den proper, scented about, flumped down and stayed there. The other two, who had not used the den before, then followed and lay down beside her. They also followed Bevy about; when she tugged at the fencing with her teeth, they did so too. They copied many of her actions, such as the way Bevy would pick up a rabbit skull and run round with it. The other two picked up bones and trotted about with them too. Sometimes they swapped bones, running up to each other, letting them fall, then each picking up the bone the other had carried before trotting round again. I never saw them fight over food. Each fox would take a piece of meat and then go a few paces away to eat it.

One day at dusk Moobli went on the alert, and I saw Elvy on top of the aluminium roof, as if keeping a lookout. I told Moobli to go ahead, and he set off up the north hill. Just then there was a movement on the first ridge above and I saw the rear end of a small dark fox with a white tail flash disappearing through the heather. It was clearly Aspen, who had probably come back after scenting the other foxes. I put some food up there for her. It was good to know she was all right.

I had to go out for the night of July 5. Afraid the foxes might escape, I caught both Bevy and Elvy and put them in the kitchen with food. To avoid upsetting them with prolonged pursuit in the pens, I waited until they had gone through the hole into the old fox pen at the end of the main enclosure, then set a rope snare over the hole and chased them back through it. The rope, too thick to bite into their necks, held them until I could get in and pick them up. In case Emvy also escaped, I put her on a collar and line but left her in the pens.

When I got back the following evening, the two foxes in the kitchen were fine but the room was smelly from their scats. I opened the window, which was extremely stiff, just an inch and set its latch. I found that Emvy had somehow undone the knot on her collar. Next morning the kitchen was empty. Bevy and Elvy had escaped. Bevy, the stronger, must have lifted the hefty brass latch and forced the stiff window open. I was now finding out that the escape abilities of foxes are horrendous, far more advanced than those of wildcats.

I never thought I would see them again, but after four days of tracking with Moobli we got them back, Moobli holding them at bay in the bracken until I could grab their necks and tails and carry each one home. As soon as all were back together they played around as if the two had never been away. At dusk that evening I found Liane on the pens' roof, growling as if prepared to have a go at all three of them! I ticked her off and fed her as usual in the woodshed. She had not put in an appearance when all the foxes were out on their 'maypole' lines during the daytime, but came through the window for a cuddle shortly after dark.

Slowly I learned more about fox behaviour. They always located food first by scent, then by sight. Hearing was highly developed, clearly as important as sight, especially when danger approached from downwind when scenting was not possible. They seemed to hear my approach first, then confirmed it by sight. Bevy still greeted Moobli's appearance with puffed cheeks, explosive snorts, the low '*urm*' sound and, when he got closer, a loud spit, which I now noticed was more a '*kek*' than a '*bick*'. She also gave a throaty '*rar*' or '*raowl*' call which again seemed a warning to the other two. She was cleverer than them too. It took only seven times for her to work out that if she ran into the fox pen she would be trapped in the rope snare. I then had to catch her by coaxing talk and a slow approach. The other two never learned. While I could have tamed Bevy easily on my own, her hatred of Moobli prevented it fully. Elvy would have been the next easiest, but Emvy remained obdurate. Taming

69

foxes which had been caught in traps and thus had experienced rough treatment from man was as hard as taming young wild-cats. And three were harder than one. If only I had got them before their eyes had opened.

When I got back from an eagle trek in mid-July I found Bevy trying to pull the pens' fencing loose. She grabbed the thick plastic-coated wires with her rear molars and tugged and tugged with strong jerks. She seemed to work in definite sessions, resting every few minutes before having another go. And sitting by, watching her like little Colditz tunnellers, and also having a tug now and then, were Elvy and Emvy. They watched the master cracksman at work, then copied her actions. I was sure the fencing would hold and she would tire of it.

At dusk I went out with their food. Bevy had gone! She had wrenched one wire straight, had made a small hole and had escaped through it. Moobli tried to track her but could not seem to get any scent. I repaired the fencing, hoping she would return if she could not find food. That night I heard a fox barking in the hills to the north.

Each day I took the remaining two foxes out on their leads for walks to see if they would establish a territory once they got used to the area. Walks? They were more like mutual tugging sessions. In the end I decided it was a goofy idea, for they did not behave naturally. The days passed. Bevy did not return, although once Moobli showed interest in the ridges to the north. I just hoped she was making out all right. At least there were plenty of frogs, lizards and beetles about.

Nine days after Bevy's escape I was woken at dawn by loud thumps from the woodshed area. I crept out, naked but for a sweater and boots, and Moobli dashed to the gap between the shed and the cottage. I was just in time to see an animal dart into the shed through Liane's hole. I opened the door. There was Bevy, lying below Liane's haybox; Liane herself was sitting on the logpile at the far end with half-closed eyes, not looking at all angry, which was odd. Bevy let me pick her up easily, without protest. She was terribly thin, the ridges of her spine prominent. I carried her into the kitchen after shutting Moobli in the study. She had lost 1¾ lbs. Although obviously hungry, she refused to eat in the kitchen. I set her out on collar and line and, once she was sure the dog was not about, she ate like a little wolf. Then she lay in the sun, flat on her belly with her hind legs sticking straight out behind.

After two hours I put her back in the pens. The others accepted her easily, and soon all three lay asleep in the den. Later, because I knew the others would eat all the food and because she was shaking slightly, I brought her back into the kitchen. She ate and drank some more, then went to sleep.

To try and find out where she had been, I went out with Moobli and back-tracked her up the north hill, over the burn, then back across it again to the north-west. We found one scat near an old decayed deer carcass which she had clearly chewed at briefly for there were hairs in it, and also mud which meant she had found a few worms, and some dor-beetle wing-cases. She would not have lasted much longer on such fare and I was glad, despite her dislike for Moobli, that she had finally returned.

Next day I had arranged to meet a friend and stay out overnight. Bevy was weak on her feet, her eyes slightly sunken. I found a small wound on her inner right thigh. I doctored it with TCP, cuddled and stroked her a while, left her in the kitchen with milk, cheese, meat and eggs, and boated out.

When I returned the following afternoon, most of the food was untouched and Bevy was dead, her body still warm. I held it sadly, realising the wound must have been worse than I had thought, that blood poisoning had set in. I felt awful, that I had failed her. Then I recalled the fox barkings on the night she had escaped. Could she have been attacked by one of the resident foxes, maybe Aspen herself? Or perhaps even by Aspen *and* Cedric. Our trackings had already revealed that foxes are extremely territorial animals, except towards members of their own family. Thus, to some extent they control their own numbers. Weakened by days of hunger, Bevy would have been no match for a dominant resident fox successfully living in the wild. I laid her to rest near the west wood.

The theory that she had been attacked by another fox, or foxes, was confirmed three days later. At 1,400 feet, on a trek to check an eaglet was flying safely from an eyrie far to the north, I found some tufts of white-flecked sandy hair. They were certainly from Bevy's distinctive fur. And there were three big fox scats in the area. Poor Bevy had been a mile above the cottage when she had been attacked.

When we returned I fed Elvy and Emvy like fighting cocks. As usual with excess food, they buried the left-overs under hay. On August 7 we had our first encounter with Aspen in the wild. We had just landed the boat when Moobli did two of his 'huff' jumps, and I felt sure some animal was in the woods. I told him to go on. He tracked up through the north-hill bracken as I chased after him, turned east and then back along the top of the burn. I kept on the edge of the sloping gorge, when suddenly – *plop*. I looked down and there was Aspen in the burn. I saw her come up after being totally submerged, climb out on the far side and disappear in the herbage. We went down the almost sheer ground, Moobli following the scent. But he could get none on the far side. Obviously Aspen had de-scented herself by her plunge into the pool. It seemed clear she had come to visit our foxes. I later took one of Moobli's big sausages up to the spot, in case she was hungry.

Now we had a problem. I had to go to London, to get films processed, visit publishers and do vital biological research for my eagle book* at London Zoo's library. I could not release Elvy and Emvy on my neighbouring farmer's land, especially after what had happened to Bevy. For the same reason I could not release them on the vast sheepless forestry ground on the far side of the loch, for I often heard foxes barking there too. They would have to come with me.

I telephoned friends in London who earlier had offered me their beautiful flat on the Regent's Park canal, near the Zoo. They told me that the flat had a huge balcony overlooking the canal and that if I made a suitable pen the foxes would be quite welcome to live on it during my stay! I made a portable fourteen-foot by four-foot pen, and with that and the foxes in the best den box, boated out on August 9. I left a huge supply of cooked and sterilised meats for Liane in the shed. (She was catching most of her own food by this time.) My friend at the farm agreed to boat down once a week to see that she was all right, and also to let in three friends from Edinburgh who wanted to stay at Wildernesse

Golden Eagle Years

for a weekend. I camped overnight in a wood near Wigton. The foxes had night and morning runs on their leads, and I had them safely ensconced on the flat's balcony by late afternoon.

Despite their new confines, they settled down well and constantly played and mock-fought each other. If Elvy got too boisterous Emvy mewed at her, just as Elvy had done at Bevy. They slept together in the den box but usually woke up around 3 am and woke me up by scratching at its wooden floor, carrying their water dish and playthings about and dropping them, and yickering at each other like giant mice.

One day I looked up from my desk to find they had escaped by chewing through the wire netting, and were now free on the balcony. Both were perched on its edge, looking down at the canal. Suddenly I heard a woman shout from a boat below.

'Oh, there's a fox on that building!'

Then the boat's engine started up and off they went. I had a deuce of a job retrieving the foxes from the balcony without either taking a suicide leap onto the concrete below. Eventually I got them back into the repaired pen.

The night before we were due to leave London I took the foxes down to the private garden below the flat and tied their leads to a drainpipe, so that they could run and scratch about among the earth and vegetation. Later I fed and watered them and put them in the den box to sleep overnight.

At dawn, I went down sleepily, still half awake, to let them out on their leads again before we set off. I took hold of the lines poking out of the ventilation holes and opened the lid. I just had time to glimpse that Emvy's collar had come off before both foxes bolted. Only Elvy was halted by her lead. Emvy was free. Clearly Elvy had somehow undone her collar. She crept along uncertainly, looked as if she was going to crouch down and allow me to pick her up, then casually wandered through a seven-foot spiked iron fence that was impossible for me to climb.

I could only watch in dismay as she trotted away down the canal towpath. She looked with brief interest at some unalarmed ducks, one of which had only one leg, and then vanished among some privet and thorn bushes. A search with Moobli for much of the morning failed to reveal any trace of her. Emvy had escaped – into the 'wilds' of London. Well, there were plenty of wild areas along the canal and round Regent's Park, with mice, beetles, insects, grubs and worms, and many open-mesh rubbish containers. I did not give much for the chances of the one-legged duck when Emvy got hungry. I just hoped she would survive.

It was when we camped out in the wild area of Loch Lomond on our way home that disaster struck again. I got up early to give Elvy a run on her lead before the final driving. I tugged the rope and it felt firm. I opened the lid of the den box and – whoosh – off she went. She had, for the first time, chewed through the rope near the collar. It had *felt* firm because she must have been standing on it.

'Track the foxy!' I commanded Moobli, and off he went.

Within minutes he had cornered her in thick undergrowth and I got her back. I tied her up again, with *double* ropes this time, and went back into the truck for a brief final snooze. When I got up Elvy had gone again. She had chewed through both ropes, having finally learned how to do it.

We tracked up to 800 feet, where Moobli got strong scent from the root tangles under a huge stump surrounded by dense bracken and brambles. There was no way we could get her out, even if she was still there, and I had no live trap with me. I may have reared two broods of wildcats, even tamed one, but at taming foxes I had failed miserably. It was not so much failure as fiasco. I drove home with a heavy heart. I had nothing to blame but my own ineptitude.

That was not the final disaster, however. On our home loch, the reliable boat engine which had been put in for servicing refused to work. I had to row all the way. I later found out it had been wrongly re-assembled. Furthermore, Liane was missing, and my friend said he had not once seen her. He had stopped coming down when he saw the food untouched, and then had fallen ill. He told me, also, that instead of three people taking over Wildernesse for that weekend, a party of eleven had been in my home. Maybe that had caused Liane to leave. As the wildcat had come into oestrus three times earlier in the season; had stayed away then for several days at a time, I could only hope that at two-and-a-half years of age she had finally left to seek a mate in the wild. I would never know. We never saw her again.

The complete lack of any signs of her in the ensuing weeks was acutely depressing.

Occasionally we found Aspen's scats and a few scent trails in the woods, but we did not see her. The run of bad luck continued. In a storm the four-foot tip of a silver fir was broken off and crashed to the ground less than a yard away from me in the west wood. An old alder fell on to my water pipe, holed it and sent it hanging over the thundering waterfalls in the burn. On October 4 I was chasing after Moobli on a scent trail when my right foot hit a tussock the wrong way, tearing ligaments so badly that I could not move the boat for nine days. Eventually I got out and went for hospital treatment, then hobbled with the aid of a stick for several weeks. The bad luck turned to nightmare in mid-October when friends boated down the loch with a cable saying that my stepmother was dying and my father had become incapable in Spain, where they were then living.

I rushed out to Spain to look after my father, finally managed to get him back and into a nursing home in Worthing, and did not return to my disrupted life until late February.

It is impossible to record in the space of this book every fox trail Moobli and I covered. It is enough to say that from scats, fox scent and visits to carcasses it was clear that Aspen *was* covering the same territory as Cedric. Once we came back from a supply trip to find his huge droppings actually in the porch. On February 23 I saw her heading up the ridges above the west wood. Two days later either she or Cedric were in the high hole den in the rockface to the north-west, and there were many big and small scats above the cottage on an east-west line. On March 11 I heard a sharp '*raowl*' bark in the eastern woods, the alarm call Aspen made at Moobli's sudden appearance. I looked up and saw her slipping along the top of a cliff above us. A few yards further on Moobli got a strong scent, and we found one of her dens below a recess between two embedded granite slabs. The thick carpet of oak leaves was all trodden down, the scent so pungent it almost made me choke. I avoided treading on the area and we left quickly. It was a den on the eastern edge of her territory, less than a quarter-mile from the cottage. From snow tracking on March 22 we found Cedric's huge tracks in the east

75

wood, circling here and there where he had urinated on old stumps. They went to a deer carcass in the front pasture, showed he had scraped at it but not eaten anything, then on through the west wood. But once the snow broke up, melted in the marshy area, Moobli could not follow any scent. It seemed that Cedric had headed for the long woods to the west.

We went to check the new den we had found to the east but it seemed unused now. Well, it *was* very close to the cottage, Aspen had seen us near it and they probably would not use that one again. Three days later we checked the long woods to the west and found Cedric's huge scats near the eleventh dead deer of the winter. Sadly, the two old dens of Sylvesturr's remained as empty as they had been before the winter. I had to admit the old cuss was now probably dead.

We had no visits from foxhounds that spring, though I heard that two foxes had been killed on the ground above the far end of those woods. Long treks revealed that there were still foxes in the dens of the four territories we had established, so it appeared the Hunt was probably killing off surplus animals, the less aware young or the old and unfit.

Twice in April Moobli huffed on getting outside at dusk and each time I saw Aspen heading up to our rear fence. Once her eyes, close together, flashed green light in the beam of my torch. She seemed little scared, however, and I felt sure neither she nor Cedric were really put off by Moobli's scent around the place, though they had clearly decided it was safer not to come down until he was in the cottage for the night.

For months I had been working on a most complicated book, trying to wrestle many species over several years, through all four seasons, in the main environments of mountains, woodlands and loch, into a meaningful narrative.* At times I felt close to despair. One May evening, mind reeling, I wandered along the loch shore. The sun was going down and I was not thinking where I was going. I crossed the burn and ambled on between the trees of the eastern woods.

Then I heard movements above, a sort of scraping of leaves. I bobbed down, cautiously stalked upwards and peered round a

A Last Wild Place

tree growing right beside a great slab of granite. Two fox cubs were frolicking in the golden light, running up a large flat rock covered in dry moss. They jumped on each other, clutched each other with little paws and, playfully biting each other's muzzles, tumbled down, rolling over until they reached the bed of crackly oak leaves. There they scooted about, throwing up little showers of leaves, rose on their hind legs and boxed until they tumbled over again. All the time they made high yickering squeaks, dropping their absurdly big ears back in mock aggression. Their tails were still in the spindly stage (they could have been no more than five weeks old) and here they were playing immediately below the new den we had discovered in February. Because the den had been empty on March 22, and also because I had been away, I had not checked it again.

Suddenly there was a sharp '*raowl*' yapping from above. The two cubs shot into the den, one after the other, like small brown torpedoes, and there was – Aspen. She glared down at me briefly, and as our eyes met, she drew back and disappeared. She must have given birth after all in that den, the nearest one to the cottage, and obviously Cedric was the father. How marvellous! I left quickly.

It rained heavily overnight. When the clouds rolled away next day, I waited until the sun would be shining in the den area before stalking back with my camera, heart beating eagerly. I waited downwind for two hours, but there was no sign of movement anywhere. They must have gone. Aspen had taken the cubs elsewhere. I fetched Moobli. Although he found a scent trail leading north-west towards our burn, he could not track far on the wet ground. We checked the other two dens we knew to the north-west and found nothing.

All through the rest of May and June I worked hard on eagle treks and from a new hide on a precarious ledge in a cliff-face. After a freezing night of rainstorms on June 28, I loaded a new film into the camera with great difficulty, using only my left hand, as the right was braced to stop me going over the edge of the cliff. The sun came out and I got eleven glorious photos of the eagles, one of the male glaring at me, his legs wide apart as he turned to leave, his wings open wide.

With this film still in the camera, I set off on the hardest trek of all, sixteen miles involving 12,000 feet of ups and downs. It was a cold showery day, so we were not dawdling along. After a hard climb we tramped over peat-hagged meadows at 1,600 feet. Suddenly I noticed Moobli was no longer with me. Had he gone after a deer? He hadn't disobeyed like that since he was a pup. I cursed his lapse as I approached some sheer cliffs above a deep dramatic glen. Suddenly I spotted something red-brown ahead. It was sitting in the lee of the wind on a small black peaty ledge under a turfy overhang. Well, just a piece of brown rock, or maybe a deer calf sleeping while its mother grazed. I raised the fieldglass. It was a huge fox.

I stalked it, got to within seventy yards, and from behind a boulder took a picture. The fox heard the click and looked up as I froze, just the top of my bush hat and the end of the lens showing. Then it stood up. It was Cedric! I took another picture. He looked back, walked off a bit further and looked back again. I dared not try for another just then, although it would have been a fine photo, his great white-tipped brush curled beside his belly. Then he walked slowly round a small bend, still in the peat hag, and vanished.

I had the distinct feeling he would not go far. I got up, stalked again on hands and knees, making a wide detour because of a depression in the ground between us, then moved towards a rock I had memorised which would give me the correct angle from which to see where he had gone. I crept round the bend, trouser knees soaked, to the rock and saw Cedric lying down asleep further round the overhang. I took two more photos as he opened his eyes and looked up. I waited until his head was down again. I was not close, about forty yards away. I used every skill I knew to creep silently to the north-west, then back south to a much nearer rock. He was still there! I was just moving the camera round the side of the rock when he shot up and slipped round the corner with a flash of his tail. I looked round – Moobli had just appeared on the close skyline. After tracking me down by scent, he had scared Cedric away. I am afraid I clouted him hard, for he had ruined a wonderful fox stalk by his rare disobedience.

Weeks later I discovered that somehow in the eagle hide I had failed to fix the film correctly to the winding spool. Developing showed that as a result I had missed every one of the superb eagle shots and the first three of the fox. Miraculously, perhaps after being shaken up on the trek, the film had caught itself up on the spool in time to make the last photo of Cedric the first on the film. Angry as I was with myself, I was delighted to have at least one good picture to show for the best fox stalk I had ever made.

7 · Incredible Meetings in the Wild

The bad luck changed on July 22. We were heading for the high plateaux to the north-east to photograph red deer, and had only gone half a mile when Moobli scented something and wanted to rush ahead. I hissed him back as I saw what looked like two small red deer a quarter of a mile ahead. But these were *slinking* along over heather and boggy areas. They were foxes, with white tips to their tails, and I wondered if one was Aspen. Then I realised these were much lighter in colour than Aspen's dark auburn. Not only was the camera in the pack but the standard lens was on it, as I had been photographing flowers. By the time I had put on the telephoto lens the foxes had worked downwards to the south-east and into a bracken-flanked and tussock-strewn gully.

Keeping Moobli back I kept stalking, went through some high bracken and then saw one of the foxes resting on its belly on a sloping piece of turf. It was grabbing away with its paws, hooking into the long grasses below it, cupping its claws like a cat does, ears forward and head down. It was catching grasshoppers. I waited until its head came up and took two photos. Then the fox jumped down into the bracken, and I kept quite still. Sure enough, wanting more of that game, it ran back up the sloping turf and jumped off again as my camera clicked. This time it did not return.

We were pressing on when suddenly a fox appeared on a ridge

to the right of where the other two had gone, a huge fox with a great white tip to its tail. Cedric! He saw us, swerved away as my camera clicked a shade too late, and disappeared in the wake of the other two. We tracked them for an hour but in the full summer vegetation did not see them again. Nevertheless, I was delighted, for these were clearly Cedric and Aspen's two well-grown cubs, and they had been out learning to hunt with their father. Obviously they had been following him when I had first seen them. Possibly, after giving birth, feeding them milk and later regurgitated food, and guarding them closely for the first nine weeks, Aspen was taking a well-earned rest.

Greg Hunter told me on a beautiful day in August, as we camera-stalked a bachelor herd of fourteen stags on his estate, that he had killed twenty-three adult foxes (mostly vixens) and thirty cubs in a 180-square-mile area in the past year. He thought the area could easily stand such culling. I put to him my theory that surplus foxes from unhunted areas spilled over into those where foxes were hunted, and so dominant resident families were broken up. The newcomers could not then be 'controlled' by the residents, for they would not know the best marshes to go to for frogs or waders, nor the finest vole areas or most prolific river banks, nor where best to hunt and forage in rains, moon-light or heavy snows, and would have to resort to killing anything they could find, especially farming stock. Greg said I was probably right! We would never change each other's minds on the fox-killing issue, and so there was no point in squabbling about it.

Later in the month, as I was passing a moss-covered rock on which Aspen and Cedric often left their 'visiting-card' droppings in winter, I found the remains of a honeycomb. It was only about three inches across and looked too small for bees. There was a fresh fox scat on the rock. I searched about in the undergrowth, but Moobli found it first, his head deep into a tuft of rushes. I went over and picked up the remains of a destroyed tree-wasps' nest. In it were two lone wasps trying to repair the damage. I knew that badgers devoured wasps' nests, eating both grubs and honey, but a badger would not bother to carry it away. I remembered that foxes like to look around them while eating.

Eight days later the two wasps, which came to rasp fibres from my porch logs to make a malleable paper pulp with which to repair the nest walls, had completed the job. Some of the new tubular cells were sealed, apparently containing grubs. Three days later I went to see how they were getting on.

There was a fresh scat on the rock – and another abandoned piece of honeycomb. I had forgotten the excellent memory of foxes, one of which had returned to demolish the nest for a second time.

We did not have another close encounter with the foxes until January 27. That day as we were walking through the frozen tussocks in hazy sunshine on a trek westwards, I saw a large brownish animal looking at us from above some heather on a hill near the long woodlands. I raised my fieldglass. It had broad jaws and looked like a wolf. As I tried to get the camera from my pack, it turned, flashed a great white-tipped brush, then slipped into the wood. It was Cedric, in his darker winter coat, grown even bigger. He was a really hefty beast now.

Moobli picked up his scent and we followed it through the trees, zigzagging about over the steep rough terrain until he came to a halt overlooking a ridge. Some sheep below were all that could be seen. I cuffed him and sent him on. He picked up more scent. On we went, losing and finding the trail, until we were three miles from home, and I was sure Cedric had eluded us. Suddenly I heard crows calling on a higher ridge, and saw them diving and swooping. And there, between bushes under some birch trees, was Cedric, just looking calmly at us. The crows were mobbing him. I failed to get the camera on him in time and he slipped away, this time to the north-east. It was good to know he was still alive.

On a supply trip in late February, I went to have a drink with Greg who, after the usual joshing about bringing the hounds down my way, said a vixen with cubs already inside her had been shot in January. This indicated the dynamism of the suppressed population trying to adjust to persecution. He then introduced me to the new huntsman who had taken over the local hounds. I needed the information these men could give me so I put forward no hard views; hunting with hounds seemed cruel to me, but then nature is 'cruel' too. Maybe human beings should be above such red-toothed laws. I simply proposed that the manpower wasted on hunting foxes might be more usefully employed in looking after sheep better, especially if *they* were right that sporadic killing kept the species as a whole fit and healthy.

The huntsman had an open honest face and turned out to be a purist. He disliked the system here, where locals went out with shotguns during a Hunt, especially as some of them didn't go far on the Hill, but just stood about and seemed unable to fire a single shot when the fox appeared! He said real hunting was about a well-trained pack after its natural prey, and when done well the fox was killed only by the hounds. He had once been on a stag shoot when a dog fox had got up from a solid den and stood looking at them. The shooters had fumbled with their guns while he waved his hat from behind them to scare the fox away – so that he could hunt it cleanly with the hounds later. In the end the fox had been shot. When the Hunt Chairman had heard what he had done, he had told him off, saying that their main task was to kill foxes, control their numbers, and that was the reason and mandate for the Hunt.

The huntsman declared that he had given up a comfortable home in England, partly because more landowners there were refusing permission for fox-hunting, but chiefly in the hope of finding better hound-hunting in the Highlands. He said he hunted because he *liked* it.

The fact is, many men just *like* hunting, enjoy pitting their wits against a legendary, cunning, so-called 'wicked' creature, which will give them a good run for their money. Some young-sters feel they have proved themselves by killing their first fox, in much the same way as an Eskimo boy proves himself a hunter by killing his first seal.

Greg thought the Hunt Chairman had been right. It was their job to kill foxes, by all legal means possible. The huntsman persisted that hound-hunting should be a clean sport, with no guns involved. The two men fell to arguing with each other more vehemently than with me. Although referred to locally as the 'Hunt', what they belonged to was in fact a Fox Destruction Society, formed to control fox numbers after the gin-trap was banned. Not only is it a perfectly legal Society, but in 1982 it received an annual subsidy of some £4,000 from the Department of Agriculture and Fisheries. In addition, all local landowners

were expected to be subscribers, the recommended annual subscriptions being: big estates with some forestry, £120; farmers
and crofters (per 100 ewes), £14; deer forest proprietors, £60.
While foxes do no harm in forests, the Forestry Commission in
the region still contributes some £700 a year. The Hunt/Society's
annual reports are interesting, showing wages costs at some
£3,400 a year, vehicle costs nearly £2,000, hound feeding at
£1,400 – a total in the region of £9,000 a year. Quite apart from
the man-hours expended by all those engaged in chasing after
foxes, this would seem to be a considerable expenditure.

Since no one knows precisely how many lambs are actually
killed by foxes, it is surely impossible to put a meaningful figure
to the loss to farmers. In my talk with the two men, I argued that
some 'wanton' killing could be put down to acts of revenge by
dog foxes which had suffered the loss of their vixens or cubs to
the Hunt, or to terriers and shotguns. Both men agreed there was
truth in that. But they had also known foxes to slay lambs and
then not bother to eat them – and this even *before* the Hunt had
been out, and their dens had been untouched. I learned that
on average the Hunt killed a hundred foxes a year in the Lochaber region. Much as I liked them, I was glad that the two men
did not live near me, even more so in mid-February when I
learned that the Hunt had killed four foxes at the western ends
of the two big estates in my region.

One night I was woken by two loud fox '*kahf*' screams and
hoped it was Aspen calling her mate. Next day I took Moobli to
the west wood, where we found large scats left on tufts for a
distance of almost three miles, with smaller ones left by the vixen
on higher tufts. We found more signs above the cottage in the
following two weeks, then a fine lay-out place with a huge scat
by it at just over 1,000 feet to the north-east. It was in the tip of a
triangle formed by two high rockfaces and gave a wide field of
vision, commanding the whole of the valley below and the
woods round us. In fine weather foxes often rest in the open and
like to see all round them while feeling protected. The scent was
still strong, and a huge scat indicated that Cedric had been there,
had seen us coming while still far off, and had spirited himself
away.

Signs continued to appear in the area, but fewer of them, until they ceased altogether in early May. I heard that the Hunt had been out in April and had killed two foxes. The farmer and a keeper had also worked dens with terriers on both estates and had got a vixen and three cubs, but these were on his far grazing lands to the north. I found an occupied fox den on May 18, three miles to the north-east, probably one of the family that lived up there. I wondered if Aspen and Cedric had fallen victim to the Hunt, for a ewe with twin lambs was surviving unmolested in the middle of their hunting range.

In June on a trek to photograph red-deer calves, Moobli surprised a dog fox out in the open. After it vanished over the highest ridge, we circled the deer-calving grounds in the hope that our scent would keep the fox away from the calves. As we came back round the mountain, I managed to photograph a slim long-legged vixen before she dived into a tangled cairn of rocks where she had cubs. It was interesting that this family had established itself on what I had always believed to be the north-east part of Cedric and Aspen's territory. Were the two still alive?

Before long I was at my busiest, working from a hide with the nearest pair of eagles, which had twin chicks in their eyrie. I was keeping watch on the nest from half a mile away on July 2 when I saw the great dark form of the mother eagle drifting over the eyrie cliff. Suddenly she half-closed her wings, dived downwards, went into a fast glide and landed with a rush beside a large rock. Instantly she began flapping her long wings and leaping up and down, and I could see a browny-red animal at bay which seemed to be snapping back at her. The fight was obscured by the rock, but then the eagle jumped hard, bounced back into the air with her wings beating strongly, and flew into her nest with what looked like a deer calf or fox in her talons, though I could see no dangling brush.

After my stint in the hide I climbed up to the nest and found a fresh quarter-eaten fox cub on it, its tail still in the spindly stage. I went down to the scene of the fight and found a new fox den in a nearby jumble of rocks. There were certainly foxes in it, their scent strong, and round the entrance of the den, among the scats, were three legs of a lamb. The foxes might have found it dead, I could not tell for sure. As this new den was in the west end of

Cedric and Aspen's territory, it seemed possible it contained their second family, but I did not see either of the adults.

On July 5 I hiked back, to find the eaglets both flown and perched just below the nest, which now contained a second fox cub. I did not check the fox den again as I was too busy following and photographing the eaglets. Four days later I found one eaglet back in the nest and the other perched on a ridge. Both adult birds were flying nearby. The fox den had now been vacated. Not surprising, after losing two cubs to the eagles. The treks to the hide also revealed why the foxes (if they *were* Cedric and Aspen) had not come so often round Wildernesse in late winter and spring. For once, there was as much deer carrion in the open glen below the eyrie as in the small conifer woods around us.

In rainstorms in late August we had a sign that Cedric might still be alive when we found a huge scat, still warm, near the west wood. Moobli was most agitated, tracked him far into the eastern woods, but ran out of scent. Four days later at dusk I saw a dark fox-like form race through the bracken in east wood. On August 31 we found a hind carcass that had been torn about by foxes 700 feet up the burn. On September 18 I glimpsed a dark fox sneaking through the heather on a ridge above the cottage. It stopped briefly to look down, a white-tipped tail showing. It *was* Aspen! More heavy rains, it seemed, had made her come back to the rich food of the woods. At dusk Moobli wanted to go out. He huffed and ran into the east wood – and away over the burn, giving a light screech, went Aspen. Although he only wanted to get close and play with her, I called him off. On a stag trek ten days later we found that the high buttress den four miles to the north-west was again occupied by foxes. So there were now five groups of foxes in the nine-by-four square-mile area.

By mid-October foxes were shifting the skull and bones of a deer-calf skeleton in the east wood to different places at night, but we never saw them in daylight. Clearly a family playing. After dusk on November 1 Moobli made his '*huff*' bark, scenting on the east wind, and we saw a fox slipping over the loch shore to the west.

In late November winter began its first real onslaught with hail, sleet and snow all in one day. Next morning we found huge scats on the north hill, some overlaying Moobli's of four days earlier. It seemed Cedric was still about. Confirmation came three days later when we found the first track in the snow above the west wood. Each print was a full two-and-a-half inches long. Smaller tracks across our front pasture from the east indicated Aspen, or one of their cubs, had been passing below him.

On my next supply trip I found a dead sheep near my truck. When I went to tell the farmer's family, I was told they already knew about it. It had been accidentally driven into the loch by a sheepdog on a gathering and had drowned.

That day I met a farmer acquaintance who was having second thoughts about the efficacy of the Hunt. In England the 'sporting' Hunts were grateful to farmers for letting them go over their lands, he said. But here the Hunt, which existed to *destroy* foxes, expected the *farmers* to be grateful that they went after them. Apart from the subsidy from the Department of Agriculture and Fisheries, and the subscriptions from landowners, farmers and crofters, the Hunt expected donations and for folk to organise dances and whist drives to raise funds for them. He now thought it was better to have one good man with terriers and gun to get foxes at dens, rather than have a pack of hounds running over his land, disturbing wildlife, stock, and often getting nothing.

I long ago realised that, even if I wanted to, I could change nothing by high-powered rhetoric concerning the rights and wrongs or the 'immorality' of hunting foxes. It would take many years to assemble all the facts and evidence for a fully researched book on the subject – and it would be a very long book indeed. However, the argument of the fox-hunting lobby that, but for hunting, there would be far fewer foxes about than there are today is not a specious one.

Before fox-hunting started to become popular in Britain in the early eighteenth century, the animal was far from plentiful, particularly in the Highlands as the many accounts of early naturalists prove. Up to this time, and for some years afterwards, foxes had to compete with other powerful predators like the wolf and the wildcat. When hunting took hold and put strong roots down into the social fabric of country areas, providing new employment for many people, thousands of foxes were imported into Britain and released in many areas from the

Highlands to the coasts of Hampshire. Over a thousand were imported annually into the main distributing centre of Leadenhall market. These foxes came from Spain, Holland, Germany, Austria, Italy, Sardinia, Russia and Scandinavia, and imports were kept up until the middle of the last century. For over two hundred years it was considered socially unacceptable for individuals in lowland areas (farmers, keepers, stock-keepers) to shoot, trap or poison foxes. They were to be left for the Hunt to chase, and because the Hunt preserved woods, coppices and other habitats in which their quarry could breed, shelter was provided for many other forms of wildlife too. Also, so the argument goes, since just as many foxes escaped as were caught, the persecution from hunting was far less than if every Tom, Dick or Harry was also having a go.

Even today between 50,000 and 60,000 foxes are killed every year in Britain and yet there are more foxes in the kingdom now than there were 250 years ago. No wild creature has better adapted itself to civilisation than the wily fox. It has survived our roads, railways, electrification and urban sprawl. It is difficult to be sure whether the fox 'came to town' because the myxomatosis epidemic among rabbits in the 1950s reduced its main natural prey, or because it knew it would not be hunted there, or because it found plenty to eat in the high food-wastage economy of town life. Certainly it has invaded many of our major cities (there are estimated to be 1,300 foxes in London alone), and in the towns this nocturnal creature has so lost its fear of human kind that frequently it can be seen by day. It is far easier to watch foxes behaving naturally in Richmond Park than it is in the wild Highlands.

Just what damage do Highland foxes actually do? The Animal Breeding Research Organisation in Edinburgh has found that 17 per cent of all lambs born on Scottish hills are either dead at birth or die within twenty-four hours, due mainly to poor ewe nutrition in the winter months. And this figure can shoot as high at 40 per cent in some of the harsher sheep runs in the north and west. Many of the lambs taken by foxes (great carrion eaters) are already dead, or come from the ranks of the doomed weak.

As for game birds like grouse, a Nature Conservancy Council study shows that the birds most predated upon were surplus grouse, driven into marginal areas by the territorial behaviour of their own kind. As in all predator–prey relationships, it is the weaker, less wary, least intelligent, diseased prey that are taken first. These less-nourished birds, carrying more parasites, are by far the main victims.

Few ask what 'good' foxes do, but since they cannot prey on lambs or game-bird chicks for more than a few weeks in the year, it is a legitimate question. Their main Highland food consists of rabbits, hares, weak birds (including crows and ravens), grouse, deer calves, mice, insects, beetles, many earth-worms in winter, large quantities of lamb, sheep and deer carrion, and many field voles. By clearing up carrion, they rid the Highlands of thousands of blue- and green-bottle flies, and nasal bot and warble flies, whose larvae feed on and pupate in it. And apart from helping transmit 'louping ill' to sheep, voles compete with sheep and deer, each vole eating up to 120 grammes of best grasses a day. A study by Drs J. Lockie and W. N. Charles showed that a predator force of owls, weasels and foxes can reduce voles from ninety to forty-five per acre in winter.

It is true that some foxes will occasionally kill lambs, some-times from a revenge motive. Just as one or two will break into an insecure poultry house and kill far more birds than the one they need to eat. Surrounded by squawking flapping birds in an artificial, confined situation the instinct to kill becomes highly aroused. The answer is to lock the birds up at night in a *secure* hut. One crofter I know had a fox break into his run and kill four ducks. The fox took one with him but 'cached' the rest in the nearby woods, burying them so their webbed feet stuck up like markers for his eventual return. I did not blame the crofter for going after that particular fox.

The most efficient fox-killer in my region of Lochaber, Greg Hunter, has destroyed 153 foxes and cubs in five years over a 180-square-mile area, and that does not include those killed by the Hunt. His tally: Year One, 27 foxes; Year Two, 15 foxes and 7 cubs; Year Three, 14 foxes and 16 cubs; Year Four, 18 foxes and 3 cubs; Year Five, 23 foxes and 30 cubs. He is convinced total fox populations have not been affected; if anything have been strengthened. 'When I first began I was getting thin, mangy, scruffy beasts,' he told me. 'There were just too many on the ground. Now I kill fewer, but all are much fitter and healthier.'

The hunters' argument is that the fox no longer has any natural predators (I have found 7 fox cubs, 6 almost fully grown, in golden eagles' nests, so this is not strictly true) and so man should take over the predator role. In doing so he helps to keep the species healthy, for it is the least fit, the old, sick, weaker, less wary animals that are killed. Thus, the fittest are left to carry on the race. There is some truth in this: a suppressed population is a vital one, tending to bigger and more frequent broods, constantly adjusting, with guile, to thrive against persecution. The Highland fox is so far managing very well.

While intensive control certainly keeps *local* fox populations below normal levels, over the Highlands as a whole, fox-hunting is uneven. So what are the negative aspects of such sporadic killing, apart from the emotive charges of cruelty? I will try to show one possible negative aspect here.

The Highland vixen comes into season in February, but can only be fertilised over two to three days. She calls loudly at this time, attracting mature males who often fight over her with loud 'yickerings'. Usually, the dominant vixen mates successfully with the dominant male; she then ceases to call, and the pair stay together during the birth and rearing of the cubs. Dens can be in enlarged rabbit burrows, an empty or unused part of a badger's sett, a hollow tree, sand or earth holes in banks, or (most often in the Highlands) deep in the tunnels below a rockfall of giant boulders. Litters, born after some fifty-two days, vary from three to six, sometimes as many as eight, and more dog cubs are born than vixens. The vixen lies up, giving milk to the cubs, whose eyes open at about ten days old, and the dog fox brings in most of her food. After about three weeks the vixen resumes some hunting, lies out in the open more often but usually near the den, and starts weaning the cubs on regurgitated food at about four and a half weeks. The cubs now venture outside the den, playing for long periods in fine weather, ready to bolt below at the first parental warning of danger. By seven weeks they are fully weaned, and begin to eat mice, voles or rabbits brought to them. By nine weeks they are able to kill small prey for themselves, under the vixen's watchful eye. By three months the cubs are hunting with their mother, learning the use of all their senses. By mid-November quarrels are frequent and the family begins to split up.

It is my belief, gained from my field studies, that foxes are extremely territorial and will not tolerate strange foxes in the central parts of their home ranges. While some vixens are tolerated longer in a submissive capacity, the young dogs and a few vixens are driven off before winter. It is a tough time for them, for they have to find their own ranges in peripheral areas, and only the most resourceful individuals survive.

One effect of sporadic killing is to break up the stable resident family groups, which largely exert their own controls over numbers. Surplus foxes from the unhunted areas join up with foxes from the disturbed, more persecuted areas. These displaced foxes are forced into new terrain, often ranging many miles. They become itinerants, unfamiliar with marshes where they can catch waders, the rabbit meadows, the best vole banks, streams for frogs, where best to hunt in moonlight, rain, mist, snow, ice and so on. Hence they are far more prone, or rather are *driven* to find easier prey such as poultry and lambs. They must kill what they can find.

In a 1971–6 study on the variation in Scottish fox diets, Drs R. Hewson and H. Kolb (both employed by the Department of Agriculture and Fisheries for Scotland) suggested that in north-eastern areas, the fox, eating many rabbits, was beneficial to agriculture. Their effect on sheep was negligible, and even game birds did not form a large proportion of their diet. However, in Argyll and west Perth, lamb remains (*in the spring only*) accounted for 35 per cent of their food, and in the Lochaber area as much as 45 per cent.

What remained unknown was how many lambs had been actually *killed* by foxes and how many (in such high-mortality areas as Lochaber) had been scavenged as carrion. It is to be hoped that detailed studies of lamb mortality and fox behaviour, now being conducted, will reveal the answer.

Forestry, both Government and private, is increasing in Scotland. It is often claimed by stock-keepers that forests, especially younger plantations, harbour too many foxes – that the foxes shelter in the woods, then go out to prey in the open hills on lambs and farm animals. A year's study in west Scotland (Argyll) by Drs Hewson, Kolb and A. Knox in 1975 showed that the main prey items of foxes in Argyll was field voles. This applied equally to foxes from the forests and the open Hill, even though sheep and deer carrion was common on the Hill. Not only were forest foxes finding most of their food in the woods, but the Hill foxes were also resorting to the forests for food. Hill scats contained more sheep and deer, but these did not make a large contribution to the diet.

Percentage frequency of food items for forest foxes were: 32 per cent rabbits, 65 per cent small animals (mainly voles), and 7 per cent sheep; for hill foxes: 35 per cent rabbits, 58 per cent small animals, and 13 per cent sheep. A similar study for north-east (Kincardine) forest foxes showed: 72 per cent hares and rabbits, 19 per cent small animals (mainly voles), and 4 per cent sheep.

In a study of fox control in Scottish forests the previous year, Hewson and Kolb, while admitting *local* control can be effective, suggested from an analysis of bounty figures over the previous twenty years that it is doubtful whether foxes are effectively controlled over Scotland as a whole. Like other animals, foxes produce offspring surplus to their annual breeding density. It seems inefficient if control merely removes this surplus, and comes into competition with such natural controls as a reduction in the supply of rabbits due to myxomatosis. Furthermore, natural controls operate mostly in mid-winter, when foxes do least mischief. The report suggested a need for experiments in which fox control would be relaxed over a period of years so that the effect on performance and predation can be measured.

And this came from two expert *agricultural* scientists. Their suggestions have not been put into practice.

On January 20 we found a stag calf dying in the woods. I removed its haunches and hauled the rest up to 300 feet as food for the eagles. By February 5 the carcass had been well chewed, a huge fox scat lay beside it, and Moobli tracked fox scent up to the high hole-den in the rockface to the north-west. I felt sure that Cedric had paid us a visit. Twelve days later I found another big scat, still warm, beside the body of a hind which had died near the remains of the stag calf.

Towards the end of the month I found last year's breeding den south-west of the twin-chick eyrie to be empty, but Moobli located a new den below the eyrie, near a dead calf that had been ripped apart and rolled downhill by foxes, the stomach neatly removed so as not to taint the meat. As we hiked back home a dark fox with a white tip got up and lolloped slowly over a crest. Believing it to be too far away, I did not take out the camera, but as we came over the crest it was just slowly hoppity-hopping over the next ridge. It was almost certainly Aspen, though she looked older now. Later that evening Moobli gave a '*huff*' growl. I shut him indoors and went out – to hear a short '*kraik*' yap from the hill above. It seemed that Aspen had tracked us back to the cottage. I let Moobli out, hoping he might corner her. Off he went and I heard his play growls and a few yaps. Then he let her go, cocked his leg on a tuft and looked at me as if to say, 'Yes, it's her again.' Next morning we found that one of Moobli's droppings east of the cottage had been covered by one of Cedric's, again asserting his and Aspen's territorial rights too.

Not until March 2 did foxes break into the hind carcass above, first taking just the ears. After three days they had hollowed out the top ribs, apparently working with their rear ends up the hill. This must have been awkward, but they no doubt wanted to keep watch on the cottage area while feeding. Five days later I found a new den a quarter of a mile from the twin-chick eyrie in a jumbled pile of huge boulders, and from Moobli's scenting I reckoned there was a fox in it. We left quickly. By March 10 the hind carcass had been ripped to bits and hauled thirty yards down the hill.

On an eagle trek in early April we found the new boulder den near the eyrie was still occupied. Moobli whined agitatedly, scraping at the moss on the rocks with his great claws. I took the camera out – just in time to see Aspen, looking scraggy, run from the back of the boulders and bound slowly up the hill. Her lips were drawn back from her teeth in what looked like a smile of terror, as if expecting to hear the crash of a gun. I managed to focus the long lens on her as she wended her way between rocks and got one photo before she disappeared over the ridge. At

125th of a second in cloudy light, however, it would not be much good. I could hear slight scrapings below. Moobli was still interested and was making loud huffing sniffs. There were certainly cubs in there (Aspen's third family) but, though I crawled about and got into tight places, I could not see any. That day we found five dead deer within half a square mile of the eyrie and the dens – enough food to feed an army of foxes and badgers, as well as the eagles, yet the eyrie was not being used. We also found two new fox holes, one freshly scraped out, in soil on a slope half a mile to the north-east. The fox-hunters knew of two of the dens in this area, so would they now discover where Aspen had her new cubs?

Over the next few weeks we found that one of the two dens in the big corrie to the north-east was occupied by a small fox, probably a cub from last year. Another fox had made a new den below the raven cliffs to the east. The high buttress den to the north-west was also occupied. So was the remote den in the long glen three miles to the north-east. So there were still five lots of foxes in the nine-by-four square-mile area. In late April Cedric laid several scats over Moobli's droppings and tugged the carcasses about.

After a hectic trip to London, during which I bought some expensive new binoculars, I arrived back in mid-May to an idyllic scene. Bluebells, thicker than I had ever known them, flooded the front pasture and halfway up the north hill. The double lilac and crimson rhododendron flowers were breaking out and the trees were sprouting new leaves. On May 18 I went outside in golden evening sunlight and saw Aspen on the high ridges to the north-west. With her white-tipped tail flashing, she was slipping through the grasses between three ewes and a big lamb. As she got near the lamb, one of the ewes made a swift head butt towards her. She dodged with a fast sideways leap, though she was not within range, and just kept going westwards towards her den. Had she still got cubs, and had she brought them near?

Next morning I was woken at 4.05 am by a sharp fox bark. I kept watch from time to time during the day but saw no foxes. In hazy sunlight on the following afternoon I spotted something moving on the hill far ahead. I raised the new binoculars to see a huge red-brown fox with a white tail-tip moving through the grasses. It was Cedric. He lay down, looking ahead, jumped on to a mossy tuft as I took a photo (too far at 500 yards), then vanished into the bracken. I tried to stalk him along a swampy burn gully, all doubled up, as there was a long shallow dell between us, and then used the binoculars once more. There was a fox out again, but this time smaller and far darker, also with a white tip. It was Aspen! As I watched she reared up into the air, pushed both front paws out, leaped and whapped down on something, probably a frog, as there were many about that spring. Then Cedric appeared again and they put their muzzles together as if both were eating the same frog. They rolled over twice, biting and cuddling with their paws. This only lasted a few seconds before they darted into the bracken. Then I saw two other foxes above them, far smaller – cubs. Only one of them had a white tail tip. They both jumped up briefly before also vanishing into the bracken. I climbed up high to the east, hoping for another glimpse. As they crossed our burn I saw one of the cubs pause momentarily, as if afraid of even the shallow slow-flowing waters. Then they vanished into the herbage on the far side, heading west.

I was delighted then that I had saved up and paid £340 for the new binoculars. I should have bought them years before. They had helped me to achieve something rare with wildlife – to see a fox in the open before it saw me! I was also glad that Aspen and Cedric had reared two more cubs. One of the fox-hunters had told me that they had found a new den in that area, but he thought the terriers had only got one or two cubs. They did not see the vixen at all. It seemed the two surviving cubs had been successful at squeezing into rock crevices, and thus had escaped.

On the way home I found a small stag calf that had tumbled into a steep burn gully at the top of the west wood. It was dying. I lifted it out gently and carried it to a comfortable spot among short heather on a shelf just above the trees. Next morning the calf was dead, its upper eye already missing, and ravens were flying above. They had pecked a small hole in the lower gut and pulled out some small intestine.

That evening I went out before dusk and saw a single lamb leaping about on the north-west ridges. It was racing back and forth, a good thirty yards each time, while its mother grazed placidly in a gully. Then I saw Aspen crouching down, her lips peeled back in what looked like a smile, her forepaws braced on the ground, as if trying to entice the lamb nearer. The lamb seemed confused, unsure whether this strange animal was a playmate or not (there were no other lambs near) and kept darting towards the fox and away, fascinated by it yet afraid at the same time. As the lamb dashed away Aspen got up, only to crouch down again as the lamb returned, as if to make herself look small.

I was too tired to storm up there, and was about to give a shout when Aspen swerved away and vanished over the tops. She did not return. The lamb still dashed across to where she had been and ran back again. Eventually it stayed by its mother, which seemed to have been unaware of the fox. I removed the haunches from the stag calf to feed to Moobli and to release fresh meat scent into the air.

Sure that foxes would not yet have touched the fresh carcass, I went round the west wood next morning with just the 300mm lens on the camera, for I was hoping to photograph wood warblers. I climbed the rock escarpment in the centre, Moobli well behind, when I spotted the stag carcass; it appeared to have been shifted two yards to the right. Then *it* appeared to move by itself! No, there was a huge fox there, its head buried in the calf's chest. It was Cedric. I signalled Moobli to stay back and poked the camera round a tree.

I took several photos of Cedric tugging at the carcass. After a few bites he looked up nervously towards the cottage and straight at me, though he did not see me. He appeared not to hear the camera clicks, nor to know that I was just below him. Once he tugged so hard at the meat that he half-somersaulted backwards when it came away. He also walked about slowly, clumsily, as if extremely fatigued. I slid back down the slope and moved sideways, keeping a rock and a heather tuft in sight as indicators of the fox's position, and then crept up again behind a thick red-barked pine, out of Cedric's sight. There was no point in wasting time. I edged the camera round the tree trunk.

He was still at it, his face covered with blood. I took more photos, winding the film on slowly. Then the film came to an

above: Bevy liked to leap on the window–sill and watch me working at my desk.

below: I took the foxes with me on a brief trip to London, where Elvy and Emvy escaped from their pen on to the first-floor balcony of the flat. It was difficult to round them up safely.

One May morning I was astonished to find Cedric feeding avidly from a deer–calf carcass near the west wood. He looked up suspiciously but did not see me. Full of meat, he plodded back towards his den, stopping once to relieve himself on a tuft.

above: The most successful fox stalk in the wild resulted in this picture of Cedric, the big dog fox, lying fast asleep in a peat hollow.

below: One of the cubs from Cedric and Aspen's first family catching grasshoppers on a heather bank.

end. Surely I could not get down, along the shore for 300 yards and back to the cottage, change the film, put on the 640mm lens, and get back to find the fox still there? I decided to try it, and reached the pine again to find that Cedric had gone. I moved slowly up to the carcass. He had eaten some of the lungs, liver, heart, and some of the kidney – a good 5 lbs of meat. I stayed dead still, searching the hillside, trying to employ the 'all-seeing eye'.

There he was again! He was not running, or even walking, but sneaking along slowly, even *plodding*, about 300 yards further up. His gut was so full of meat it occasionally brushed the ground. I followed, taking photos of him scent-marking tufts, and even of him stopping to leave a big scat, as if to relieve himself of a bit of weight, his tail up and pumping, and once looking back at me. I lost him for a while after that, but went on, clambering up some almost sheer slopes, until I judged I must be just past him. Then I climbed up a short rockface.

I was just in time to see him wandering between the lamb and three ewes. The lamb saw him and performed an odd pirouette, but Cedric barely glanced at it. One of the ewes made a weak, almost symbolic bunt, but he just kept going, hopped heavily on to a rock and disappeared over the far side. There was no panic among the sheep. It was as if they *knew* this old fox. He would be at least seven years old now, a good age for a Highland fox considering the persecution it suffers.

For a full mile more I followed him, taking photos and watching him through the powerful binoculars. It was clear that he was heading for one of the western dens, where doubtless he would regurgitate some of the meat for Aspen and the cubs. Well, I would leave him in peace to do just that.

As I watched the old-timer plodding doggedly home to feed his family, I just raised my hand in silent salute.

PART THREE

8 · Knowing the Wild Tawnies

It was one of those hot and cold, bright and cloudy days of mid-April when, once it does break through, the sun shines with a baking heat that fires the earth into new life and brings all nature intensely alive. The searing heat through the window made my desk work impossible. It was my first spring at Wildernesse and I was anxious to learn the secrets of the wild-life round my remote home.

'Come on Moobli, we're away for a trek,' I said to the patient Alsatian, then a six-month-old pup. As we headed east through the lochside woods, great tits were belling '*tootsie tootsie*' in the budding hazels and birches, coal tits joined the chaffinch choirs with high-pitched cries of '*me too, me too*', and a great spotted woodpecker drummed a tattoo on a larch snag.

Higher we climbed, snapping off occasional snakehead shoots from the first bracken, emerging above the woods at about 600 feet. We mounted a 1,700-foot crest, dropped down a steep killer of a hill filled with tussocks, and then continued along the wide river valley. We came to a dilapidated old barn and found white splashes on the floor and many 2½-inch pellets, doubtless cast by tawny owls. The pellets were filled with fur, bones and tiny jaws of voles and a few woodmice. Knowing the tawny to be an early nester, I wondered if they had a nest nearby. If there was a breeding pair here, the female

99

should by now be sitting on eggs, but I found no nest in the barn.

On the way back from photographing stags which had dropped their antlers at the head of the valley, we were doused by the odd cold shower, so we kept to the riverside trees. As we emerged from them I saw a huge old dead oak-tree snag standing all alone in the fields. Suddenly a large dark brown bird seemed to appear from nowhere, beat away with rapid flaps of its long wings, then it curved and vanished into the trees further ahead. An eagle? No, it was too small; too small even for a buzzard. I noticed it had a chunky body.

We made a wide circle round the snag. About eight feet up the great trunk I saw a large recess, with a level edge in front of it. Curious, I placed a piece of thick broken branch against the tree and stepped up. Three large and almost round white eggs lay close together on a bed of old wooden chips in the recess. It was a tawny owl we had seen, and this was her nest. What luck!

Rapidly we left, retraced our steps and waited behind the thick green foliage of a stunted holly tree. It was nearly ten minutes before the tawny returned to her nest, and it was a good thing I kept a close watch for she flew back at such an angle that she kept the trunk between us and her flight path. All I saw, to know she was back, was a brief wing flip at the side of the snag.

Telling Moobli to wait by my pack, I stole cautiously to behind the snag, focused the camera lens at three feet and judged the exposure against the dark bark on the shadowy side of the snag. I climbed on to the piece of branch, raised the camera slowly, waited until a gust of wind caused a rustle in the nearby trees, then clicked off a frame.

Nothing moved. Had I been mistaken? Was she there? Sides and stomach aching with the strain of balancing on the branch, I raised myself up painfully until my head came level with the female tawny sitting on her eggs, her eyes more closed than open, fitfully dozing! I had never been so close to a wild adult owl before. As she had not noticed the first camera click, I took another photo.

This woke her, she came out with her black eyes staring at me and for a second I feared I might suffer the fate of bird photographer Eric Hosking, who lost an eye to a nesting tawny. But she turned away as I jumped down and beat a hasty retreat, then flew into a riverside alder. We left quietly and I saw her fly back to the nest when we were 200 yards away.

It seemed odd that the great hole should be on the east side of the snag, away from the corroding weather of the prevailing south-westerly winds and rains that swept the valley. I imagined she found it cold work in the wintry north-easterlies we had recently experienced, because female tawnies do all the incubating of the eggs.

This was not, of course, my first experience of tawny owls at Wildernesse. The previous autumn I had frequently heard the sharp '*wick*' calls of one bird and the mournful but musical hooting of its answering mate, as the adults sought to re-establish their territories, and any young owls reared that year looked for areas of their own. Sometimes I went out and, through the two thumbs atop my cupped hands, hooted back in fair imitation. It is fun to 'hoot up' owls in this way, for often they will come nearer and nearer, making '*wick*' cries, and once I hooted an owl into the ash tree beside the cottage. On a winter supply trip in deep snow I had seen two tawnies perched on telegraph poles, hoping for a traffic-crushed rabbit or mouse.

They called a lot in March too, during courtship and before mating. I took a morning off to make a proper owl nest-box, which I installed in an oak tree in the east wood, beneath a broad sheltering branch. Some nights I managed to hoot them near it, but they did not use it to nest in. One misty morning in late April we trekked over to check the tawny in the oak snag and found she was still on the three eggs.

Much of May was spent making a BBC television film. Then on a glorious day towards the end of the month, the oaks now thick with leaves, the beeches well covered in their bright spring dress, Moobli and I set off in the boat for a big river valley, to trek up and check the tawny's nest. As it was my birthday I thought I would take *them* a gift, so in my pack were two trapped woodmice which I would leave on the edge of their tree hollow. While the female tawny does the incubating, the male does most of the feeding of the young; today he would have to work less hard.

As we were leaving the shore I swung the pack off my

shoulder to lay it down in the boat. There was a loud plop. The top half of my valuable 640mm lens had fallen into the loch. It floated for a few moments but, as I desperately reversed, it sank in fifteen feet of water. I tied fishing line round a plastic box, weighted the other end with a rock and left it there as a marker while I boated back to change into my rubber wet suit. I had to dive three times before I managed to locate the lens. I grabbed it from where it lay wedged between two rocks, and then had to swim hard after the drifting boat and clamber aboard. Back home I went again, to change and dry out the lens. When we set off once more, delayed by two hours and with another little lesson learned, the male cuckoos behind the cottage were answering the loud cuckoo calls from across the loch. As I recalled that the great slapstick team of Laurel and Hardy had adopted 'The Dance of the Cuckoo' as their film theme tune, the music of their calls seemed hugely appropriate to my idotic escapade.

We moored the boat in the river and trekked to the owls' snag. Making Moobli wait by the pack, I went with the camera and stood on the ruined wall of an old sheep fank thirty yards away. Having had luck hooting up owls in the autumn, and wanting one photo of the owl in flight if possible, I gave a low hooting whistle. I thought I saw movement in the hole. Levelling the camera, I hoot-whistled again. Up came the female tawny's head, then with a jump and a brush of her wings, she launched herself as my shutter clicked. With her broad blunt head and twin-dialled face, its staring blue-black eyes thrust forward, she flew silently on long broad wings to the riverside alders.

The eggs had hatched successfully and the three youngsters already had most of their feathers, but their wings were short and their tail feathers not grown at all. They were not near flying stage yet. They crouched in a corner looking like wise old monks, clopping their great grey-yellow horny beaks in fear, holding their light-blue third eyelids, or nictitating membranes, half-closed as if sleepy. It was as if they were trying to block out the sight of the human face, or to pretend to themselves the obvious threat was not really happening. Unlike the semi-grown young of many birds of prey, they made no threat movements, and I thought they were among the loveliest of all young birds.

How hard it was, having kept a young tawny as a boy, to resist the temptation to take one home. But of course they were protected birds. And like all wild creatures, unless injured or definitely abandoned by their parents, they were best left alone. As I took some quick photos the mother called '*wick*' from a large alder. I put the woodmice on the ledge and left.

Almost a week later I trekked back over the hills to check the owls again. As I came down the steep tussocky slopes I saw a pair of hooded crows hunting, doubtless to feed *their* semi-fledged young. One crow was sneaking cautiously through the high tufts beside a small burn after tasty young frogs, while its mate sat very still on a high tussock, perhaps watching the movements of nesting birds, as does the cuckoo, but for quite different reasons. Crows are partial to other birds' eggs, or even their young, which is perhaps one reason why ground-nesting pipits often pull grasses over their nests when they leave them. Hoodies also clear up carrion in which many pest flies breed; and I have seen pairs of them eating maggots off carcasses.

There were two young owls left in the nest, and while their wing feathers were longer, the tails were mere brownish tufts. Of the third owlet there seemed at first no sign, but after walking in widening circles I found three downy feathers heading in a straight line to the north-west. Either fox or wildcat could have leaped up to the nest (a fox can climb almost as well as a cat, especially if the bark is rough to give purchase for its claws), but then there should have been feathers scattered around the nesting hollow. And the other owlets would probably have been taken too. It was possible the youngster had fallen out and been taken by a fox or wildcat when stunned, so that it did not struggle and lose its feathers. I returned on June 7 and the hollow was empty. As there was no sign of any struggle, I felt the young owls had flown safely.

A few evenings later I was startled by a sudden shrieking commotion from the nearest islet to the cottage where some common gulls had a small nesting colony. In the hastening dusk I hurried down to the wooded land spit opposite the islet with my fieldglass. I then heard tawny owls calling from the stunted pines. It was hard to see what was going on but the ghostly shapes of the gulls showed that they could see well enough to fly. They appeared to be diving down and sheering off from the branches of an outer pine.

It seemed a pair of tawny owls were after grabbing a gull chick or two; but why did they hoot at the same time? It did not make good hunting sense. Then, when I heard one owl calling '*kwik*' and the other hooting from the other side of the islet, I realised what was probably happening. The pair were working together. One owl would call, thus attracting the mobbing attacks of the airborne gulls, yet remaining safe in the densely needled branches, while the other tried to sneak down and snaffle an unguarded chick!

Presently I saw one of the tawnies rising from the nesting rocks and wing away eastwards like a grey-brown ghost, and I was sure I saw something in its furred talons. Instantly, the second owl shot from its tree and followed the first at a speed I would not have believed a tawny was capable of. Would they share the prey? At any rate, it was an interesting discovery. I heard the owls on the islet twice more after that.

There were the usual owl calls in our woods that autumn as the birds re-established territories. On Christmas Day I trekked up the big river valley. There was no sign of the tawnies near the oak snag, nor in the barn, and I wondered if they had taken to the shelter of the long woodlands where there would be more prey in winter. When I heard owls' courting calls in our woods in mid-March I spring-cleaned the nest-box I had put up for them and covered its floor with dry wood chips for additional encouragement.

On April 4 we went to check the oak snag again. The river was swollen with recent heavy rains, so I had to cross it by leaping along the tops of boulders. Moobli, who did not mind getting wet, just bulldozed his way across the rapid current. There was now grass growing on the edge of the hollow, which made me think it was not being used. But as I put the thick branch against the trunk to climb up, out came the female tawny. There were two eggs on the wood dust and chips, both oddly dirty. It appeared that she was still laying and had not yet started full incubation. On April 11 we checked again: still two eggs and they were still dirty.

I did not return until May 28, when I was sure any young

104

would be fairly well fledged. The river tawnies had had a bad year. There was no sign of them at the nest, in which I found one addled half-empty egg covered in debris, plus some wax-sheathed feathers that had clearly come from a youngster or two. Some of the quills had been neatly clipped above the tips, which I felt must have been the work of a fox. As we trekked further up the river both parent owls flew out of the alders as if unable to break the bond that held them to the nesting snag. I felt even sorrier for them when I found no new nest in the old barn.

That autumn, and again in the early spring of our third year, tawnies hooted often in our woods. When, at 7.30 pm on March 18, I heard loud hooting in the east wood I went out and hooted back. Suddenly a tawny landed on the porch roof above my head with scratchy clinks of its talons, glared down at me, made two loud '*kik kik*' calls, then flew off again. I had thought it was much further away. It seemed almost to be telling me that while I had the woods to myself all day, at night my place was indoors. I kept hooting to see if it would come back.

It did – and flew past quite close, from right to left. It was wonderful to see it gliding silently along, its broad round head, dark eyes staring from the twin dials of its face, long wings straight out and slim as pencils. It went past again from left to right, then soared into the west wood. There it made a few more '*wick*' calls.

In the hope that it was looking for a good nest site, I climbed up next day to check the owl nest-box. It had been half-filled with moss, pine cones and old thick-budding oak twigs, which suggested it had been used as a food cache by a red squirrel pair. I cleaned most of them out and again put in some wood chips.

Next morning I was startled from sleep by loud '*kwick kweek*' screeches. The batteries in my torch were low, but even in the dim light that I shone towards the window I could make out the chunky shape of a male tawny owl on the sill before it flew off towards the east wood. I wondered if it had come to say thanks, or else to stage a protest. Although we heard more owl calls during the next few nights and stayed away from the nest-box area, they did not use it.

On April 3 I went to look at the oak snag again. I approached carefully, using my fieldglass, determined not to put the tawny off if she was sitting on eggs. I was dismayed to see three small rocks had been placed in the recess, apparently by human hands, as if to discourage the birds from nesting. What 'crime' they could have committed in that wild deserted glen I could not imagine, except that they often roosted in the old barn and let a few droppings and pellets go on some ramshackle equipment. Tawny owls do more good than harm, even to man's interests, for they kill far more mice and grass-eating voles than any other prey, but there are still a few goons about who hate anything with a hooked beak.

When I climbed up I saw the hollow snag would not have been used by the owls anyway. The winds and rains had finally worn through the back of the trunk and rotting chunks of wood also lay over the nest bowl. On an eagle trek two weeks later I found the old snag was still deserted, but an adult owl flew out of the barn. At least it had not been shot.

In February and March of our fourth year, tawnies again courted noisily in our woods but they still did not use the nest-box, nor could I find any nest. In March Moobli sniffed out feet, pelvis, and some wing feathers of a tawny stuffed under rocks by an otter holt a mile to the west. What little flesh was left was still red, so it had died in the last ten days. Then we discovered the remains of another not far from where the wildcat had killed the barn owl in the lochside woods to the east. When we trekked to the oak-tree snag on April 16 we saw no signs of owls, either in the barn or the trees. The hole at the back of the nest hollow had been even more opened up by the weather, and an eleven-foot section of the top of the great snag had snapped off and lay in large orange chunks of rotting wood about its base. Even without human interference it had now definitely come to the end of its days as a nest site for owls.

That autumn there were no hootings or calls in our woods. The two dead bodies I had found must have been those of our resident pair. This was the first intimation I had that in our sort of terrain, where the woodlands were sparse and the trees fairly far apart, tawnies would range over two miles to hunt. While this was interesting, I felt sad, for it seemed things were not looking at all good for the tawnies in our immediate area.

Imagine my feelings, therefore, when on a supply trip on

October 11 my local butcher friend Dugald told me that a family I knew had found an injured owl on the road. It had been hit by a car. One side of its head had been knocked in but it was eating well.

'They want to release it, but I told them you would look after it and would be up to see them,' he said. 'Are you interested?'

Was I! I could have hugged him. I wasted no time after shopping and went round to see the owl.

I was greeted by two lovely little girls who said they knew owls did not like daylight, so they kept it in a darkened room and fed it mince and water. I followed them in, and we found the owl perched quietly on the back of a chair.

Even in the gloom I could see it was a tawny owl. While rather squat and short, its plumage was fully grown. Its breastbone was thin and the right side of its head had been badly damaged by the car, though the eye seemed to be working all right. I told the girls I would fetch it after an overnight visit I had to make to a friend.

On the following day I bought four mousetraps and a supply of meat, and then went to fetch the owl. There was no one at home, but a note on the unlocked front door said 'Mike. Owl is in kitchen.' I coaxed it into a box stuffed with dry bracken, and drove and boated it home.

Arriving back, I carried up the supplies and swiftly made the owl a good strong perch. To do this I nailed a thick straight hazel sapling to a heavy round butt of larch, which made a secure base, and to the sapling I nailed a hazel crosspiece about three feet long and an inch thick. I set this perch in my fourteen-foot-square kitchen. Then I lifted the box, opened its lid, and held it near the perch. To my delight the owl stood up, looked at the crosspiece, immediately hopped on to it, then turned round to face me as if it had been used to that perch all its life.

9 · A Highland Victim

Now that I could see the owl in full daylight I was surprised at the rich beauty of its plumage. Oranges, bright browns, fawns and dark browns mingled delicately, and down its light tan chest were an array of superb dark-brown anchors. Its long thick legs were encased in soft downy fur which reached over the toes to the black talons, and its feet were zygodactyle like a woodpecker's, for it perched with two toes forward and two to the rear of the crosspiece.

As I saw again the squat short shape, I knew it was a male, for female tawny owls can be up to a quarter as big again as the males. No one dislikes cosy anthropomorphisms – giving to animals human attributes they cannot possess – more than I do, but I could not keep calling him just 'the owl'. As he perched there, looking wise, regarding me with half-closed eyes, I decided to call him Wallie – in honour of a wise, talented novelist and journalist by the name of Wallie Clapham, who had first encouraged me to start writing about wildlife.

Right from the start Wallie was so tame and tractable that I felt sure he had been a pet owl, perhaps taken from the nest as a youngster; either he had escaped or had been released because he was not house-trained. And there he had sat in the road, waiting for one of those kind two-legged giants to shove some meat into his wide gape, but he had been hit by a car instead, and had the right side of his face bashed in.

I held up chunks of steak and kidney. He reached down with his beak, took them from my hand, tried to jerk them back down his throat, stopped, looked perplexed, and dropped them to the floor. When I cut them up small, however, he jerked them back without difficulty. This would not do. Eventually I wanted him to go into the wilds and he would not find neatly cut-up meat there. By holding the bigger chunks near his feet, touching them with the meat, I finally induced him to stretch out one set of talons and grab them. Then, holding each chunk down on the branch, he bent down and rended it with his beak in the natural way. It took an hour, but finally he got the hang of it, and by nightfall he had eaten a quarter-pound of meat. When I held out water in tin lids he quibbled his beak in it, lifted his head up and let the drops go down his throat. What was interesting here was that when I held the water out in a red container, he nibbled at its edge and did not drink, yet he never nibbled at a lid of unpainted metal. He could clearly see the colour red and must have thought it was meat. It was the first hint I had that tawny owls could distinguish colours.

Next morning, after he had again eaten well, I decided to exercise his wings. To do this I made a broad leather jess for one of his strong legs, tied this to a line that ran off freely from a fishing spinning reel, and tried to get him on to my hand. At first he clung hard to the perch, but when I pushed against his chest with a finger he fluttered his blunt broad wings and finally climbed on to it. *Ouch.* Those talons were sharp indeed.

I took him outside and worked my arm gently up and down, making him flap his wings. Finally he took off and flew quite well but when I saw he was heading for the ash trees along the shore, I applied slight pressure to the line and brought him down in the grasses. His eyes then went wide, blue-black like two great sloes, and his head turned round a full 180 degrees as he stared up at me from the ground. Although his plumage was composed of tans and browns, all I could see from a few yards away were his two huge black eyes. Like a wildcat, his eyes opened fully in daylight when he thought he might be in trouble. I now saw his irises were in fact dark brown. He had two more flights, then I took him in and put him back on his perch.

He spent most of the day dozing. When I went into the kitchen he looked at me by squinting with one eye open or the other. Whenever I put my face near his, far from being alarmed or attacking, he shrank back with a blissful look and gently quibbled his grey hooked beak against my nose as if bestowing little kisses. When I gave him a piece of bread, to see what he would do, he held it in one foot, tugged bits off with his beak, appeared to taste them with his tongue, then tossed them up into the air. But he kept pecking at the bread in this way, as if hoping to find meat underneath. He showed no fear of Moobli, just gazing down at him with a contemplative air, but the dog did not like the sound of his beating wings and so mostly stayed on his bed in the hall, his favourite place in the cottage anyway. While an owl can fly silently when hunting, due to the velvet pile on the fine-fringed edge of its pinions, its wings can also make loud woofing noises when flapping hard in a confined space.

Wallie could definitely taste, but whether with his tongue or some sensory organ in his beak, I could not know. He liked kidney, beef, liver, in that order. If he had eaten enough and I gave him more, he just held it in his beak tip, nibbled it a few times, then dropped it. He nearly always rejected mutton in this way. He liked to keep his beak clean. He could feel meat fat left on the outside of the bill, and would bend down to wipe his beak on the hazel branch, first the left side, then the right. The first time I saw him do this he went on wiping and wiping so long, like a man stropping a razor, that I was afraid he would wear off the basal feathers. I cleaned his beak up with a cloth and, as if knowing it was now clean, he stopped. I noticed he always held food with his left foot, yet when he scratched his chin he did it like a little dog, amazingly accurately, with just one talon of his right foot.

An owl needs roughage in its diet; fur, feathers and bones of its normal prey, and as there were many mice and voles round the place since Liane's disappearance, I started setting the traps. Wallie looked at the first woodmouse with wide-eyed surprise, reached down and took it from my hand with his beak. He seemed to weigh it, realise it was too big and heavy to gulp back,

110

then grabbed it with his left foot and held it down on the branch. It took him eighteen tugs to dispose of the mouse, sometimes pulling so hard his foot came up by his head. But for furious wing flapping, he would have overbalanced backwards. He always ate the heads of prey first, swallowing the skull and the brains before the other parts. It was comical later to see him produce his first pellet, the ball of fur and bones that all birds of prey disgorge during digestion. He reached up into the air with his head, made bowing motions as if trying to be sick, then up came the pellet. As it dropped to the floor he seemed to gaze down at it in great surprise. Maybe he had not been fed a mouse before.

One night, after I had left my supper simmering on the bottled-gas stove, I went in to find the flames were out and a smell of gas everywhere. Wallie had clearly been flying around and the draught from his wings had blown them out. I had to watch that in future.

Over the days he seemed so utterly tame I wondered how I would ever, to use the falconry parlance, 'hack' him back to the wild. When it was raining and I could not take him out for wing-stretching flights on the fishing-reel creance, I devised little games to keep him alert and occupied. If I ran at him from across the room and stopped with my face just an inch from his, he would only bob up an inch or two, as if in slight surprise or he had not seen me coming. His great black orbs, slightly oval, gazed into my eyes, then he went 'soft', assumed a blissful expression and reached forward to nuzzle my 'beak' with his. He really enjoyed this. If I suddenly put my hand over his face, however, he swivelled his head round 180 degrees and stared at the wall! He loved being tickled under the chin, stretching himself to his full height of just over a foot, his eyes half-closed sleepily.

At night, if I left all the doors open, he would fly through the kitchen and hall and into the study and land on my shoulder as I sat typing at the desk. He would stay there for up to two hours at a time, deliberately leaning in close and keeping that side of my neck and head warm. If I turned my face his way slightly he nibbled gently at my lips. He also nibbled up and down on my ear which, as anyone knows from love nuzzlings with humans of the opposite sex, send you quite gaga! These were definitely expressions of affection. He was the friendliest creature I had ever known.

By the end of the first week he could dispose of a mouse or vole in four hard tugs. If he was not really hungry, he would just hold the prey in his left foot, then gaze rapturously into space for long periods, as if anticipating the easy meal ahead. I noticed, too, that he did not appear to have a frontal crop like most birds. Instead the food travelled to a special sac in his belly under his tail, from which it was presumably digested. Dissection of a dead owl would be interesting. To check he had eaten enough I could just pat this odd 'container', feel the weight there. Oddly, his splashy white droppings caused little trouble. He had just three favourite perches and newspaper spread under each of them took care of the problem.

Wallie's pre-dusk flights continued and his wings grew stronger. Then the boat arrived from down the loch with the telegram that told me my stepmother was dying and my father had become incapable in Spain. I could not release Wallie into the wilds as I was sure he could not hunt and kill yet. After a frantic phone call, a friend in Worthing kindly agreed to look after both Moobli and Wallie. I left Wildernesse and drove south, installed Wallie in Margot Wallis's town-house kitchen, and dashed off to Spain. After a nightmare month, my sister flew out to relieve me for a further month while I hurried back to Britain to sort out our father's tangled affairs and to finish a book by its Christmas deadline.

When I collected Moobli and Wallie, Margot said the owl had been no trouble in the house, apart from the mess he made. He had enjoyed games with her children. The only troubling moment had come when they took him to some allotments for an outdoor flight. He had flown a long way and landed on the roof of a garage, from which he refused to come down. Margot was a skilled amateur mountaineer, however, as she had proved on a visit to Wildernesse, and after a little 'rockface' work without pitons she managed to recapture him.

A brief visit to London on the way back to the Highlands gave Wallie the chance to save me from a parking ticket. When I emerged from a lawyer's office in Holborn after sorting out a *right:* Holly, the London tawny, was found shot through the wing in a Putney park. Before it healed, she held the splinted wing out to the side like a barn door.

below: At first it seemed Holly and the emaciated female kestrel would get along well together. One night I heard screeches from the kitchen, and found Holly holding the kestrel round the neck with one set of talons. Luckily the kestrel was well enough to fly free a few days later.

above: Hacking Holly back to the wild, I left her on a stump with a mouse. I gave her a final goodbye chuck under the chin before I released her, but she did not appear to know her jesses had been removed.

below: Crowdy, the most beautiful young owl, was the only one afraid of Moobli. She perched on the kitchen door and glared towards the study, checking on the whereabouts of *that dog*!

above: Crowdy often flew round the kitchen showing her beautiful wings before landing on her favourite perch of deer antlers.

below: She had an astounding ability to separate every individual feather of her wings and tail after a bath so that they would dry more quickly.

above: When I put a vole on the floor Crowdy landed beside it with all the grace of a ballet dancer. With exquisite delicacy, she bent down and picked it up with her beak before flying with it back to her perch.

below: She loved to nibble affectionately at my knuckles while making high chittering squeaks. Almost ready for freedom, she went for a swing on my Spanish chandelier and glared at the world of darkness outside.

legal problem for my father, two traffic wardens intending to put the ticket on my illegally parked truck were so entranced by Wallie on his perch that they completely forgot to write it out. They asked me many questions about him, then with a laugh waved me on my way.

As we drove home I felt more relaxed and had a chance to study Wallie's behaviour. He often flew from his perch to land on my shoulder, nuzzled close, then returned the astonished stares of other motorists with weaving movements of his head. An owl's eyes are fixed immovably in their sockets, unlike those of humans, so it makes those bobbing and weaving actions as an aid to focusing.

When we camped for the night outside Fort William, he fought strenuously with his strong legs and talons not to be put in his bracken-filled box. He wanted to be part of the action.

He perched on the driving seat and peeped round the curtain to watch me cooking, first one side, then the other, peering at me with one eye at a time. Then he flew into the bowl of washing-up water. After I put him back on his perch he again hopped on to the driving seat, peeped round the curtain and flew again – this time into my cooked soup! I had to use all the rest of my water supply to clean him up. Once he landed on Moobli's back; he just groaned loudly and put his head out flat with resignation. It was natural Wallie should be more active at night but we could not have him flying about as we tried to sleep – so into his box and under the truck he went.

Back in our kitchen after a stormy boat trip home, Wallie looked round with his great dish of a face, seeming to remember everything. Then, just as I was hearing over the radio that it had been the mildest November for twenty years, the first snow blizzards began. Wallie thrived in the kitchen. He was far more active at night and woke me several times with noisy flying and knocking things off shelves. He took to tearing my carrots to tiny fragments, scattering them all over the kitchen table and floor. It was further proof he could distinguish colours; the red must have looked like meat to him, for he never tore up other vegetables in this way. When the weather improved, and I was not on snow treks for eagles and red deer, or pounding away at my book, I took Wallie out for flights. And I fed him mice and voles on the level mossy branch of a plum tree, as part of his rehabilitation back to the wild.

I had to fly back to Spain to relieve my sister on December 9. I still felt that Wallie would be unable to take care of himself in the wilds, especially in what was now proving to be an exceptionally harsh winter. I felt I could not inflict him on Margot again, although she had agreed to take Moobli. So I telephoned Roger Wheater, Director of the Scottish National Zoo Park in Edinburgh, to whom I had given one of my wildcat kittens for breeding purposes.

'Certainly we will take Wallie,' he said. 'I am sure the kids who visit here will love him. And there'll be no charge!'

When the time came, I drove Wallie to the Zoo and with the help of keeper Eddie Clarke installed him in a parrot cage for the night in a heated warehouse. He bore it stoically, and as I left him a dead mouse and kissed him goodbye, he wrinkled up his eyes and returned it with a gentle beak nibble on my nose. I felt quite sad as I drove away for Worthing and Spain.

After more nightmare weeks, I managed to get my father back and into a nursing home in Worthing, where he had once worked and had many friends to visit him, and returned with Moobli to my disrupted life in the Highlands in February. I did not pick up Wallie as there were still legal problems to sort out in Spain and I would have to go back again in April to sell my father's villa. In March I wrote to Roger Wheater, explained the problems and hoped the Zoo could take care of Wallie a little longer. His reply was most reassuring:

> I am sorry you are having such difficulties over your father's affairs in Spain, but rest assured that your loss is our gain because Wallie has endeared himself to all the Education staff, has been the most marvellous education aid in that he is totally free-flying all the time in the Unit and reacts very gently and nicely to the children . . . Please do not concern yourself about our looking after him; we are delighted to do so and I know there will be a lot of disappointment when he finally returns to the wilds in Argyll.

A trek on April 8 revealed no sign of the river tawnies. The top of the oak snag had broken off even further, just above the old nesting hollow. I wondered if they had been shot.

It was May 31 before I returned from selling the villa and arrived at Edinburgh Zoo to claim Wallie. I was greeted by the Curator, Miranda Stevenson, and the Education Officer, Rob Ollason, who had Wallie in a fruit box, ready to leave.

'He was a great favourite here,' said Rob. 'The kids who come here from the schools in the Lothian region loved him. They all thought he was a stuffed owl at first – until he flew! He flew free in two big rooms, had his own perch and was wonderful with the kids, allowing them to handle him. He seemed to enjoy whirring round above their heads, almost as if he was showing off.'

Apparently Wallie had shown great interest in some gerbils, who had been so terrified by his goggle-eyed stares that they had to be covered up when he was flying about. He paid regular visits to some chipmunks, staring at them through the glass of their enclosure; he perched by a pair of ferrets with five young, looking at them for up to an hour at a time, and was also fascinated by the tank of axolotls. He had, however, shown no interest at all in the Education Unit's tortoise!

We boated home in sunlight and soon had Wallie safely back on his kitchen perch, where he spurned the day-old chicks the Zoo had given me and gulped down chunks of liver and kidney. Over the ensuing weeks, as I began working with eagles again from a hide, I noticed Wallie had undergone a slight personality change while at the Zoo. Although he still affectionately nibbled my nose, he sometimes pecked quite viciously at my hand when I went to stroke him. He seemed to have become a bit of a townie! Maybe, having had lots of kids handling him, he had learned to be defensive, and how to make it known when he did not want to be touched at any particular moment.

This viciousness, small though it was, only occurred when my hand approached him from the left side, however. When I touched his right side or his right foot, he was as gentle as ever. Well, it was his right side that had been damaged; maybe he had less feeling there. In mid-June, I brought back a dead rabbit, which a pair of eagles had repeatedly ignored (frustrating my attempts to photograph them at it) and left it on the kitchen table. Next morning I found Wallie had opened it up and had eaten meat and bones from its upper shoulder. Later he brought up a pellet with rabbit fur and bones in it. It was the first intimation I had that owls would eat carrion.

By this time we had invented a new game – Footsie. I would extend a crooked forefinger, he would stand high and grab it hard with his right foot, then I would make gentle backward and forward tugs, and he would look down, really enjoying it. Sometimes he put his head back, looked dreamily at the ceiling and fluttered his whitey-mauve eyelids. He liked being rocked and swayed about in this way, sort of dancing on his perch. If I pulled my hand out too far, he held on until his leg was at full stretch (I was astonished to find it extended a full six inches), then removed his talons. We played this game every time I returned from checking eagle eyries or from visits to the hide, and he seemed to look forward to it. As I felt the strength in his thick leg I realised one possible reason why it was so long – an owl can thrust its talons well in front of its face when hitting into prey while flying, and thus avoid possible injury to its eyes.

On June 28 I was woken up by noisy splashing sounds from the kitchen. As I went in, Wallie flapped to his perch with great difficulty, his wings and tail soaked. He had been taking a bath in the washing-up bowl in the sink! After that he seemed to like a bath every three or four days. I put my hand near him one afternoon, to try and get him on it for an outdoor flight, when he bent down and pecked it hard. I withdrew my hand and tried again. This time he flew out, hit my face and transfixed one set of talons two inches below my right eye. Instinctively, I swiftly brushed him away hard, but he kept flying and started flailing at the window. I went to get some meat to calm him down and saw my face in the mirror. Blood was streaming down my cheek. Those talons were even sharper than I had thought. I did not think it was a definite attack, more that he was using my face to bounce from as it was in the way of his sudden flight. Later I had him in the study, talked to him while I was typing, and he was soon his old self. I noticed now that the kitchen window was often misty in the mornings, a sign he had been trying to get out.

Obviously, he was maturing quickly and would need to be released fairly soon. I began trying to train him to 'catch' moving prey. I tied dead mice or voles to thin fishing line and tugged them about the floor in what were meant to be natural darts and runs. Although he looked down with wide eyes he never flew down to chase them. Within minutes of my going out and shutting the door, however, he would have them up on his perch for eating. When two woodmice were caught in the traps, one dead, the other just trapped by a rear leg and still alive, I gave the dead one to Wallie, who shot his left foot out for it. He stared blissfully into space, dreaming of the meal ahead, as he usually did when not hungry. The live woodmouse I put into a box of hay with cheese and bread, and set ox kidney chunks on the floor.

When I got back next day from an overnight eagle stint, the box was upended, hay was all over the floor, the mouse was gone. Wallie's rear-end food sac was nicely full. The ox kidney remained untouched. Owls have unusually large ears under the feathers on the sides of their heads and hunt by hearing as much as by sight. He had clearly heard the mouse rustling about and had contrived to get it out of the haybox. At least it seemed he *could* catch a live mouse. And on his pre-dusk flights now his wings beat with considerable power.

I often kept watch on him when he did not know it, by sitting in the study at dusk and keeping my eye glued to a monocular. I then found he had two main methods of stretching which he never used when I was in the kitchen with him. One was to stretch one leg and foot down as far as it would go, then extend the wing on the same side down past the leg. He held this pose for a few seconds, brought the leg and wing up again, then repeated the procedure on the other side. The other way was to lift his wing shoulders high in double bows way over his head and fan his tail out downwards, so he looked like a Hottentot.

It worried me that he never made any vocal sounds, which he would surely need in the wild. For weeks he had been the Owl That Couldn't Hoot. So I started giving him some 'hoot' training. Each night, for a quarter-hour or so at a time, I made whistle hoots with my mouth, and also the cupped-hands hoot through my thumbs. He looked at me with his head on one side but never tried to imitate the sounds. One night I gave up in disgust and went to bed.

At 4 am I was woken up by extraordinary noises, like an

animal being strangled. High-pitched breathy screeches were followed by attempts to make an '*oo*' sound. I got up, crept through the hall and opened the kitchen door slowly, just in time to catch Wallie's first fully-fledged hoot. It was higher in tone than that of any tawny I had ever heard before but it was a hoot nevertheless. Wallie glared at me from the window catch where he was perched, as if annoyed I had interrupted his first attempts to make owl songs, then flew back to the hazel crosspiece.

After this I often found him on the window catch, gazing at the world outside. He clearly wanted to go. I set him on the hazel perch in late afternoons in front of the kitchen window. I intended, once he was free, to leave food there for him, so I now fed him there too.

On July 14 I took him from this perch for one last fly before bringing him indoors for the night. I carried him down to the open front pasture, sure he would head for the east-wood trees and that I could slow him down on the reel if he looked like going too high. Off he went, beating strongly, and I kept his flight under control, gently applying pressure to the line, until he landed on an oak branch some fifteen feet up. That was fine.

I walked towards him reeling in – then came to the end of the empty line. It had somehow snapped, just before an old knot join. I ran for my longest rod, and made a loop of line at its tip, went back and managed to snag and twist the end of the line that hung from Wallie's jess round the rod's tip. Then I gave a slight tug to make him fly so that I could bring him down. To my horror the line snapped again, right by his jess. He took off and landed high in the ash trees on the shore.

Wallie was free – by accident. And it was my fault for not testing the line. At least it had snapped off right by the jess so it could not get him tangled up in a tree. And he had a full gut, as he had eaten well that day. He was so tame that I felt sure he would come back when he was hungry. I set some meat out near his perch and on the kitchen table and left the window open. At 10 pm I went out again and saw him higher in the ash, sitting with his feathers fluffed out, ready for the night.

Before dawn next morning I heard wings whirring and slight crashes in the kitchen, but when I got up he was not there. While having breakfast in the study I heard another crash in the kitchen. I hurried in. No sign of Wallie, but the bits of heart had gone and many great tits were in the willow bush by the cottage wall, making the chirring alarm notes they use when mobbing an owl. I saw that some of them were youngsters. It seemed that Wallie *had* been there, that the parent birds were showing their young the 'enemy', but though I searched the woods until midday I could not find him.

Four days of misty drizzle followed. Only a few bits of heart meat had been taken from below the perch on the second, and further searches failed to reveal him. We were coming back from a trek in the eastern lochside woods on July 22 when I found a long soft breast feather, with the telltale anchor-like cross at the end of it, lying on a bracken frond. I was sure it was Wallie's. If so he was nearly a mile from the cottage. I looked round but could not find him, nor, thank heaven, his body. Further searches also failed. On August 5 I saw a buzzard constantly circling low over the north-east corner of our east wood. Had it spotted Wallie or his body? I went out but found nothing. Next day I did find one of his feathers in that same area. Well, he was free now, there were many mice and voles about; he would just have to take his chances. At least it was summer. What surprised me in view of his exceptional tameness was that he had not returned. It never happened like that in the story books and certainly not in wildlife movies.

10 · An Owl Shot in London

The owl now on the kitchen perch was bigger, heavier, and possessed a temperament quite different from Wallie's. A full three inches longer, clearly a female in her prime, she was stately, dignified – and wild. She had been found shot through the left wing in a London park and had been taken to the RSPCA animals' hospital in Putney. The wing had been set and now had a broad plastic clip on it, but was still so stiff she held it out to the side like a barn door.

A yard away from her on the same perch stood a female kestrel. She had also been found in a London park, weak, emaciated, but not injured. A friend of mine who worked at the hospital, knowing I lived in a wilderness area, had asked me to take these two Cockneys home, try to nurse them back to health and release them back into the wild.

Now, when you're taming owls, or at least trying to keep them friendly while they are in your care, it is important that you talk to them. As with most birds and animals, quiet soothing words, especially when you are about to feed them or handle them, help to calm owls down. For that reason you have to give them a name they recognise. When handling him I had felt the word Wallie on its own was a little stark, so I had called him Wallie Owly which, by some perverse process of my mind, had become Wallie Howly! Now, as I observed this female's prickly disposition, I called her Holly. Reverse the onomatopoeia, and what do you get? Two very soothing words when spoken in a low tone – Holly Wowly!

At first it seemed the owl and the kestrel would get along fine together; in fact they appeared to ignore each other's presence.

I soon discovered the differences in Holly's disposition. If I put my face close to her in the way Wallie had so enjoyed, she hissed with alarm and made loud clops with her beak. She did not mind the hand so much. By gently speaking her double name, and always giving her a little titbit from the hand first, she slowly permitted me to stroke the feathers on her broad cowled head. Whereas Wallie had been an unusually brightly coloured owl, with reddish orange tints among the varying browns of his plumage, Holly's dress was much more sober. Her browns were dark, almost chocolate coloured, as were the anchors down her chest, which was more light grey than tan. Despite her wing injury, she could fly a few yards, even up to the perch from the floor, but I tried to keep her as immobile as possible so that the wing would set properly.

At first she ate little, but when I found a newly dead thrush in the garden – which the kestrel immediately opened up – I stuffed steak into its breast and left it near her. She soon hopped down, grabbed it in one set of talons, flew with it to the wood-chopping block and tugged away at the meat. Then, one by one, she tore each of the thrush's main wing feathers out and let them drift to the floor. She had considerable strength.

She was much noisier than Wallie after dark and went to investigate things all over the kitchen. I was woken up by loud clangs and bangs on the second night. When I went to investigate Holly was on the floor surrounded by condiment containers, tea-bags, two broken saucers and three pans. She greeted me with an innocent stare in her great dark eyes, and a 'Don't blame me' sort of look. Luckily she had not hurt herself, and after that I kept hefty shelf items like pans upturned on the floor. Once she disappeared. She had gone into the chimney and was perched on a shelf three feet up it. I got her down and wired the chimney off.

At first she would not take raw meat from my hand. She just quibbled her beak on it and stood upright again. When I touched her foot with it, she lifted the foot up and I slid it beneath. She

121

felt the squashiness then, and holding it down with the foot, she tore it into pieces to swallow. When I gave her the first trapped vole she held it in her beak, knew instantly it was her natural food and tried to gulp it down whole. But it was just too large, considerably bigger than a mouse. She reached up with her left foot, a great hairy prometheus of a foot, and delicately pulled it out of her throat again. Then she tugged at it normally, and got it down her gullet after five pulls.

After a long trek one day, she must have worked up quite a hunger for she grabbed the mouse I held out with a ferocious strike of her left foot, then took it down to a dark corner on the floor. When I bent down to try to take a photo she hissed, clopped her beak, crouched low with all her feathers puffed out, moved her wings sideways and forwards, pinions tipped up, and fanned her tail out in a semi-circle below her body. Like a cat, she was presenting a fearsome front, making herself look bigger, to forestall any attempt of mine to take back the mouse.

After a week I decided to put Holly into the wildcat pens and to get some sleep free of all the bumps in the night. It was also important she did not become too tame in the kitchen. Although she had recently begun to clamber on my hand for food, she wouldn't right now. I had to catch her by the legs and she fought hard with her talons until I turned her on her back. Then she seemed to go into a dreamy catatonic state, as if hypnotised. Her eyes half closed, her wings hung loose and she stopped the hard clutchings. I got her into the pens and just left a mouse on the den roof as she had eaten well during the day.

Next day I found her standing on a rock by the den, looking at me with half-slit Japanese eyes. As I came nearer she did her hissing 'cat crouch', then hop-jumped into the shelter of the huge hogweed leaves by the side of the den. Shortly before dusk a torrential downpour began, so I got her into the den itself and left a chunk of ox heart beside her.

She was again standing beneath the leaky hogweeds on the following morning. She had clearly spent the whole night in the open and was drenched. She looked half size, her tail no longer a fan of soft broad feathers but straggly curved spines instead. As I went to catch her she clopped her beak, but once her talons took hold she walked up my arm to my shoulder, scrunching up my flesh painfully with each climbing step, and stayed there. As I walked back to the kitchen, she did her 'cat crouch', as if daring me to turn my face any nearer. I dried her wing and tail feathers lightly with a soft cloth and fed her. She soon dried out to her normal shape.

At the end of her second week I took her outside on a fine but breezy day and set her on the tall bow perch from which I was giving the kestrel its daily creance flights. As she looked around with black-eyed interest I saw there was a little pus under her plastic wing splint. I left it a few days longer than the RSPCA had suggested because the wing had not looked strong; now the splint had to come off. Oddly, Holly let me hold the wing and snip through the stitches with scissors as if she knew I was doing something for her own good. Then I treated the area with antiseptic. There was nothing much wrong with the joint but when she flapped her wings I could hear it creak slightly as if the joint was made of metal.

I left her there while flying the kestrel, but when I looked back I was horrified to see her fly two yards to the bird table, from there to the porch roof, then taking advantage of a stronger gust of wind, she flew high into a birch tree just east of the cottage. I tried to reach her with the fishing rod's tip but she just hop-climbed higher. I got out my old ladder and had climbed to ten feet, when a rung broke. The ladder slipped off the branch and I had a hard job to thrust it away as I fell so that it would not land on top of me. By dusk she had moved into an oak tree and was forty feet up. As Wallie had not returned, I feared Holly would not either. Since she had not seemed to have the sense to get out of the rain during that wet night in the pens, and as she could not fly as perfectly as Wallie could when he escaped, she could not possibly hunt as efficiently as a healthy strong owl. Even with the effort to overcome a big vole she might damage her wing which was still weak. It was essential to get her back.

The next day I set out with Moobli on the hopeless quest to find her. All round the woods we went, I glassing up and down every tree. After an hour Moobli found her – sitting on a rock near the burn, looking like a piece of stump. I crept slowly towards her, gently repeating her Holly Wowly name, as she regarded me with her huge sloe-black eyes. It was not a time for

messing about. I was afraid she would fly off into trees again, so I
did what one should never do with a bird except under such dire
circumstances – I made a swift grab with both hands. Her talons
and beak fought like windmills and I felt one talon go right
through to the bone of my middle finger. But as soon as I turned
her on her back, she relaxed into the same catatonic state as
before, and I carried her gently back to the kitchen. She was very
hungry, grabbed a piece of meat and took it to eat under the
table. *Phew!* That had been a near one.

I do not believe we have the right to keep any wild creature in
captivity unless its surroundings approximate to its natural
conditions in the wild. This applies even when we breed rare
species in order to re-stock the wild. The only exceptions are if
the animal itself chooses to stay close, if we are looking after
young which have truly been abandoned by their parents, or if
nursing a sick or injured animal back to health, as I was doing
with both Holly and the kestrel. While Holly's wing would take
a fair time longer to heal fully, the uninjured kestrel was eating
well and quickly replacing its lost body flesh. After a few more
daily flights on the line from the fishing reel, it would be fit
enough to go free into the wild.

Holly had never flown to land on my shoulder as Wallie had
but that night I was startled at my desk by a loud woofing of
wings, a rush of air, and when I looked round there she was,
sitting on the sweaters on my sea chest, calmly regarding me
with smiling slit eyes.

By the third week the kestrel had fully regained its strength,
was flying strongly, and tucking away more meat than the
bigger Holly. On three occasions I saw it trying to filch meat
from her as she tugged at it on the floor. The first time it landed in
front of her and made two fast snatches with its foot, but Holly
just held on, seeming to look at it with disdain. The second and
third times, the kestrel looked at the meat Holly was holding
with one foot, opened its beak, lifted its wings and tried to drive
her off it. Once it actually held on to the meat too, with one foot.
Holly again looked disdainful and shoved the other bird away
with a body movement, then fluffed her own feathers up and
took the meat into the wall corner behind the butt of the perch. It
surprised me that she did not once try to peck the kestrel, which

was less than half her weight. I felt sure the kestrel would not actually attack Holly, except for these attempts to filch her meat, which I could supervise. And it seemed Holly had no aggressive feelings towards the kestrel.

One night, however, I was startled at my desk by loud high-pitched squeals from the kitchen. I dashed in. Holly was holding the kestrel round the neck by her right foot at the fully extended reach of the long leg, while clinging on to the perch with her left. She seemed to be taking no notice of the kestrel's squeals and wildly flapping wings but just staring dreamily into space. I managed to get the kestrel free, noted it was unhurt, and shut it in the rear workshop. That was the end of the first fighting between them, and of any possibility of the owl killing the kestrel, for three days later the kestrel went free.

By the end of her fourth week in late September Holly's wing was being held in a normal position like the other, and I began taking her out for creance flights. After the first she seemed tired and went to sleep on her perch, close to the projecting tip of the upright sapling. I noticed she had an astounding ability to change her shape. In sleep she had elongated her body, her rounded facial discs had narrowed and were curving upwards and the patterns of their plumage now looked like twigs. Her body and tail, also narrowed, were pressed close to the sapling. It was obviously a camouflage technique a mature tawny owl possesses to make it look like a piece of stump, decayed wood, or a piece of bark that had split aside from a tree trunk. Wallie, far younger, had not yet had this ability to change his structure.

That day I came back from the shore in torrential rain, having hauled the boats higher out of the loch's rising level, to find the kitchen stinking of Calor gas. Holly was staggering round on the floor like a drunken parrot. She had somehow landed on the rubber pipes between the Calor-gas bottle and the cooker and they had come adrift. Neat gas was hissing out fast. I was terrified the leaking gas would reach the pilot light of the gas fridge and BANG – farewell to half of the cottage and no doubt to Holly, Moobli and myself.

Careful to make no draught, I switched off both gas canisters, opened the windows, and got Holly into the clean air of the workshop, where she soon recovered. I felt pretty groggy myself. I made sure the pipes were well protected after that.

As the days passed I became more and more fond of Holly. She would now climb on to my hand and stay there, allow me to fit her jess without protest, and never fly until I raised my arm high. Her nightly bangings ceased; she had learnt not to land on movable objects like tempting pan handles, and as she only messed in three places I toyed with the idea of keeping her as a pet. Only rarely did she take early morning baths like Wallie. I went in once, and she flew with difficulty to the perch looking like a scarecrow, her feathers rattling loudly. By late afternoon she was dry and fluffy again.

An extraordinary incident occurred at the end of September. I found a sick heron down by the shore and brought it into the kitchen in the hope it would recover while we went on a stag trek. I was just getting on my boots when I heard some loud thumps. I rushed to investigate and found three oranges lying near the heron. Holly was flying about in great agitation, clearly scared of the huge bird beneath her. The oranges had been in a deep plate on the shelf above the fireplace, yet the plate was still exactly in its place. Holly had clearly picked the oranges up and had been trying to bomb the heron with them! I shut her in the workshop, fed the heron slivers of meat, and when we returned from the trek put it into the wildcat pens under a fine starry sky.

From then on Holly liked perching on a bracket in the workshop as much as on her normal perch, and spent most of her days on one or the other imitating old stumps. On October 6 I found a freshly killed rabbit on the road, brought it home and left it on the kitchen table. When I went back in to cook supper, Holly was on it, had pecked through the skin and was tucking into the meat. Further proof owls will eat carrion.

Five mornings later I was woken at 5.35 am by odd calls from the kitchen. They started gently '*wooee ... ooeey ... oo ... ooe*', and built up to a crescendo '*oowhee, whee, wheeick, wheeick*, WICK!' It was not so much hooting as a slow build up to the full '*wick*' calls. This was the time of year when wild tawnies seek to re-establish their territories, calling frequently, and I felt she was now feeling lonesome for her own kind. At precisely 8.14 pm in the dark that evening, she gave a loud and perfect '*kee-wick, ko-whoo*' call, thereby confounding many naturalists, myself included, who believe Shakespeare was wrong when he wrote one owl can make both sounds together! I noticed the second part of the call was much deeper than Wallie's.

After that she spent much time on the window catch, or on the bench in the workshop, looking through the windows at the world outside. I knew then I should not keep her any longer. I took her for more daily flights, left her for periods on the bow perch outside, and then she began to flail at the windows at dawn, frequently making the double '*kee-wick, ko-whoo*' calls. I wondered if she had seen Wallie. Though I had looked out for him on all our treks, not once had I glimpsed him.

October 22 was a gorgeous sunny day, the first of a typically fine spell at this time of year. By now I loved her so much I knew I had to do it fast or I would never do it at all. In late afternoon I got her on to my hand and held her to my chest for a last stroking. As always, she stared upwards, eyes narrowed looking into mine, head shrunk into her shoulders, a little ball of trusting owl. She clopped her beak as I carried her out and she saw again the pasture and the little woods. I put her on a natural hazel perch, stroked her beautiful head and chucked her under the chin for the last time. She stayed on the perch for several minutes, as if not realising she was free, swivelling her head to the west wood then back to the east wood. Then she flew on her great long wings, her flight perfect now, and landed in a greengage tree on the edge of the east wood. I took what I felt would be the last photos and went back indoors. Half an hour later I went out again. She had gone into the oaks and with so much foliage it was impossible to see her any more.

Holly was free. As I cleaned up the kitchen and set her main perch outside in the porch, I felt sad, knowing I would miss her as much as I had Wallie. At least I had restored her birthright. Friendship with wild animals must never be possessive.

I began setting out bits of meat on the porch logs at night, but as nothing seemed to take them apart from chaffinches, great tits and coal tits, I stopped doing it. Instead I baited the whole area in front of the cottage with chicken corn and meal, hoping to increase the mouse and vole populations. This certainly worked, for within a month both species were climbing up the porch

walls and thundering around inside my roof, sounding like a
herd of small elephants. They must have come from the surrounding woods to the food bonanza, but whether Wallie and
Holly were taking any, or were even still alive, I had no idea. I
heard no hootings, and on our daily trek round the woods saw
neither of them.

Things changed on November 24 when I was woken in the
eerie light of pre-dawn by loud '*wick*' calls and also deep hootings, almost certainly made by Holly. I stole to the window and
through the fieldglass saw her perched on a broken branch of the
foremost ash tree on the shore. It was good to see she was doing
all right but why would neither she nor Wallie, if he was still
alive, come back to *me*?

Rainy dark days followed, so dark that once I had to light the
paraffin lamp at 2.45 pm. In December I had to dash south to
sort out a major problem for my father and to agree a contract
on a book with a new publisher. Before I left I cut up the carcass
of the first dead deer and distributed the meat round the woods,
hoping the owls would feed from it if they were in need.

We boated home in mid-January and soon were engulfed in
major snow storms. Although the deer meat had been partly
eaten by foxes, ravens and crows, there seemed to be no owl
pellets or droppings in our woods. On a snow-tracking trek
on February 3 to the eastern river valley, we found the old oak
snag even more broken down, the section containing the nest
hollow had gone, and there were no signs of owls in the old
barn. If Wallie and Holly were still alive, they had not taken over
that area.

It was on a ten-mile return trek from the west a fortnight later
that we had final proof Wallie *was* still alive. Half a mile into the
long wood, there was a sudden woofing of wings above my
head. I looked up to see Wallie's broad dished face, the dark eyes
staring down, and away he went on blunt brown wings from
where he had been perched in an ivy-covered tree. His body was
as squat as ever, his plumage the same bright browns. It was him
all right. He must have seen us coming from a long way through
the leafless trees, yet had waited until we were right below before
taking off. He had been perched near a deer-calf carcass, and
some small pellets containing deer hair were under the tree. He

128

above: A wild tawny owl dozing fitfully on her eggs.

below: Looking like little cowled monks, two semi-fledged owlets blinked sleepily in the nest hollow in late May.

above: Wallie, a wild Highland owl found injured in the road, loved to play 'footsie'.

below: Wallie used to take a bath in the washing-up bowl in the sink – usually when I was not present.

above: Wallie liked to perch on a chair in the study, watching me work at the desk.

below: When hacking Wallie back to the wild, I often left him perched outside to survey his new territory.

above: Wallie always held prey in his left foot before tearing it up.

below: I did not see Wallie at all during his first winter of freedom. But in May he returned to perch above me in a larch tree, gazing down without alarm.

was over a mile from the cottage. On February 22, I heard Holly's deep hootings in the east wood. When I trekked round later I found her white splashes under a huge old larch, but I could not spot her in the trees. I hoped at least she was getting some mice or voles nearby for I was still baiting the area with corn.

Four days later, having seen an eagle at a new deer-calf carcass just over the ridges to the north, I built a camouflaged hide forty yards away and went into it at dusk, hoping to photograph the eagle, or even a fox, on the carcass. It was while I was waiting in it that I received evidence of an astounding possibility regarding the two owls.

11 · The Owls Return

After three and a half hours in the hide the cold seemed relent-
less. Although I was in a sleeping bag, its zip had broken and I
had to keep turning as one side froze worse than the other.
The cold crept from my feet, up my thighs until even my rear
end felt numb. As I shivered away, not daring to sleep in case I
went into a coma from which I might not wake up, I heard an
owl hooting from the west wood below.

  The hoots began wheezily, as Wallie's had of old, then went
into the same high-pitched tones I knew so well. Then another
owl started up, with a much more positive and deeper voice,
from the wood past the bay to the east. I was sure it was Holly.
Wallie answered and came nearer to the east edge of the west
wood. Then I heard a slight rushing *woof woof* of wings as he
flew straight over the hide. Holly kept calling from the far wood,
then Wallie, who sounded as if he had landed in our east wood,
began making '*kwik kweek*' calls in return. The two owls seemed
to get closer and closer to each other, with Wallie now sounding
more positive and Holly just issuing shy single notes. Then
both appeared to take off to the east, their calls slowly dying
from my hearing.

  It was always probable the two would meet but was it also
possible they might even mate together? Were the sounds I had
heard part of courtship? I endured 15½ hours in the bitterly cold

130

hide, round which snow had fallen heavily, but no eagle or fox put in an appearance. I went down to the cottage again and hand-sawed two six-foot logs for firewood to warm myself up.

On March 5 and 6 I heard Holly's deep hootings in the east wood at dusk, managed to hoot her fairly near and even recorded our odd 'duet'. A week later I went to fell a huge, dead, dry old larch snag that towered to sixty feet and leaned over our daily path in the west wood at an alarming angle. I wanted not only its dry firewood but to drop it *between* two silver firs that stood in its path, rather than have it mow them down when it fell naturally. I power-sawed in the wedge-like undercut, then piled the noisy saw into the back of the tree. As the tip made its first shiver, I stepped back to take a final look – just in time to see Wallie's bright short form shoot out of a larch close by to my left, wing north, then east and vanish into the top of the wood. He had stayed there during all that noisy clatter of the saw! I went back to work, the great snag shuddered and cracked as I leaped back out of the way. It took its time to go down . . . crack, crack, CRACK – a loud swishing and an earth-shattering thump, with dead branches breaking off and bouncing in all directions. It was like a huge skeleton being thrown to the floor, the bones scattering on impact.

At dusk, as Moobli and I were returning through the wood, Wallie hooted at us from the trees above. I hooted back and we had quite a 'conversation', as he followed us almost to the cottage, hooting all the way. Later we heard Holly calling from the east wood. I marvelled at how easily both owls had returned to the wild. Owls like Wallie are programmed to spend all day alone in a tree, then launch out at night and kill. They can know nothing of love. Yet when with me he had insisted on snuggling up close, nibbling my 'beak' with his affectionately. It seemed a hint that at least part of man's duty is to impart love and harmony, not only among men but all other creatures.

A few days later I was making a new bookshelf complex when a slim volume fell out – *The Prophet* by Kahlil Gibran. Idly, I turned the pages and came upon the line, 'The owl, whose night eyes are blinded to the day'. I love Gibran's hazy meanderings in the realms of philosophy but felt he might have

131

done more research into the world of owls, for they can see perfectly well in the daylight.

More nightly hootings followed, then at the end of March I went to cut firewood from the felled larch. I power-sawed three large bolts from its base, chopped them up and carried several heavy loads back to the woodshed. Back from the fifth trip I noticed some white splashes under a larch some twenty yards away. There were pellets there too. I looked up.

There, only forty feet up, perched on a small spiky branch beneath a larger one with a flat base, which made a perfect shelter from rain, was Holly. She was gazing down at me with half-closed eyes that seemed to be smiling. She had been there all the time I was sawing and chopping the firewood, no doubt interested in what her former mentor was up to and making her silent smirks. I sneaked away for the camera and got three photos of her. To get a really good one I leaned against another dead larch snag. Its tip moved, I heard a mere whisper, looked up again and she had gone. It was wonderful actually to see her. She looked fat and healthy and so must have been hunting well. She had clearly made the transition from Cockney park owl in London to being a wild Highland owl quite easily.

Next day she was in the wood again but in a different tree. It was windy and I noticed she was perched on its leeward side, close to the trunk and doing her best imitation of a chunk of loose bark. At dusk she was still there and when I talked to her as I had in the kitchen, she looked down as if interested and showed no alarm. On April 1 she was in yet another tree, as usual a larch. That night I heard her hooting from the wood and Wallie's higher hoots from the east wood. I wondered again if they had mated.

Two days later there was a large white splash over the porch logs and a family of woodmice which had taken over the nesting-box on the bird table was gone. As they used to eat the corn on the table after dark, it seemed possible the owls had taken one or two of them and the others had fled. For several more days I heard the two owls' different calls from both woods, and one morning there was a white splash down the kitchen window, as if one of them had tried to get back in.

I decided not to make a hard search for any nest they might

have for it would disturb them. Anyway, as I had to go away on a work trip, now seemed a good time to head out and leave them in peace. On the very day we arrived back in early May I saw Wallie fly south through the trees from the north edge of the west wood, but he went too fast for me to take a photo. White splashes and pellets outside the study window showed my baiting the area for mice and voles had worked well while we had been away. There were many pellets in the west wood too.

Next morning I saw Wallie in the wood again, seeming shyer now for he dropped low through the trees as if to avoid being seen, his body as blunt as that of a big bumble bee. I also found on the ground a superbly made chaffinch's nest which contained owl feathers, sheep wool and many of Moobli's moulted hairs. Now what had caused that, for it appeared to have been torn from its high tree-branch site? Later in the day I was digging manure into my vegetable garden, when I saw Wallie fly from the wood and into an ash tree on the shore. He stopped a few seconds, as if taking a good look at us, then flew on into the east wood.

Before long I heard him hooting, the same weak hesitant calling I knew so well, and he was coming nearer and nearer. But each time I went to the wood with my camera, he was not there and the hooting was then coming from further away. It was as if he liked to watch me at work, and was playing a game, to get me to stop work and go looking for him, then retreating again to 'hide'. The little beggar! At 5 pm I heard him again. I'll foil the fates this time, I thought. I'll leave the camera behind. I'm bound to find him then. And damned if I didn't.

He was perched high in the thickest tallest larch on my south-east land spit. He looked down with friendly interest, twisting his broad head to one side. I went back for the camera and took my first photos of Wallie in the wild. I hooted back at him, made the old crooning talk songs he had liked when living in the kitchen, and held my hand up. He glared down, hopped to a lower branch, another, stared intently, then looked at the other trees round him as if wanting to fly off. I left him then. On the way back to the cottage I found a new but empty mistle thrush's nest on a broad larch branch at the top end of the east wood which had been ripped about. What had caused that?

All this time I had not heard any calls from Holly and I was beginning to fear she had left the area, a fear that ended abruptly on May 8 when I again heard her deep mournful hooting from the east wood.

Two days later I was browsing along the west edge of that wood when I saw something white among the pine needles. I picked it up – a piece of eggshell, white and thick. Then a bit further on I found a bigger piece. They had come from an almost round egg, without any doubt at all a tawny's. I looked up and there, some forty-five feet up a Scots pine, was a big nest. It looked like a hooded crow's but it had some new twigs in it, which could surely not be the work of tawnies for they do not build nests. I climbed on to several ridges but because of the surrounding larch trees I could not see into the nest at all.

I then began a systematic search of the wood which took all the morning, scanning up and down every trunk with the fieldglass. My gaze was travelling up the grey-green bole of a three-foot-thick silver fir when it came upon a deep crotch thirty feet above the ground. The crotch had been formed by the breaking off of a large branch. Suddenly, I saw a movement. I focused the fieldglass better – and saw the rounded fluffy grey top of a young tawny owl's head. I could not see if there were any more young as the fallen branch had left a long sliver that blocked my view. Filled with delight, I quietly withdrew. Not until I reached the meadow below the cottage did I release my feelings in a brief mad dance of joy. Moobli looked at me as if I had gone crazy.

Despite all the problems, Highland Wallie and Cockney Holly had survived their injuries, had met, mated and were now successfully raising a youngster or two. What I could not understand, however, was how that eggshell had come to be forty yards away from the nest tree. Had some animal taken it there after being driven off by the tawnies, or had the owls themselves dropped it there?

Three evenings later I had more evidence that the owls were ranging a good mile and a half on hunting forays. I was trying to photograph badgers at a 600-foot-high sett when I heard Holly hooting in the west wood. It was a still night and I heard Wallie's higher answering hoots from the long woods west of our home. Then Holly's calls came closer until she must have been perched in one of the small trees along the shore below us.

For several nights I had noticed the owls making new kinds of calls. The normal hoot turned into a trilling hooting 'song', with a series of breathily intonated high '*oh-oh-oh-oh*' sounds before ending in another normal hoot. I was sure these were either courting songs or to do with pair bonding while away from the nest. I heard Holly hooting once more on May 26 and after that, as usual in summer, the tawnies fell silent.

Imagine my surprise, therefore, when on July 11, as I was walking back from the shore at dusk, Holly hooted at me from the top edge of the west wood. I immediately hooted back. Then Wallie started. I hooted him too. Finally I saw them flying round the top of a pine tree, and in the branches was a young owl with much paler plumage, flapping its wings gently as if soliciting food. Had they broken the 'summer silence' rule in order to show me the youngster? Or were they hooting like that to show it, or alert it to man the enemy? I preferred the former theory. Well, it was wonderful to have had such final proof that they had successfully raised at least one youngster, and that seemed to be that.

In late August, however, a third tawny came into our lives. One of my readers had written to say that she had been to Glasgow Zoo to pick up a Soay sheep from which she wanted to breed and had fallen for a young owl that had been found in a city park by children before it could fly. The Zoo had given it to her to rear to maturity and to try and hack it back to the wild. The trouble was that she and her husband lived in an urban area, and now that the owl was full-grown, they felt they could not release it successfully there. Would I be interested in training it to hunt and let it go round Wildernesse?

Naturally I was, and on August 22 her doctor husband drove to my nearest village and handed the owl in a box to me. I soon had it home and installed on the old perch in the now empty kitchen.

It was the most beautiful tawny I had ever seen. Bigger even than Holly, clearly another female, its plumage was filled with varying chestnut browns, not as dark as Holly's nor as light as Wallie's. Searching for the right sort of soothe-talking double name I feel one needs when looking after owls, I hit on the name Crowdy. It rhymed well with Owl, and it was a good Scottish name, as befitted her Glaswegian birth. The name could also be extended to Crowdy Wowdy, to be intonated gently when feeding or handling her. She had a superbly broad cowled head, an orange-brown moustache, and long black lustrous whiskers round her bluey-grey beak. Her wing feathers were long and soft, perfect and undamaged, as were those of her wide tail.

At dusk on her second evening I was startled at my desk by loud calls and hootings. When I went into the kitchen I was just in time to see both Wallie and Holly fly off from the window-sill! I went out quietly and heard Holly hooting loudly in the east wood, then making '*kwick*' calls. I kwicked and hooted back and she came nearer, making strange agitated noises, '*kikikikikik*', as if she *knew* the new owl was in the kitchen. Yet Crowdy was nowhere near the window and as far as I knew never had been. Then behind her I heard the half-strangled hooting of Wallie. I hooted him nearer too. Holly then flew right past me over the bird table and landed in hazel trees by the path where she began hooting again. There was no doubt the two owls knew Crowdy was in the cottage, but how? Had they come so close to welcome her in some odd way, or, because tawnies are believed to be extremely territorial, to try and drive her out of their area? I had no intention at that point of releasing Crowdy in order to find out.

Apart from refusing to eat during the first twenty-four hours, Crowdy soon settled down. Just as Holly had shown different characteristics from Wallie, Crowdy exhibited over the ensuing weeks considerable variations in behaviour from the other two. When I got her on my hand and brought her close to see if she would crouch into a ball and look up with her huge dark eyes, as the others had done, she clawed her way up my sweater like a parrot and stayed on my shoulder. As I walked about preparing supper, she clambered from one shoulder to the other, whickering and crooning in my ears. Whenever my hand went near the food she made loud high-pitched chittering squeaks, took it with her beak, then clamped it under her left foot to tug at and eat. If my hand went near without food she still made the squeaks and nibbled vigorously but gently at my fingers.

She was far more frightened of Moobli than the other two had been. Before feeding she always flew to the top of the kitchen door, crouched down so that her big round face was well below the level of her feet, and with a fearful but comical expression peered along the hall and into the study to see if he was coming in. Her favourite perch soon became a big stag's skull and antlers above the fireplace. Here too she would hold a mouse in one foot, then twist her neck sideways a surprising distance and peer into the hall for the whereabouts of *that dog*!

Unlike the other two, Crowdy *would* chase a mouse or vole if I tugged it about over the carpet. She glared down, flew to land on the sink, glared again, flew to the lower back of a chair, glared again, then went down to chase after it like a winged cat, striking out with her furred talons. When I just put a mouse on the floor she landed by it with long upraised wings and all the grace of a ballet dancer. Then she folded her wings, bent down, picked it up very gently in her beak, and flapped back up to the antlers with it.

When I came back from the next supply trip, she was in the washing-up bowl, taking her first bath. She saw me come in and flapped with great difficulty, spraying water everywhere, up to her perch. It was then I noticed she had an extraordinary ability I had not noticed in the others. She puffed her chest and back feathers out until she was a great round football, then somehow managed individually to separate each pinion in her drooping wings from its fellows. She could do this with her tail feathers too, not so much spreading them out in a fan as separating each one from its neighbour in an up and down fashion. It was a perfect technique for drying newly washed feathers quickly, most useful in the wild when an owl cannot afford long periods with soaked feathers which hamper its flight abilities. It also showed extraordinary muscle control.

Once I saw that she had eaten the head of a mouse but had apparently cached the rest of it far across the room between bowls on a high shelf. When I picked it up I could feel a presence, a distinct feeling of animosity. Crowdy was glaring across at me with murder in her eyes. When I put it into the gas fridge to keep it fresh she became most agitated, clamping her talons up and down as she moved about on the perch the better to see what I was doing with it, glaring, and even clopped her beak twice. I put it back on the shelf in exactly the same position, with its feet showing upwards, and she subsided. I was sure then she *had* cached it there, for eating later. This could well be something owls do in the wild.

A few days later I secretly watched her preening through a monocular from the study. I found she could twist her rear neck feathers right round to the front, for intricate combing through her beak, by sheer muscular action. She could also part her long breast feathers into two definite 'beds' on either side, so she could quibble at her close thick furry inner coat. It was like watching the parting of the Red Sea. When she scratched her head she used one talon like the other owls but when scratching near her large hidden ears she bunched the talons into a fist. She flew superbly and often went for circular flights round the kitchen, nearly always landing back on the antler perch. I noticed that she always held her legs backwards, tucked under the tail, and at the last second they swung down and out like grapnels for a safe landing.

On September 1, about to leave for a trek, I put a mouse on the floor. She flew down to it as I left the room. I went back but she stood her ground, grabbed it from my touching finger's reach and flew with it back to her perch. I tugged one end and she tugged hers back with surprising strength, crickering her protests loudly. This became a kind of game in later days. If I pulled really hard she would let go, with a look of surprise and resignation on her face as if thinking, 'Well, you pull harder so you need it more.' When she was really hungry, however, she fought hard to retain her mouse and could support the entire weight of my arm yet still hold on to the perch with her other foot.

When Crowdy decided to give her feathers a shake she first looked extremely serious, intent, even worried. Bit by bit she fluffed them out, then gave them all a terrible shaking that sounded like a pile of cardboard boxes being flung down some stairs. Then she put her head right down as if saying no, no, no, shook it hard from side to side but oddly slowly. It must be a very serious business, shaking your feathers, if you are an owl.

Like the others, she always ate the heads of mice and voles first. Maybe the brains helped make her wise. It is believed owls gained their reputation for wisdom not only because they look wise, with their forward-facing eyes and sombre mien, but because in the heyday of Hellenic culture the Greek city of Athens was infested with them, and the Hellenes chose owls as their emblem.

At this time odd things began happening in the woods and inside the woodshed. One by one the traps I set down for mice and voles vanished without trace. At first I thought a fox had found mice in them and had carried them off, removed the mice, and left the traps where I could not find them. Then a long owl flight feather in the shed helped me to solve the mystery. From its colour it looked like one of Holly's. She had been finding the full traps and had carried them off. This time she must have hit the door frame with her long wings, so losing the feather. As a result I had to drive to the town forty-four miles away to buy new traps, which I then tied down.

I came back from a trek in mid-September and before entering the cottage I peered cautiously through the kitchen window. Crowdy was perched on the sink, twisting her beak up sideways and drinking from the dripping tap. I wasted hours trying to photograph her doing this but, as when she took a bath, she never did it when I was in the room.

One night I was typing my diaries with all the doors open when there was a great rush of wings and in came Crowdy. Moobli, who disliked her beating wings, gave a fed-up sigh and quietly took himself to his bed in the hall. She had invaded for the first time the last bastion in his territory. I stayed still. Crowdy flew to perch on a picture, which tilted up, flew to a pine round I had nailed up for decoration, clung on, then landed on the books of the top shelf. Still I ignored her. A few minutes later she went for a swing on my Spanish candle chandelier, stretching down and peering out of the window, her throat rapidly going in and out with her fast breathings.

In late September both Holly and Wallie came calling every night and again before dawn, and Crowdy made loud '*kee-wick*' calls and hootings back to them. When she took to perching on the window catch and looking out at them, I almost let her go. But knowing this to be the time owls re-assert territories, I feared they might be wanting to kill her rather than adopt her. As time went on, however, I began to have the sneaking suspicion that perhaps tawny owls are not as aggressively hostile towards each other over territories as they have been made out to be. Maybe they just like to meet up, and somehow sort out what territory goes to which owl between themselves. There had never been any aggression or revenge motive in anything I had done with the three, even when I took Crowdy's mice or voles off her by pulling stronger than she could.

On October 2 both owls came hooting strongly at 5.30 am. Crowdy stayed quiet, but after twenty minutes she started replying and further sleep was impossible. That day she flailed at the window twice, something she had never done before. I began to hack her back to the wild, putting her out on jesses on the bow perch and feeding her there during the day so she could get her bearings in the outside world. I also gave her long flights on the creance line. But before dusk I brought her in again as I was still not sure the others were not hostile.

By the end of October the two wild owls had stepped up their noisy campaign to get in to Crowdy, or else get her out with them. On November 3 they came in the near dark at 6 am calling loudly with '*kee-oo*' and '*kay-oo*' calls, and rolling shuddering '*oo-oo-oo-oo*s' which sounded more like singing than hooting. I sneaked out and opened the kitchen door. By the light of my torch I saw one of the owls fly from the window-sill. I was still half asleep but felt if *was* time, time to give Crowdy her chance. Surely, if the other two were aggressive she would not go out to them, and surely they would not now come into the kitchen. I put a mouse on the table and opened the window.

There was a tremendous cacophony of owl calls as I fell back into bed. I heard Crowdy making loud '*kee-wick*' calls and singing hoots several times. A long silence followed then I heard loud rolling '*ooo*' calls in the ash tree in front of the kitchen window. I felt I had been too hasty, heard more crooning noises, then the long squeaking chitters Crowdy made, followed by a loud, drawn-out '*weeeek*'. I got up again. All the calls were now coming from outside. The kitchen was empty. Crowdy had gone.

All day the mouse remained untouched on the table and at dusk I heard all three owls calling from the west wood. Next day I could find none of them but at night heard hootings from the far side of the loch, for the first time ever. Were Wallie and Holly showing Crowdy a new territory? A three-quarter-mile flight across the loch would be nothing to long-winged tawnies. It had seemed obvious to me those two were going to make my life hell until I let her go, and I was tired of losing so much sleep. Much as I loved them and wished they would all come back into the cottage at times, they were better off making their own way. Owls are not capable of gratitude; only a fool would expect it.

At 6 am I was woken by Crowdy's rolling scratchy hoot right by my window. She was perched on my house-painting ladder. I went out into the year's first frost stark naked and showed her the mouse, shrew and bits of meat I had left on the kitchen sill. Later they were all still there but a fresh moist vole pellet was left on the table indoors. The cheeky cow! It was as if she was telling me she could catch her own food now.

It became obvious over the next weeks, even months, that Wallie and Holly had *not* meant Crowdy any harm, I often found her up trees and took photos of her many times, as I also twice photographed Holly. Indeed, as Crowdy stayed in the immediate vicinity more than they did, it seemed as if they had given her the easier territory round the cottage. On Christmas Day she actually landed on the study window-sill as I was typing at my desk in the gloom, and left a large white visiting card.

From mid-February I often heard the three owls' distinctive calls in the woods, Holly and Wallie making their musical trilling courting songs, mostly from the woods across the eastern bay, and sometimes from across the loch. These courting calls continued until early May and by then Crowdy was also making them. I hoped she too would find a mate, maybe with the youngster the other two had reared the year before, if it had been a male – but I found no owls' nests that year.

Since early winter, however, I had seen odd dark twisted scats, like a wildcat's only smaller. When I first found them, on mossy rocks along the shore and also up the burn, I thought they might have been left by a young otter. A few similar scats appeared on the tops of old windfall trees that had fallen over other trunks so that they were a yard or two off the ground. Perhaps they had been left by an unusually small fox. In the autumn I also found several little piles of rowan berries, up to a dozen or more, which were sometimes left over the droppings.

They looked like little offerings, as if a small fox had left them as pacification gifts to another fox. These, too, were puzzling.

I was also perplexed at finding several disturbed birds' nests. A hedge sparrow had hatched four of its five bright blue eggs in a nest built in the bramble bushes below the study window. Two days later the nest was damp from overnight drizzle, the last egg was cold but still there: the pink naked young had vanished. A blackbird's nest with five young in a mossy stump in the west wood lost them all overnight; the nest had been slightly disturbed. A robin's nest on the ground below one of my caged sweet chestnut trees lost four young in the same way, though I found a lone semi-fledged survivor crouched under grasses two yards away, and one of the parents was in a hazel bush with a caterpillar in its bill to feed to it. I found the great tits' nest in my best nest-box on a huge oak in the east wood had been torn out through the hole. Again the young had gone.

One morning Moobli scented out a pressed-down patch in the grasses on the loch shore. Again I thought a small fox or wildcat had lain there, perhaps watching the young mergansers that were swimming round that area. Then I heard loud strangled hootings coming from the waterfall in the north-east corner of the east wood. I went over, heard a cock chaffinch making insistent *'pink pink'* alarm cries, and looked up. In a larch just above us, looking down with huge alarmed eyes, was Wallie. He stared down at me for a while as I softly hooted back to him, then flew to an oak across the burn. As I got near again, he took off and flew right across the eastern bay into the woods on its far side. He was not so tame now. Could it be the owls which were raiding the nests? I suppose it was possible that with their long strong legs one of them could have performed the grab act on the great tits' nest in my bird box. Yet I had never found such raided nests in the first years at Wildernesse when there had been other wild tawnies about us.

On June 12, a bright but windy day, as we approached the animal lie-out place we had found earlier, Moobli made a brief 'huff' sound and darted forward two paces, pointing his nose. Suddenly I saw a dark-brown animal with a long tail dash from a stump and up the trunk of a larch tree. As it stopped to look back at us, I stared with amazement as I realised what it was.

PART FOUR

12 · *Enter a Rare Pine Marten*

Clinging to the rough larch trunk and only about twelve feet up was what looked like a giant chocolate-coloured squirrel, but this animal was three times the size. It had lustrous rufous-brown fur, a long bushy tail, a broad head topped by two huge radar-scanner ears, and it clung to the welts of bark with long sharp curved claws that looked as if they belonged to a bird of prey. The winds were swaying the trees backwards and forwards so that sprays of leaves from a nearby beech kept obscuring my view, but I managed to take two photos before it scrambled rapidly upwards and came to rest on a cradle of four small branches. As it then peered down, I saw the broad creamy orange throat and chest patch which was the final clue to its identity. A pine marten, one of Britain's rarest mammals, was now in our woods!

Now I knew the cause of the few raided nests and the owner of the small dark twisted scats that had been appearing on the tops of fallen trunks and on mossy rocks lining the burn for over a year. Trembling with excitement, I ordered Moobli to stay by the base of the larch, hoping the marten would stay where it was (in the high winds it seemed to have no intention of leaping for any of the smooth-trunked beeches nearby) and raced to the cottage for my longest telephoto lens.

When I got back the marten was still there. I dashed through

143

the burn, oblivious of my soaked boots, until I reached a position beyond the far bank where I could see the marten clearly. It was standing on the broadest branch and peering outwards like a miniature bear. I clicked off several photos, trying to time each one for when I had a brief clear view between the swaying foliage. After taking a couple of fair pictures under the difficult circumstances, for it was quite high up, I set blackberries, buttered fruit cake, bread and jam (I had heard the pine marten has a distinctly sweet tooth), cheese and an egg on a stump below the larch, hoping it would thus discern we were friendly and would stay in the area.

Pine martens date from the Eocene period. They survived the last Ice Age and their remains have been found in forty-million-year-old deposits. When much of Scotland was covered with ancient Caledonian pine forests, and there were far more woods in England, Wales and Ireland than there are today, they were both common and widespread. For centuries, however, they were highly prized for their fur and were heavily trapped. They were also widely regarded as vermin and were trapped and shot because of their alleged depredations on game-bird chicks and poultry. By the turn of this century pine martens were almost exterminated over their main range, surviving in small pockets in the Lake District, in the Snowdon area of north Wales, in south-west Ireland, with their main last stronghold confined between Ardnamurchan and Cape Wrath, mainly in west Sutherland and Wester Ross. The slaughter relaxed in the First World War when most able-bodied men were after targets of a different kind. In the late 1920s and 1930 they began to multiply again slowly, gaining another respite in the Second World War when they spread to Loch Ness and were found south of it by 1961. The new conifers planted by the Forestry Commission and private interests later helped pine martens considerably so their numbers slowly swelled in other isolated pockets too.

The first intimation that martens had spread to the area in which I lived had come two years earlier. A stalker who lived on an estate eight miles to the west of Wildernesse kept four hens and three ducks, which at night he kept locked in two stout sheds which he was sure were fox-proof. To give the ducks some air he left a top window slightly open. One February morning he found one of the ducks missing, with no sign of any tell-tale feathers that would indicate a struggle. Then his hens also began to go. He set a trap and, to his surprise, caught a pine marten, which he shot. A few weeks later I had my first glimpse of a wild marten as I was driving along a single-track road four miles south of our home. It dashed across the road between two Forestry Commission plantations and vanished between the trees.

On a winter trek in the same area with Richard Balharry, Chief Warden of north-east Scotland for the Nature Conservancy Council, we found a small twisted scat on a mossy rock. Dick, who bred pine martens and was as much an expert on them as he was on golden eagles, broke it open so I could sniff its characteristically sweet smell. He also told me martens were not as arboreal as was often believed. They could survive on the open hills if there was enough food about, and used rocky cairns for their dens. The new scats in our own woods seemed to have no smell at all, and also appeared to be larger than my memory of the one Dick had found.

The next evidence of martens in the area came the following summer from the owner of the estate next to that of the stalker who had trapped the marten. A baby pine marten fell from a tree and landed at her feet, not twenty yards from her house. She picked it up and set it back on the trunk, but it looked round as if requiring another 'bunk up' so she helped it climb back up the tree with gentle hand pushes on its backside. Word soon got around and a vanload of German tourists turned up with flash cameras to photograph the marten. This apparently disturbed the marten family, which then removed their young to a new area deeper in the woods.

I was determined that the pine marten in our own woods should stay and the best way to achieve this, I felt, was to help feed it. Over the next two days, however, all the food I put out on the stump in the east wood remained untouched. Martens are omnivorous feeders and adapt their appetites to the foods of the seasons, though the bulk of their animal food consists of field voles and mice. A study conducted in 1961 by Dr J. D. Lockie in the Beinn Eighe Nature Reserve in Wester Ross showed these small rodents (mostly voles) can form up to 81 per cent of martens' diet in winter months. Small birds such as tits, wrens and tree creepers come next and a few young hares and rabbits are also taken. They eat large quantities of berries in summer and autumn, as well as beetles, large insects, butterfly and moth pupae, small fish, and carrion from dead deer in winter. Both Dick Balharry and a mutual friend of ours, wildlife photographer Geoffrey Kinns, told me that the one food pine martens cannot resist is raspberry jam on buttered bread!

It was when I boated out on June 14, to get a good supply of these ingredients as well as normal shopping, that I became even more concerned to keep the marten close to my home. For I heard then that another had been trapped and shot, this time by an acquaintance who lived near the sea ten miles west of us. He told me he had lost two hens, each had lost its head and some neck flesh, then the animal had apparently slaughtered another. Thinking it was the work of a fox, he had set a trap and had caught the marten.

Like some other conservationists, I had long campaigned on radio and in newspaper articles and books to gain legal protection for otters, wildcats and pine martens. Naturally, I was gratified when these three creatures were given some protection under Schedule 6 of the Wildlife and Countryside Act, 1981, but the fulfilment of that Act was over a year and a half away from the period I am writing about.

When I returned from the supply trip I set some raspberry slices out below the bird table and kept watch from my desk but no marten showed up. That night I was woken by loud thumpings from the woodshed. I dashed to the rear workshop window but could see nothing moving. Had wildcat Liane finally returned? In the morning I found that two tree-wasp nests which had been hanging from a rafter in the shed had been demolished and their honeycombs taken. A piece of plastic guttering that had been lying on the top of the door frame had been thrown on the floor.

Hoping to solve the mystery, I took the old box-cage live trap I had used for catching my wildcats and set it carefully below the workshop window. It was a four-foot by two-foot contraption like those I had learned to make on a project to radio-collar cougars in Canada, where similar but far larger traps were used. When an animal takes the bait, it triggers off a mousetrap on the top of the cage. As the mousetrap's spring shoots forward, it pulls a nail out of a wooden door at the rear of the box section, and the door promptly drops down, imprisoning the animal harmlessly inside.

An hour later I wandered idly into the workshop. Suddenly I heard a snap and a loud thump as the wooden door fell down. I caught a glimpse of a brown furry body leaping to the left, then the trap's nail on its nylon cord bounced off the window. I hurried out. I saw no sign of the marten and the trap, of course, was empty. Had the creature the intelligence to work out that if it sprung the trap from outside, it would not get caught? Or had it just tugged at the nylon line out of curiosity?

I never received the answers to these questions for although the food I had set out on the stump in the east wood had now all gone, further titbits remained untouched. Apart from finding a marten scat in the west wood on July 3, no further signs of it appeared. That season I noticed that while there were still a fair number of young willow warblers, wrens, robins, tits and chaffinches being fed by their parents in the woods, numbers were lower than in previous years. Well, that was the way of the wild. Predators are controlled by the availability of food and prey, not the other way about, and there were certainly enough young left to maintain stable resident populations of all these birds.

It was clear that pine martens were highly secretive animals, mainly nocturnal in their habits and hunting. It was not until mid-September when again I found rowan-berry 'offerings' in the woods that I knew the marten was still about. Some of the berries had been partially digested but all had obviously been regurgitated by the marten. Often they were far from any rowan trees so had been carried many yards, and again they were sometimes laid over or beside the animal's droppings. I felt certain they were left as a food gift to a potential mate, to an actual mate or even for youngsters, but not a glimpse of any marten did I catch. I still occasionally put out raspberry jam on bread but, as far as I could see, it was only taken by birds and a few voles and mice.

In late December ferocious gales lasted for days, and gave me the worst boat journey of my entire life, during which I narrowly avoided being sunk. Rain, sleet and snow replaced each other with boring monotony. The daylight hours were so few I felt I was living in a dark tomb. For the first time ever I thought of going away for the winter, of taking my father from the nursing home and looking after him in Spain, which his few letters were begging me to do.

Eventually two brighter days came. I spent the first sawing two fallen larches into firewood logs and backpacking the lot 300 yards back to the woodshed. Still tired from the labour on the next, I decided not to trek over the mountains but to take an easier route through the lochside woods to look for wildlife. But first, as my water system was frozen up and I would be fatigued on my return, I went to fill my water containers through the ice on the burn.

As I reached the spruce grove, a huge switch-horned stag – without tines to its antlers – leaped to its feet from its bed of conifer needles and looked as if ready to charge. Unfortunately with oaks on each side of the spruce, I had him cornered and I did not think a clout with a plastic bucket would be much of a deterrent! But after a few steps towards me he dodged to my left, bounded to the burn, soared over it with an easy fifteen-foot leap, looked round briefly as if to be sure I had really been there, then trotted off into the woods.

I carried the water back with thudding heart, grabbed the camera and with Moobli tracking the fresh scent, set off in his wake. It was dry for a change. In the cold east wind the few leaves, now withered and sere, still clinging to the oaks, rustled faintly. After half a mile Moobli began to step high, his broad black muzzle dilating like a bear's. Sure our 'quarry' was not far away, I was glad of the tinkling of a burn up ahead for it would hide any sound of our approach. Then suddenly something happened which made me forget all about the stag.

There was a rushing noise in the trees above us, as if a large bird had suffered a heart attack and was still beating its wings as it tumbled through the branches. I looked up to see a red squirrel, its bushy tail streaming like a banner, hurtling through the tree tops. About ten yards behind it came a much larger, darker animal, also with a great brush of a tail. At first I thought it was a small fox, but that was impossible.

148

The squirrel, ears back so that even at such speed its face looked rat-like, leaped frantically from tree to tree, its four feet spread wide like stars to make a gliding surface of the skin between them and its flanks. It clutched desperately at some insubstantial twigs, then fell to the branch below. Quickly recovering, it shot off again. The pursuer also 'flew', its longer legs sticking out even further than the squirrel's, but with tail held high in the air. Because of the creamy orange throat patch, I knew it to be a pine marten. It made a longer leap, landed successfully on the branch the squirrel had aimed for, but muffed its next jump – for a mossy fork on the far side of the tree so it would avoid hitting the tree trunk. Its claws scuttered on the dry moss; for a moment it swung to and fro like a monkey, then it twisted its body and rear feet back on to the fork, re-positioned itself, and set off after the squirrel again as my camera clicked on empty space.

I was sure the squirrel was one of the pair which inhabited our woods. While I was glad to see the marten still around I did not want it to kill a squirrel when there were plenty of mice and voles about. Without thinking I yelled a loud 'Hey!' This appeared to have no effect whatever and the animals disappeared from sight, leaving a shower of dead twigs falling to earth behind them. I dearly hoped the squirrel would escape, for it had gained valuable yards from the marten's mistiming.

I recalled then how I had once seen a similar treetop chase in western Canada, only that time the pine marten had been the quarry, pursued by the powerful fisher. The fisher is second only to the wolverine in the hierarchy of North American mustelids, but it does not exist in Britain. My shout had ruined any chance of catching up with the stag, but that mattered little after such an incredible sight. I did not know at the time, of course, but it would be the last time I saw a red squirrel in or near our own woods up to the time of writing three years later. Whether the marten killed them (certainly I found no squirrel remains) or just drove them away by his presence I could not know.

The odd thing now was that I saw no more trace of the marten in our vicinity through the rest of the winter. Dick Balharry estimated a pair of martens occupied a territory of some 3 square miles in the breeding season, the area naturally varying according to the food supply. Other naturalists quoted in *The Handbook of British Mammals* give the average total hunting territory as from 5 to 23 square kilometres, and winter range might even reach 30 square kilometres. In Finland snow-tracking revealed that resident martens could cover 8·6 to 10 kilometres per hunting trip, while non-residents, such as roaming unpaired males, could cover 16 to 65 kilometres in a night. The British naturalist H. G. Hurrell, who has bred martens and studied them extensively in the wild, believes they travel from den to den round mountain massifs many miles in circumference. If the marten scats I found in March 2½ miles from our home in the long lochside woods to the west were from the same animal, it certainly seemed to indicate it was ranging far and wide.

On April 18 I was delighted to find the marten was back. After a long spell of unusually fine weather, I was outside doing my annual count of the wild daffodils, when I saw it loping along slowly through the north-east corner of the west wood. Like a huge slow squirrel it bounded over some mossy banks, jumped on to a Scots pine, embraced the trunk with wide-apart feet and claws, climbed up, crossed sure-footedly along a branch to a silver fir, then humped itself slowly to its top. I went over quietly, the telephoto lens on the camera, but a mass of foliage surrounding an old crow's nest obscured the marten. It was probably lying up there in the warm sun.

For two days I had been hearing two of the owls I nursed in the cottage hooting in the woods. I found Crowdy perched up a tall larch but later heard her hooting from a tree-covered recess in the hills some 250 feet above the west wood. It was possible she did not want to take unnecessary risks and had moved out after seeing the marten. I put raspberry slices on a fallen trunk near the fir but they were still there next day, and again the marten seemed to have gone.

No further signs occurred until late June, and apart from two ruined small bird nests, there seemed as many young in the woods as in any previous season. On June 24 I found a marten scat near the boat bay and next day three new ones on mossy rocks on the far side of the burn. One of them was half the size of the others. While I hoped it had been left by a youngster, I did not accept it as conclusive evidence. Just like humans, individual animals can leave droppings of various sizes, depending on the food eaten, general health, and interruptions in the digestive process. Pine martens, like some other mustelids and even roe deer, enjoy delayed implantation of the blastocyst, the fertilised egg, into the wall of the uterus. This means they can mate in the late summer months of July and August, when the female comes into oestrus, yet the young are not born until late March or April, after a gestation period of about a month. The young first venture outside the den at eight to nine weeks old, so it was possible the small scat had been left by a youngster.

I kept watch on the area, saw nothing, and left raspberry slices and an egg under a wooden slab, hoping to prevent them being taken or pecked by birds. Two days later the slices had gone but the egg remained. I searched the almost sheer sides of the burn gorge for a den, knowing martens like rock fissures on steep faces for breeding dens, as if knowing they will be inaccessible to animals like foxes. I found nothing. More raspberry slices disappeared over the next few days. Then I found the culprit – a large brown rat which had temporarily taken over the empty nest-box on the bird table! I stopped putting them out after that.

In late July I had to journey south, not only on business but to sort out more urgent problems concerning my father, whose capital was now dwindling because of the high nursing-home fees. I took him to look for a property in which I could look after him, then promised if he was well enough in the winter I would take him back to Spain, where he dearly wanted to be.

When I returned in mid-August there were marten scats all over the west wood, some showing where all our ripening gooseberries, raspberries and blackcurrants had gone. On several days I waited, hidden behind the upended tangle of roots of a fallen larch, camera focused on raspberry slices thirty yards upwind, but still I had no glimpses of any martens. In early September the rowan-berry 'offerings' began to appear again, mostly along the shore, and kept appearing through most of the month. With so much autumn food about, the titbits I set out were only taken by voles, mice and birds. Then, towards the end of the month, the raspberry-jam titbits began to disappear rapidly from the area in front of the cottage. I would watch for an hour, then go into the kitchen to make supper and return a few minutes later to find them gone. But as the pieces I set actually *on* the bird table were left, I could not be sure it was the marten taking them.

In late October I was astonished to find a perfect large four-toed wildcat track in mud on our path through the east wood. Had Liane come back, or had one of my other released wildcats found its way back to its old home? I disinterred the old box-cage live trap from the herbage now growing over it, rebuilt it completely and put it below the bird table just under the study window. I put bits of flank mutton in and round it but did not set the trap. How wonderful it would be to see Liane again, to be *sure* she was still alive. But if it was her, I wanted her to trust the trap before I set it seriously.

Next day all the bait was still there, and I heard faint hooting on the forestry track on the far side of the loch. BBC reporter Ted Harrison had arrived, wanting me to do a programme on wildcats for the 'Living World' natural history series, which seemed a strange coincidence. We recorded the programme in a few hours, part of it while standing by the wildcat print, then I boated him back to his car.

It was on Hallowe'en evening at dusk that I found a new pine marten scat in the west wood, and also a larger one that looked like a wildcat's. I was determined to solve the mystery now. As I carefully set the trap on the oddly warm night, a few pipistrelle bats from the colony in my roof were flying, catching newly emerged insects and building up reserves for their winter hibernation. They looped, rolled and dived down close to my head but as always with bats not a sound of their webby wings could I hear.

At 7.50 pm I was making a minor repair to my biggest telephoto lens when I heard a soft *clunk*. The door of the trap had fallen. I looked out and saw with amazement that I had caught not Liane, or any wildcat, but the pine marten.

How surprising it was that it had approached so close when my paraffin lamp was blazing away, when it must have seen me sitting at the desk, and had gone into the trap for the meat. I felt sure now it was the marten that had taken my titbits over the weeks. Perhaps it recognised me as their provider.

152

My first reaction was to let it go again but then I had second thoughts. For months I had been trying to photograph it up close and here was an ideal chance to do so. I had heard that pine martens can become quite tame and confiding in time. Indeed, the Romans kept them as we today keep cats, to control mice, voles and rats.

When I went out it did not panic and rush up and down inside the trap. It kept looking at me curiously, then moving about with snake-like grace and in complete silence, searching for an escape hole. It looked rather thin. I decided to bring it indoors for a while, feed it well and try partially to tame it, or at least prove to it that I was friendly. I laboured to carry the heavy box-cage contraption into the cottage, through the kitchen to the rear workshop, which I had now converted into a bedroom, complete with a four-poster bed made from logs. I set the trap down and lifted the solid wooden door.

Just as I thought it would, out the marten came and, keeping low, scurried across the carpet and under the bed, from which position it again regarded me with curiosity, still showing no signs of panic. It was quite a big animal, about 2½ feet long, including its long bushy tail, with a broad head. I was sure it was a male. I set down more meats and raspberry titbits and left it for the night.

13 · *A Marten in My Bedroom*

The weather changed abruptly overnight. The first hailstorms of the coming winter battered our tin roof and woke me up. I felt at least I had saved the marten from a rough night. I certainly did not intend to detain him long from his natural freedom.

I spent all the next morning with the marten and what a fantastic little character he turned out to be. He behaved so cheekily I dubbed him Mickey. When I went into him I found he had chewed three-inch-long splinters from the window-frame and some from the bottom of the door of the bathroom, which adjoined the former workshop. Small jaws or not, they clearly had plenty of mustelid power. He had eaten the meat which was still attached to the trap wire, which meant he had gone back into the trap itself. A good omen. He had also eaten the bread from which he had just licked the butter and jam the previous night.

He was hiding behind the box of books under the bed and watched with apparent interest as I put small pieces of meat on the bed itself. I sat down with my camera and flash unit on a chair three yards away. I stayed there quietly for nearly four hours. Slowly he began to peek out. He ran behind the curtain on the far side of the four-poster bed, occasionally peeping out round it. Then he climbed up the right rear bed-post, a rough peeled log, peered over the top, round its sides and even looked at me from upside down.

His chocolate brown coat, I now noticed, had a reddish tinge, his ears were huge and rounded and fringed with cream-coloured hairs. His big creamy-orange throat and chest patch, which varies from marten to marten in size and shape, was most attractive. I kept talking soothingly to him, telling him I liked him very much, trying to make friendly sounds.

Not until an hour had passed did he make any noises in return. Then he made odd '*chhrem*' sounds in his throat, like the subdued barks of a small terrier, but just opening his mouth a little each time. '*Chhrem, chhrem*' he said as he looked out at me, and at times he also made a sort of little snorting cough, then pulled his head back again as if unsure of his own temerity. When he 'barked' his ears went back slightly, his tail flicked and his whole body jerked with the effort.

After a while he got bolder and finished his barks with high rolling growls, similar to those made by young wildcats, a high trilling sound which I thought indicated anger, that he resented me just sitting there. Then he became braver, showed more of himself, growled and often made short sharp aggressive moves towards me along the rear bed rail, like a child saying 'boo', as if trying to scare me away. Once he ran along behind the curtain, lifted it up with his head, grabbed a piece of meat, dashed to the top post with it, and chewed it up with relish. After eating another, he walked along the far-side upper rail that ran the length of the bed, then stopped to make a few more aggressive 'boo' gestures, pushing himself forward on his broad dark-brown paws, from which the lighter coloured claws showed prominently. Sometimes too he looked at me, poked his ears high, grabbed the top blanket in his teeth and with high growls began to show how tough he was, hauling it up with sharp tugs, then down below the bed, as if saying, 'Look what I could do to your hand!'

Strangely enough, he did not seem to mind, or even notice, the flashes of the camera. Often too, he yawned, which I felt was a displacement activity induced by natural fear of a human, yet perplexed by my apparent friendliness.

After I left he located a warm spot on a top shelf between the wall and wicker basket and went to sleep. I went in several times but he stayed there, looking down at me and making the odd yawns again. I decided to let him go. I made an ostentatious show of opening the window to its widest, put meat on the sill and left him again. But when I went back at 2.30 pm he was still there, dozing.

I felt sure now that he would stay around, so I decided to make a new bird-table complex. I knocked down the old table, a round of larch which was sagging over its centre post like a soft mushroom anyway, and set a large five-inch-thick slab of pine on a stout log post only two yards from my study window. To the slab I nailed a six-foot length of half-round larch, still with bark intact, and supported the far end of this with another log post. Against this cross strut I leaned a heavy eight-foot-long Y-shaped larch branch which the marten could run up and down instead of having to leap on to the table from the ground.

When I returned to the bedroom at dusk Mickey was still in the same place! And at 6.30 pm, two hours later, he still had not gone. The overnight hailstorms had been replaced by gales and heavy rain. I wondered if he had scented the fresh air, taken a step outside and had decided it was fine and warm where he was. At any rate, the piece of meat on the window-sill had gone.

I closed and opened the window several times as he looked down, trying to show him he was free, and put down some mince, a piece of mutton flank, some raisins and some more bread and jam titbits. He watched me do this, looked up at the ceiling, back again to me, yawned, then put his head down again and went to sleep. At 10.30 pm the mince had gone, along with one jammy piece but he was back up on the shelf, reclining like the Queen of Sheba, with the window still wide open. Well, he had the choice to go or stay as he pleased.

Next day he had gone but left the piece of mutton. That night I put a thick slice of bread and jam on the table, as well as a piece of meat nailed down, so that Mickey would have to tug hard at it and thus stay on the table a few seconds, enabling me to take his picture. I went back inside, typed diaries for a few minutes and then looked out. The raspberry slice had gone! He must have taken it in a second. The meat remained there all night. Clearly he preferred jam to meat. I set it all up again the next evening, camera on tripod, remote release bulb on the desk, and waited an hour. Nothing happened. I went into the kitchen to pour myself a drink, and returned just in time to see him tug the meat from the nail and drop off the table with it. My grab for the release bulb was a fraction of a second too late. He must have been watching me, waiting until either I was out of the room or my head was turned the other way. This was not going to be as easy as I had thought but it was wonderful that his twenty-four-hour incarceration in the cottage had not put him off coming back for some food.

For two nights he failed to appear. On November 6 I found a fresh scat on the top west edge of the west wood, as if left as a marker before he headed for the long woods a mile down the loch. It seemed he was a rover, staying a few days in our woods, then moving to another hunting area for a few more. The odd thing was that the owls came back, hooting loudly in the woods. I felt they had been inhibited by Mickey's presence, yet H. G. Hurrell tells the story of a tawny owl that actually attacked a marten. He was passing a hollow tree in which a pair of owls had young. The owl swept down, overtook the marten from behind and knocked it head over heels. But that of course was when the tawny was defending young. Tawnies can be fiercely territorial during their breeding season.

On November 9 Mickey returned, tore the meat from the nail and ran off with a raspberry slice too, all while I was in the kitchen. Next night I outsmarted him. I kept a weak torch-light shining on the bait, and propped up a mirror so I could keep sneaking looks at the table's reflection while I was making supper. I saw the ghostly white of his throat patch, dashed quietly back to the study, and got my first two photos of him heaving at the meat. Rain had begun to fall, spotting the window, but the shots proved quite interesting. I was glad to note, once he tugged the meat free, that he was running up and down the Y-shaped larch logs with which I had made him a runway.

He came back two days later, when my flash unit refused to work, was away four days again, then returned to filch the food when I was in the kitchen and not looking in the mirror.

These interesting games came to a temporary end later in the month when the problems concerning my father reached a crisis point. The nursing-home fees were going up again and his capital had dwindled further. I decided to grant his last wish and take him back to Spain. With Moobli staying with a friend in Chertsey, Surrey, I managed to get my father back to his beloved Puerto de Mazarron in Murcia, and to find a former nurse, a woman he liked, to look after him there. Moobli and I did not return to our disrupted life in the Highlands until late March. Almost the first thing we found, right in the middle of the top of our path, was a twisted marten scat. Mickey had clearly survived the winter, a tough little hombre.

We checked round the woods and found two dead hinds, one almost all chewed away by both foxes and badgers, the other hardly touched, plus two dead calves, one of which had also been providing Mickey with nourishing meals. Around the carcass were a few dark, wet, greenish-black scats, the result of digested raw flesh, which also contained deer hairs. Although Mickey preferred raspberry jam on titbits of buttered wholemeal bread to anything else I put out, he had been ready enough to take flank mutton when natural wild foods had decreased the previous November.

I started putting titbits on the bird-table complex again and within an hour chaffinches and tits were honing in from the woods to demolish the rich new food in minutes. Although I left titbits out overnight the marten did not come for them. The owls returned to make the woods resound with their springtime 'kik' and 'kweek' calls. I could hear their hootings and tremulous courting 'songs' at dusk most nights. Once Crowdy came to within twenty feet of me and I thought she would land on my shoulder, though she didn't. Mickey might have taken up new quarters in the long woods to the west for I found his scats there. As I now tramped the loch shore and the hills checking eagle eyries I found red-deer mortality had indeed been high this season. Enough carrion lay dotted about in the lower hills and woods to allow Mickey to roam at will, and maybe he was doing just that while searching for a mate.

On April 14 I found a fresh scat in the west wood but again he didn't come for titbits. Ten days later he left another, mostly filled with dark-blue beetle remains, near my boat runway but still he did not come for my food.

As I trekked high next day to check Eyrie 28 in fine but misty weather, I kept an eye open for possible marten dens. I did not find any but as I approached the eyrie crag I found two fresh fox holes that had been dug out in the dark peat. One only went in for two yards, where the fox had come up against bedrock, so it had made another ten yards further along. I bent down; the ammoniac scent of fox was strong. As this was not far from the den that Cedric and Aspen had last used two years ago, could it mean they were still alive?

I was disappointed to find my nearest golden eagle pair, the huge dark female of which I called Atalanta, were not using the eyrie this year either. I hiked back down past a vast conical rock, the top of which eagles had used for dismembering prey when using Eyrie 27 lower down two years earlier, and went to check the old fox den in a big cairn of tangled boulders from where Atalanta had killed two fox cubs that season. To my surprise it was now occupied by foxes again. They must have shifted back to it after deciding the peat holes were not satisfactory, maybe too damp. When I found Eyrie 27 was not being used either, it seemed possible the foxes knew the eagles were not breeding in the vicinity that year. All round the rocks the grasses and earth were well trodden down and bits of carrion, deer skin and hair had been left outside the numerous crevices between the boulders. The fox scent was even stronger here than it had been at the peat hole, but I still did not know if Cedric, Aspen, or both, were the occupants.

I turned for home and plugged over the tussocks at about 500 feet, meaning to check a badger sett at that level before making the final descent. I kept scanning, re-checking rockfaces for new eyries with the binoculars when I suddenly saw a short thick-bodied animal, like a deer with stunted legs, up to the north, over two ridges. I glassed it: a huge dog fox with a greyish patch of moulting winter coat on its throat and chest, was standing high and watching me intently. His face was so thick and round, with thick short ears sticking out, that he looked like a smiling teddy bear. I walked on, watching it from the corner of my eye, and it stayed there. My camera and long lens were in the pack. *Hell!* I knelt down, extricated and assembled them, then trying to look unconcerned, wended my way upwards to behind a rock face and peeped over. He was still there so I took two photos. I could go no further without showing myself. I walked sideways, slowly. Still he stayed. Another photo. Then he took off, loped on to a sloping rock and as he turned to look back I saw the big white flash of his tail tip. It was Cedric all right, still alive at eight years old, a great age for a persecuted Highland fox. How he had escaped the hounds and the men with terriers and guns so long, for they knew of the den he was now in, I didn't know. Maybe he had just luckily moved back into it after their usual early April visit. As my film came to an end he actually yawned at me. I was just thinking he must be a really cunning old codger by now when I found a recently-born lamb's leg in the grasses, and right by it was one of his big dog-like scats, a foolish place for a fox to leave its visiting card. I doubted he had killed the lamb. Certainly he would have had no need to, for on that day's trek I found five more dead deer, two quite fresh. It had been a good carrion year for all predators – crows, ravens, buzzards, eagles, martens, wildcats, foxes and badgers; a fact partly confirmed when I found the badger sett occupied and beside the usual big dung pits were smaller ones, filled with tinier droppings of cubs. All round the sett the grass was thicker and greener than elsewhere, primroses festooned the earth, all fertilised naturally by the badgers. One can often locate badger setts on the Hill in this way.

Whether Cedric had trailed us home I did not know but knowing a fox's natural curiosity, I was not surprised next day when Moobli nosed out one of his fresh scats near the southernmost hind carcass below the west wood, then another on our south-east land spit the next day. He had chewed some rotting green meat from a carcass that was two months old, proving yet again the power of the fox's digestive system. He spent a few days holed up in the high rockface den to the north-west, then vanished again, doubtless back to his main den. If Aspen was alive and had cubs there it was clear that the dog fox could take a few days 'off' in this way, especially with so much carrion about, and that he now knew intimately the best dens and hiding places in his territory.

The mystery of Mickey Marten's whereabouts was solved on a shore-side trek on May 6, a fine sunny day after a week of heavy rains. I was zigzagging up and down the steep slopes of the long

above: A rare pine marten moved into the woods round the cottage. It climbed a high larch then stared down at Moobli and I, like a miniature bear.

below: I brought the marten into my bedroom to give him a good feed and to try and make friends. He climbed about the log structures supporting my bed and made odd terrier-like growls towards where I sat in a chair only ten feet away.

above: I named the marten Mickey, and he became a regular visitor to the bird table to eat his favourite titbit – bread and raspberry jam.

below: Despite the marten's reputed appetite for small rodents, the voles which lived under the bird table remained unmolested.

woods two miles to the west when I heard the ringing '*keeyoo*' calls of a buzzard high above the canopy of leaves. I had found a few buzzard nests over the years but only one had been in a photographable situation. Even that was not ideal because of the constant shadows thrown over it by the surrounding branches and foliage. As I walked on my eyes took in a vast dead oak-tree snag all on its own in a small clearing. My gaze travelled up its smooth brown barkless trunk, and there, in a perfect crotch open to the sky, was an immaculate nest. It not only contained three white eggs but right opposite it was an ideal ridge on which grew small leafy rowans where I could disguise a hide easily and also see *down* into the nest. Delighted, I got out of there fast to let the buzzard return to its eggs, from which it had clearly taken a safe break in the warm sunshine.

I cut down to the shore to check the old otter holt that had been unoccupied for three years. It appeared to have been taken over by Mickey now as his small twisted sweet scats were on several mossy rocks around it. With luck, when the buzzard eggs hatched safely, I could photograph the birds with their chicks, the nest and possibly Mickey in one day. Five days later, however, it was clear that this would never happen. When I re-checked the buzzard's nest to see if the three eggs had hatched I was doomed to disappointment. They lay smashed in the nest, the shells all scrunched up as if some animal had chewed them without bothering to remove them first. I had little doubt Mickey was the culprit.

Next morning I found that Mickey had moved back into our area, had chewed a calf carcass above the cottage and left two small greeny-black scats beside it. He had also been at a hind carcass east of the main burn but here one of his scats had beetle wing-cases in it.

If my delight at his new presence was somewhat tempered by the incident at the buzzard's nest, I had cause for more dismay on May 19. I was boating home from a supply trip, after an abortive attempt to hire a movie camera, so I could film a pair of eagles which were, for once, spending as much time in the eyrie as away from it, when I thought I would make the annual count of eggs laid by the common gull colony on my nearest islet. The gulls had been making more noise than usual over the last few days, but as they had always been a rowdy lot, squabbling over little territories and greeting each inflying member with loud cries, I had thought little of it. As I tramped the islet, however, I was astonished to find that while nests had been made in the tussocks, there were no eggs anywhere. The birds, which often came to my bird table for food, all seemed oddly disconsolate as they floated on the water or stood on the outlying rocks, watching me with little cries of complaint. Much of the heather on the carpet of vegetation under the stunted pines had been trampled down, and small trails had been made. Then I found a gull eggshell, then another, then three by a burrow, another burrow three yards away, another broken empty shell, then a small twisted scat, a sweet-smelling scat. The entrances to the holes, too small for fox or wildcat, too big for a stoat, were well worn, the trails well used. I now had no doubt that Mickey Marten, partial to eggs, had heard the clamour from the gulls, had worked out in his mustelid mind they would be laying many eggs, and had swum the eighty yards from the mainland for some sumptuous and easy repasts. Such a swim would be nothing to him. Then I found a dead gull, with bad neck wounds, lying on the rocks beyond the heather carpet. The little monster!

For a moment I felt tempted to trap him and send him off to a zoo in Edinburgh that had long asked me to get them one. (I must stress this was before pine martens were protected under the Wildlife and Countryside Act, 1981, a protection for which I had been among the campaigners.) I knew I would not do this, however, From near extinction at the turn of the century, martens had been slowly spreading from their strongholds in the north-west Highlands, but were still among the rarest of our mammals. The gulls had had the islet to themselves untouched for many years and such predation was natural. Their numbers had dwindled from over forty nine years ago to eighteen this year, without any interference from martens. I tried to 'persuade' Mickey to leave the islet by laying a few raspberry titbits there, to remind him of his favourite food, and some more on the mainland with a trail up to the bird table. But the gulls themselves snapped these up before Mickey began his dusk forays, so I gave up.

Two days later I was stepping over the dry gully of a small stream before our main burn when a sandpiper flipped out beside me and performed a 'broken wing and trailing tail' display over the rocks to the shore twenty-five yards away, a display some birds use to lure predators away from a nest. Sure enough, I found its little round nest, containing four reddish blotched eggs, in the grasses right below the branch of a fallen larch. I wondered how long it would be before Mickey sniffed them out too. I glassed the islet and saw another dead gull lying on the rocks, also uneaten. Was Mickey just killing those that offered some resistance?

Just then I heard a loud '*kairoo*' call and looked up to see the old female buzzard drifting overhead, followed by the smaller male. The bereaved pair circled over the islet, eyeing the dead gulls below. Three live gulls which had been standing near their nests, giving sad '*kee*' calls of hopelessness, launched themselves upwards and with dives, rolls and loud shrieks, mobbed the buzzards away. A reflex action by the gulls, for they now had no eggs to protect.

During a lull in torrential rain next day I wandered down to the land spit again. By sneaking slowly nearer and avoiding eye contact – such birds will often sit tight until your eyes actually meet theirs – I took two photos of the sandpiper on her eggs. I quietly moved away. A tree creeper landed on a small dead snag near me, spiralled up it with insects in its curved beak, vanished into a hole, and came out again with its beak empty. It clearly had youngsters there. I waited a few minutes and to my surprise both creepers flew to and fro with full beaks, apparently careless of my presence. It was even more surprising how fast they found food, just two minutes away, then back each came with insects swiftly and easily found on the trunks of nearby trees. Once they nearly collided in mid-air, dodging briefly round each other as if one were saying, 'Ooops. Mind where you're going. Try the old alders over there!' I wondered if Mickey would get their young too, for I found the cavity filled to near overflowing with four fledglings.

On May 26 I saw the big female buzzard circle the house, then land in a dwarf birch high on the steep ridges to the north-west. She stayed there awhile, immobile, a dark graven image against the rockface. Then she just dropped off, slid through the air with uplifted wings and landed like a floppy umbrella on a vole. I could see the vole clearly through the binoculars as she carried it away, though it was too far for a photo. That day I boated out to meet Ray Collier, the Nature Conservancy Council's new Chief Warden for the north-west Highlands. We had a talk about the wildlife in my area as I took him over to the islet. He too thought the devastation to be a marten's work, but there were no new egg shells near the burrows and one of the dead gulls had gone. Mickey, it seemed, was back on the mainland. But at least the sandpiper was still on her eggs and the young tree creepers were also still there and ready to fly.

For nearly a month after that Mickey seemed to have disappeared from the area. I was not only still working with the eagles but had a foliage-hidden hide on a rare black-throated divers' nest on an islet three miles away, and also one on a ridge overlooking a peregrine falcons' nest on which the Government had licensed me to keep a watch. I had no time to search for Mickey. At least the tree creepers flew safely, and the sandpiper was still on her nest on June 8. (As I watched her crouching on the deep bowl she had made under the branch, actually *in* the wood, invisible at even three yards, it seemed I was also witnessing the evolution of intelligence in the wild, for hooded crows often sat in the larches above her.) However, the nest was empty a few days later. Then I saw her with two chicks running along like tiny ostriches between the rocks on the shore. The young in two wrens' nests I had been monitoring also flew, and the numbers of goldcrest young were higher than I had ever known. Willow warblers, robins, pied and grey wagtails reared normal families; only the chaffinches seemed well down, so I reckoned Mickey had found a few of their nests. As chaffinches were the commonest birds, found all along the loch-shore woodlands, their total populations would hardly be affected. Only the islet gulls and of course the buzzards had had all their eggs taken.

On June 11 I was driving along a single-track road amid conifer forests on the other side of the loch when I saw a chunky male buzzard perched on a telephone pole. It was 'perch hunting', using the pole as a vantage point from which to peer at the grasses below for voles or beetles. I had yet to take a good photo of a buzzard on a pole so I slowed down, opened the vehicle door carefully and took two pictures. Annoyingly it kept its head pointing away from me, so I gave a loud '*wee-oo*' buzzard whistle. To my surprise the bird not only turned its head but launched itself from the pole, just as my camera clicked, and flew right over my head before disappearing between the trees. Poor light meant a low shutter speed, so the pictures would still be too fuzzy. As I had not seen my nearest pair of buzzards for over a month, I was sure they had moved over the loch, maybe to try and nest again. If so I wished them luck, for I had found marten scats in that area too!

I still hoped the islet gulls might lay a few more eggs and rear young, so I still put out titbits to lure Mickey away. As far as I could see, however, only birds took them. On June 20 I visited the islet and found Mickey had moved back. The burrows had been extended, more gull-egg shells lay at the entrances, and there were several of his scats, more liquid than usual. I set up a small vegetation screen downwind of the burrows but while I fitted in several hours in dusk and dawn watches, not a sight did I get of him. Finally the gulls gave up their fruitless attempts and left the islet to return to the sea. Mickey left it too.

One morning I was out for my usual walk round the woods when I saw a bright reddish-brown animal on the north hill. I was sure it was a roe doe, but it looked too big. Then it turned and I saw the brush with its white tip. It was Cedric. He looked enormous. I went back inside, fitted the telephoto lens to the camera and dashed out again. Naturally he had gone. I sneaked up the hill from the south-east, concerned about my scent in the cross wind from the east. Thick high bracken grew everywhere, so there was not much hope. I saw the fox had dragged the bones and skeleton of an old red-deer-calf carcass downhill. He had probably been visiting the old winter carcasses, getting what dried pemmican-type meat he could from them.

I scanned the west wood, where other carcasses lay, then the hills above. There he was, on a grassy ledge, just a hundred yards up to the north-west. He was standing high, looking down at me, bracken waving in front of his grey-white throat patch which still appeared to be moulting. He seemed not at all scared, just intently curious, his black muzzle quivering, his orange eyes bright with query. I took a photo – and the damn film came to an end. Silently cursing, I forced the lever round, tore the edges of the film but got one more shot.

I made a few gentle '*raowl*' fox calls, then turned to go. To my surprise he followed me down the ledge, hopped to another ledge, all his legs in full view for what would have been wonderful pictures, still gazing down at me. I rushed into the cottage, loaded new film, then hiked up to 500 feet, but there was no more sign of him.

While I was happy to know Cedric was still alive, I was still wondering what was happening in the world of Mickey Marten. Where had the little blighter got to?

14 · Mickey Seeks a Mate

Early one morning, as I was ambling along the shore below the west wood looking for marten scats, I noticed just beneath the water surface a huge rock with a thick metal ring in its top. Clearly it had been used many years ago as a boat mooring. Well, I did not need it for that, but it would make an ideal anchor for my tin roof. By tying a rope to the ring, working the rope over the front edge of the cottage's corrugated iron roof, and tying the other end to a tree base in the east wood, it would effectively prevent any winter storm from blowing the roof away.

The rock weighed at least 400 lbs and I could not lift it completely, but by dragging and rolling it uphill a few yards each day, I finally got it up to the west side of the cottage in two weeks. No sooner was it in place, on July 15, than I found deposited right on top of the ringstone one of Mickey's fresh scats. It was filled with raspberry seeds, so he must have been raiding my ripening crops of fruit. A sort of double 'insult'.

I spent the day scything my paths clear, cutting blackberry leaders back, bottling raspberries (though I left some for Mickey) and filing photos. Before dusk I set out bread and raspberry jam on the bird table, rigged camera and flash gun on its tripod, and waited anxiously in the gloom of my study with the air release bulb in my hand. Mickey did not show up, nor did he leave any more signs or appear for the next few nights.

167

I had just boated home on July 26 when Moobli huffed, put his nose down and headed towards two cherry trees near the west wood. I looked up – there was Mickey, clinging like a raccoon with the claws of all four feet to a slender branch. He had been after the high overripe fruits I had left. He scuttled down on to some thick hazel-bush foliage and vanished.

There was no more sign of him until late August, when again he began leaving half-digested rowan-berry 'offerings', this time under the log archway at the top of the path. By early September I was finding them a quarter-mile apart, on the boundaries of both woods, on rocks beside the burn, and along our paths. I was sure he was leaving them for a potential mate to find. Martens mate at any time from mid-July to mid-September, and copulation can be a noisy affair, as it often is among many predatory animals, with squeaks and growls from both animals. With their delayed implantation of the blastocyst, martens can mate in the warm summer months but the fertilised eggs are not implanted in the womb wall until February. The young are born in April, when the worst of winter is over. It is two more months before the kits explore the immediate surroundings of the den, and the latter half of July before they are ready to follow their mother on hunting forays.

At about this time I discovered that the nearest buzzards might indeed have laid at least one more egg in a nest across the loch, for I saw a young one with floppy plumage on a pole near the spot where I had earlier seen the male. As I approached it, giving my 'buzzard' whistle, it kept answering with weak '*pheeoo*' chick calls. It looked extremely hungry. I showed it a chunk of meat but it flew to the next post uphill. I climbed through the fence, moved in close and then dropped the meat ostentatiously. It looked, moved its head for better focus and kept staring at the mutton. As I walked back to my truck it flew down towards the meat and I am sure found the meal, though I could no longer see it through the high vegetation.

Walking round the west wood in early September I noticed that the skulls from two hind carcasses had disappeared, and some of the bigger bones of the skeletons had been scattered. Judging from Moobli's scenting reactions, I was sure a fox or two had been visiting. I also found a new scat of Mickey's, right on the west edge of the wood, indicating that he might have been roaming in from the long woods a mile away. Its purple colour showed that he had been feasting on my cultivated blackberries, a record crop of which had been ripening a few days earlier. Cedric also had been back, and he too had been at the blackberries.

More rowan-berry 'offerings' appeared during the next two weeks but still Mickey did not come to the bird table. On the drive back from Edinburgh (where I had taken part in a television programme about my eagle book) I found a fresh traffic-killed rabbit and picked it up, intending to set it out in the hills as bait for eagle or fox photographs. Carrying gear from the boat to the house, I somehow forgot the rabbit and left it in the grasses by the log archway. Next morning it had gone, but there was one of Mickey's scats, as if left in thanks.

A few more signs appeared during the following days, then all attempts to attract Mickey back to the bird table had to stop because my father had died in Spain. Hoping to keep Mickey around while I was away, I set out half a sackful of the jammy sweet biscuits which I knew he liked.

When I arrived back at Wildernesse two weeks later it was to the wettest October in thirty years. Gales and driving rain-storms lasted for days. There were no signs of Mickey, and birds were taking the fresh titbits I left out, mainly chaffinches, which even pulled the meat off the bones of mutton flank I had nailed to the table. This was the first time I had ever known chaffinches to be carnivorous.

In the gloom of dusk on October 30 I wandered quietly down to below the west wood, and was greeted by an astonishing sight. A whole family of foxes was scuffling through the dead leaves and herbage below the trees, each with a bone from the hind skeletons in its mouth. The biggest, Cedric, was weaving about with a thigh bone. A smaller, darker fox, also with a white flash on the tail, surely Aspen, was trotting about with a shin bone, and two almost full-grown cubs, one with a white tail tip, were carrying what looked like rib bones. Even if I'd had a camera in my hands, it was too dark for photos. At times one fox would drop its bone and pick up the one another had been carrying, and then drop that a few yards away. I saw Aspen shove a shoulder bone into a fissure between two rocks. Suddenly they must have picked up my scent; Cedric gave a brief high-pitched screech-bark, '*rrraitsch*', and they all vanished silently into the gloom, noiselessly as ghosts. I had often found evidence that foxes distribute carcass bones in this way, cache some into dry crevices as if to keep them away from other predators, but it was the first time I had actually seen it taking place. While it was fascinating to know Cedric and Aspen were not only still alive and together as a couple but had raised two more cubs this year, I wondered if it was their presence that kept Mickey away.

Next night I had my answer. At 11.20 pm, with the radio playing and the paraffin lamp hissing its light on to the bird table, a large dark animal suddenly appeared on the window-sill. It was Mickey, larger than before. He was licking his chops, having chewed at the piece of meat I had nailed out, and just gazing in at me.

'Mickey, Mickey, hello,' I said in a soft voice, as I waved to him in a friendly way.

He stayed a little longer, then jumped on to the table and ran down the sloping logs I had erected for him. Quickly I put out some jam slices and set up the camera, but he did not return that night, or the next three.

On November 4 I set out a raspberry-jam half-slice, and went into the kitchen to peel potatoes for supper. When I wandered back, it had gone. I put out another, called 'Mickey, Mickey, Mickey', and gave a gentle '*weeyoo*' whistle – a call I hoped he would get used to – and sat waiting in the dark. Half an hour later he was back on the sill, then he hopped on to the table and started licking the jam off the bread. I pressed the bulb. The camera clicked but the flash did not work. I tried again. There was still no flash. He was posing perfectly, long irregular creamy-orange throat patch showing as he craned his long neck, looking about. Then I found the flash wire had come undone and fumbled in the dark for its tiny sleeve. By the time I had reconnected it all the jam had gone and he was away. I set out a new half-slice, sure he would not come again, and started typing my diary. When I next looked up that too had gone! I went out, made the same calls and whistle, set out more bread and jam. In minutes he was back again. As he chewed away I saw his canines were long and white. I would not have liked those sunk into my hand. This time the flash worked and I got my first good photos of him.

After that he began coming almost every night. I soon realised I was not being too bright. Often he just seized the half slice and jumped off with it, landing with a thump on the ground that reminded me of Moobli as a pup. I estimated his weight at 3 lbs, his length at 2½ feet. From then on I cut the jammy bread slices into tiny bits. He then had to stay on the table in order to gobble them all up! He soon became used to the flash, to my presence by the lamp, and often he looked in, his dark eyes half-closed, as if saying thanks for the grub. Sometimes he stopped eating and looked out into the dark, rearing high up on his haunches, his big puddy furry clawed feet dangling like a small bear, as if looking at a mate in the darkness. And he often jumped off with a piece in his mouth as if taking it to her.

I experimented with different foods. He certainly had a sweet tooth, always eating the jammy bits before he bothered with any meat. He liked cheese, raisins, apple, all sweet jams and honey, but left Bovril and tomato, and only took sausage if there was nothing else. He also disliked black treacle. Sometimes when I set the food out and gave the calls and whistles, he answered me from somewhere in the east wood with strange breathy '*fisch-ow*' calls. Search as I did, I still could not find any den he was using. Oddly, it became apparent that he preferred to come when the light was blazing away and I was sitting at the desk. I no longer needed to keep a careful watch for him – the white flash of his moving throat patch as he snaked up the logs nearly always caught my eye. When I set the camera outside he flinched at the first click, and next time he just poked his head over the far side of the table and snitched a titbit, but he soon got used to this set-up too.

I looked forward more and more to the sudden appearance of that cheeky face at the window. By late November I could predict within minutes when he would appear. Once James Crumley, features editor of the *Edinburgh Evening News*, and a fine poetic wildlife writer himself, trekked in to visit for a weekend, and was avid to see the marten too. I told Jim, guessing, that Mickey would appear at 6.34 pm. Jim sat in my chair, keeping an eager watch. Mickey obliged, to Jim's amazement, by coming at 6.35!

Four nights later Mickey woke me up at 4 am. I heard loud high whirring growls '*chroom, chroom*', and raised myself up enough to see him on the window-sill gazing at the ground below, ears cocked as if growling at a rival, or maybe at a badger that was coming to dig up worms around the cottage. If it was at a mate, I never saw her or any other marten on the table.

His visits continued until it was time to return to Spain to tie up my father's estate there. Before I left, I distributed a good sackful of jammy biscuits in dry places, including the woodshed, which he had often entered in summer to raid the tree-wasp nests on the roof, to help keep him going. I did not get back to Wildernesse until April 12.

As I walked past the kitchen window on my return home, I saw some white bird droppings on the table inside. I looked in closer, shielding the outside light from my eyes with my hand. To my amazement, perched on my wood-chopping block and looking at me with bobbing movements of its head, was a large tawny owl!

I unlocked the doors and rushed in. It was Crowdy. She must have come down the chimney, but why? To seek shelter from storms, or food from me? She was afraid at first when I picked her up and fought hard with her furred talons, drawing blood. She was quite thin, her breastbone sticking out, but she would not eat any mince, the only meat I had brought with me. She had never liked meat that was minced, preferring whole chunks she could tear up naturally. If I had arrived a few days later she would have died of starvation.

I managed to calm her down, talking to her with all the old soothing words and croonings I had always used with her. Before long she relaxed, appeared to recognise and remember me, and with slit eyes looked at me almost lovingly, like a winged cat. She allowed me to stroke her head, wings and chest, without protest or complaint, and I managed to get a few pinches of mince down her throat. That night she sat in a 'nest' she seemed to have made in a pair of my trousers and watched me cooking supper as she had when a youngster three years earlier, letting me chuck her under the chin.

By the following morning, however, she was wild again, darting about the floor, hopping around with uplifted wings like a little umbrella, trying to find a dark place to hide. She had eaten none of the mince I left out for her. I managed to get two more pinches down her throat, carried her outside and off she flew on her broad mottled-brown wings into the east wood.

On my first walk round the woods I found four dead hinds and two calves; only one of the hinds had been partly eaten by foxes. There was plenty of carrion around for Mickey but I could find no signs of him at all. There were only sixteen gulls so far on the islet this spring. If Mickey returned I intended to do my utmost to keep him off their nesting ground by keeping him stuffed with his favourite foods!

I was at my desk in the dark on April 18 when Crowdy landed in the ash tree by the cottage and started making her tremulous hooting courting song. I went out and she flew to the big spruce and delivered it again. I wondered if she had not been able to find a mate. Half an hour later she returned, hooting normally right outside the window, looking in at me in the lamplight. I was afraid she would try to come through the window and hurt herself. I went out, hooted back loudly, and she left. A few days later I heard her giving loud '*kwik*' screeches from the ash trees along the shore, then two more owls began their high trilling courting songs from the woods to the north-east, across the burn. I was sure they were Holly and Wallie, and I hoped this year I might find their nest and photograph them at it (I did not).

One morning, while I was writing, I was startled by two men appearing in front of my study window. It turned out to be the under-keeper of the estate in which my cottage stood, a friend of mind, and a staff stalker from the Red Deer Commission. They were conducting a red-deer census of the area and told me over coffee that the local estates were at last forming themselves into a Deer Management Group, co-operating on all deer information. As I had suggested in my last book, they had started putting out winter feed and mineral licks for the animals.

The under-keeper also gave me the less welcome news that two weeks earlier he and my farmer neighbour, with others, had visited the fox den below the eagle eyrie with guns and terriers, and had shot a bolting vixen. The terriers had killed two cubs. Yes, the vixen had had a white tip to her tail. I felt sure then that Aspen had finally met her end. He said also that the hounds had been out earlier and killed a big dog fox in that area but from his description it didn't sound as if the fox had been as big as Cedric. He said that they had only been at the den a few minutes, had seen no sign of any eagles and that the nest appeared empty. Well, the men had been performing their legal and traditional duty, trying to 'keep fox numbers down' before the lambing season. I would achieve nothing by being censorious, though I observed that fox-killing was hardly necessary this year with so much fresh carrion about. Later treks proved it had been the highest mortality season for red deer in all my years for I found a total of thirty-six carcasses (nineteen within a half-mile radius of the cottage).

In later weeks, also, I found several big fresh fox scats near some of the carcasses but whether they had been left by Cedric or not I could not know. Certainly from then to the time of writing this a year later, I have seen neither Cedric nor Aspen. If both were dead, at least Aspen had lived five years in the wild, she and Cedric had reared four families to my certain knowledge, and Cedric had lived to ten, more than old enough to have died of natural causes anyway in such hard hills.

As the days passed I had more proof that Mickey was no longer in the area because some voles moved in, dug out burrows below the porch and began to vie with the chaffinches for the food I set out. They would emerge from the burrows, dart about sniffing the air for danger, then climb like little monkeys up the wire-netting sides of the old wildcat live trap below the bird table and nibble the jammy slices, tearing out chunks and holding them up to their teeth with both tiny front paws. The odd thing was that two woodmice also moved in and I often saw them go down the *same* burrows that the voles were using.

While the voles emerged during the day, the woodmice only came after dusk, so stealing the stage, soon learning there was food on the bird table too. They hared up and down the sloping logs I had erected for the marten at great speed. Only one of the voles, a cheeky broad-faced male with big eyes (which I came to call Vicky), learned this trick. At first, when a colourful cock chaffinch advanced towards the bread, Vicky would zip away to hide under a loose wooden strut on the trap. He kept poking his broad long-whiskered snout out and making short threatening darts, which the chaffinch repulsed by flicking his wings out. Vicky became more and more agitated. One day he dashed out, landed on the chaffinch's back, bounced off it, sending it flap-staggering away, and hared down the side of the trap! He often grabbed a titbit in his jaws and ran off with it. One day I sneaked out quickly to see where he was taking the food. I was just in time to see him emerge from under some corrugated-iron sheets that protected my lumber below the west wall of the cottage, and hop like a little kangaroo clutching almost half a slice. He was making really hard going of tugging it between the long hampering grasses but he got it into the old wildcat pens and vanished between some rocks, where I was sure he would feed it to his mate.

Evidently he decided this was too much of a chore, for one day I saw him feeding on the trap together with another big vole with a distended stomach, doubtless his pregnant mate. And she had now set up new quarters right under the trap, and the constant food supply. Now Vicky did not have so far to carry food to her. While he could now rout most of the chaffinches, there was one cock he seemed to tolerate, a bird that always approached cautiously and did not flap his wings. I got several photos of the two eating from the same piece of bread. It was interesting to notice this subtle difference between individuals of different species.

While I never saw the woodmice fighting, nor any battles between them and the voles, the male voles could get extremely 'ratty' with each other. Vicky's main rival was a battle-scarred veteran which, as the song goes, was 'big and fast and grey and old'. Vicky was at the bread when up climbed the old guy. They paused, looked, leaped at each other, rose up on their hind legs and swiped out with their front feet, real roundhouse clouts, like boxers, and it was Vicky who retired defeated, running down to where his mate was chewing grasses to nourish the bairns inside

175

her. Two days later I saw Vicky fight back harder, the two whirling in circles, apparently trying to bite each other's tails, or genital regions. Then he rose up, boxed furiously and bared his little teeth. The veteran then ran down the netting sides of the trap. A few days later they had another fight, over cornflakes this time. Vicky was chewing away when the other came from beneath the strut, circled out in a lightning dash and tried to bite Vicky's muzzle. Vicky bit back, they sprang apart and he went back to the flakes. The veteran circled back under the strut and came out again, then both rose up, clouting each other round the ears, snapping at the other's muzzle, and making high-pitched chattering squeaks, until the old battler fled down the netting again. Despite the apparent ferocity of these exchanges I never saw any blood or signs of real injury. Once Vicky's mate came up, much thinner having presumably given birth, and they rubbed muzzles together gently before he passed flakes to her with his front paws.

Although the marten was still away, I wondered how the voles were surviving so well because all three owls had moved back into the woods, noisy by day as well as after dark. By this time I had located Mickey's whereabouts: he had been back in the cairn above the otter holt in the long woods but as the scats were at least a week or two old and the otter was back in residence, its mossy lay-out place all wet and pressed flat, I was sure the otter had displaced him. I trekked about and found he was now inhabiting the rocky den which had once been used by my old tom wildcat Sylvesturr when I had released him eight years earlier at the ripe old age of ten. Here there were two fresh scats of Mickey's and, as I had found no sign of Sylvesturr for five years, it was clear the old curmudgeon himself was dead.

Not until May 29 did Mickey return to the cottage area. I found smaller scats than usual on the top of the path. Years ago I would have said they were stoats, but I had learned that, depending on the food eaten, individual animals can leave small- or normal-sized scats, just like humans! I set out jammy chunks and they disappeared overnight. After a hard day in an eagle hide, I wandered from the kitchen into the study. There was a huge dark form on the bird table. It was Mickey, bigger than ever, probing his nose into the moss carpet I had spread

above left: The male buzzard winged his way westward as the sun lit up the colours of his wings.

above right: Buzzards like to hunt from high perches such as telegraph poles, peering intently for the movements of prey below.

below: A female buzzard settling down to brood her young chick.

above: I was surprised when the buzzard brought an eel back to its nest. How had it caught this slippery creature?

below: A male buzzard feeds its well-fledged chick on its nest in a dark oak wood.

over the surface, looking for food. I hastily set some out, but not until I was in bed in the dark did he come for it. Again I heard him giving loud chirring growls. It was pitch black and I did not want to scare him with sudden torchlight, so could not see what he was growling at.

When I checked the gull's islet on June 1 the nineteen birds which had returned that season possessed five nests with three eggs each, three nests with one egg each and four empty nests. Outside the burrows lay only the eggshells from last year. Mickey had not swum over there yet. Every day now I laid out his supply. He came frequently, became tamer than before and I like to think this fairly costly feeding kept him off the islet, for the gulls reared seven young to flying stage. It was their best season for nine years. The sandpiper too, back on her old nest under the fallen larch branch, also reared three young success-fully. Once I found one of Mickey's scats between my gate posts which contained bits of snail shell. It was interesting martens would eat snails. I had never seen that recorded before.

On June 17 I was sitting at my desk in full daylight at 7.45 pm when I saw Mickey come bouncing up the path like a giant dark-brown squirrel. He leaped up to the table with the graceful ease of a trapeze artist, danced about looking for his food which I had not yet set out, jumped off again and squatted down to press his rear scent glands on a tuft, so marking his territory. I knew for sure he was a male then, for I could see his little testes, the hairs on his scrotum paler than elsewhere. Then he loped down and into the thick rhododendron bush by the path. It was clear now that he had a day den under the dry thick root tangles of the bush because there was a definite rounded trail through the grasses where he went in and out. I put out more food, gave the usual calls and whistle and was surprised to see him run out, rear up on his hind legs, look at me with a quizzical expression, then bob down again. No sooner was I back indoors than he was back on the table, scoffing away.

As I was walking back from the woodshed one afternoon, I saw him galloping along through the grasses in the east wood. He saw me, dodged into another rhododendron bush and watched me set out food. To see if he really did like eggs I put a hen's egg on the moss atop one of his log runways. I had no sooner reached the study than he raced up, opened his jaws wide, picked the egg up gently and raced off with it to his den before I had a chance to take a photo. I now realised he kept a watch towards dusk. When I found a dead chaffinch that had flown into the kitchen window, I put that on to the table, and he was up and away with it in seconds.

By late August he was so tame I managed to take several daylight photos of him amid the grasses in his natural surroundings. In early September he again started leaving rowan-berry 'offerings' round the woods. As I had found no evidence of another marten it seemed he was still trying to attract a mate. By mid-month with rains increasing, he no longer used the bush den and when I saw his feet were wet, as if he had crossed the burn, I went over it next day and searched about. I found he had taken over Aspen's old den by an old ruined wall across the bay. Some scats lay near the entrance hole below some broad rocks and I could see his trail through the thick dry carpet of oak leaves that had blown into the warm comfortable chamber further in. I was certain he was in there for as I bent low, trying to see beyond the entrance, I heard his high whirring growls. I did not want to frighten him from this den so I left quietly and discreetly. I was just recrossing the burn, stepping from rock to rock, when something made me look round. Mickey was loping along behind like a little dog! I got to the cottage, gave the usual calls and whistle as I set out titbits, and as soon as I was inside he was on the moss-covered table, chewing away.

Martens are well known to prey on mice and voles, and I had certainly found the fur and bones of these animals in his scats. The odd thing was that he never seemed to chase the voles that lived near the table. Not once did I see him so much as sniff at their burrows. Vicky and his mate reared three young and I often saw the family together, the young only a third the size of their parents. I did notice, however, that towards dusk Vicky now rushed up the logs, grabbed a titbit then flung it over the side to the ground. Then he hared down the netting twisting his rear legs backwards like a little squirrel, grabbed the food and took it under the trap to eat.

As winter approached, Mickey came over the burn, now swollen by rain, by using a fallen larch as a bridge. He came regularly every night. If I had failed to put his food out in time he just looked at me, at the empty table, then back at me with a comical expression as if saying, 'There's nothing here. What's the matter with you?'

My one great hope was still that he would find a mate and bring a whole family to the table. Perhaps the pairing process had already begun, for this would help explain Mickey's sudden return from the wild for food in summer.

15 · Mickey and the Nesting Buzzards

Until the marten ruined the nest of my nearest pair, buzzards had long been an intimate part of the wildlife around Wildernesse. Then, after the vandalised and homeless buzzard pair had moved across the loch, and my attempt to feed what was clearly their late-raised youngster which I had seen on the telegraph pole, I was naturally delighted to find, late in November, a young buzzard in our woods once again. From its chunky shape, I was reasonably sure it was the same young male from across the loch and that it was trying to establish a territory of its own.

I soon became worried about his survival chances in the open tussocky hills and the thin belts of lochside woodlands around our remote home. Gales had been blowing almost incessantly for three weeks, switching from south-west to north-westerlies, bringing a variety of rain, sleet, snow and hail. On three mornings running I had seen him beating along against the gales, swept sideways or suddenly upwards, buffeted so hard he sometimes had to swerve close to the ridges to take advantage of where they lessened the wind. He fought on, glaring at the ground for small mammal prey or even a beetle or two. Once he landed on a huge rock as if needing a rest but could not keep his footing against the harsh blasts, and was forced to take off again. Despite his natural aerobatic skills he was far less stable in the air than the mighty eagle.

In such gales he could not indulge his second favourite method of finding prey – perch hunting. One reason why buzzards so often sit on stable telephone poles along Highland roads is that they can locate beetles, frogs, mice or voles by sight, then drop on them from a height. They know, too, that a passing car can make a small mammal move when otherwise it would not, or run over a rabbit at night to provide carrion, or that the vibrations can drive big worms to the surface – for buzzards will certainly eat earthworms too when really hungry.

There were no telegraph poles in my area, however, and the branches of trees were swaying so much in the storms that he could not sit on them without constant shifts and adjustments of his long wings – movements which could easily be seen by his prey, causing them to hide. The frogs on which he could have preyed in summer were all now hibernating, hidden in the mud of various pools in the marshes. And the normal winter mortality of red deer had not yet started, so I could not drag a half-opened carcass from the depths of the woods into the open for him either.

He was clearly having a hard time, facing his biggest challenge since leaving the nest, for it is in their first winter that up to 70 per cent of all large birds of prey die. If the young buzzard got through this one he had every chance of survival, finding a mate, breeding successfully and living his normal span of seven to nine years in the wild. About 20 inches long and weighing just over 2 lbs, he needed roughly 80 to 100 grammes of food a day to keep himself in full hunting trim – that is about 3 field voles or 4 to 5 woodmice. A young rabbit would keep him going 2 or 3 days, but there were no rabbits in the terrain around us.

The fourth morning dawned in a dull sky but the wind had dropped, just a small zephyr from the south-east ruffling the loch's surface. I came into the study from breakfast in time to see a dark-brown mottled bird rise from the bramble bushes by the bird table, soar slowly across the pasture, then land on a bare branch of a lochside ash tree. Had the young buzzard been after Vicky and the other voles? I fitted the telephoto lens to my camera and, although the light was poor, took two pictures of him.

He stayed there, like a huge dark shadow, motionless, only his dark-brown eyes and rounded head moving with deliberate slowness above his superbly cream-streaked broad chest as he peered into the grasses below.

Then he just fell, wings almost completely shut, guiding himself skilfully through a small gap in some twigs, dropping like a stone. He thumped into something on the ground, bounced up an inch or two, then with his wings half out made several hard gripping stabs and clutches with his talons. All the time he glared straight down at the vole he was killing, squeezing convulsively.

I dashed to the door, knowing he was too preoccupied to notice, and took two more photos in the dim light as he bent down and ripped off the dead vole's head with his beak, swallowed it, then bent down again, picked up its body and gulped that back too. He looked round, his killing concentration eased, before flapping heavily away to land on a hazel branch. He stood there for a few seconds, looked down again, and seeing nothing of interest glided on into the edge of the west wood.

Twenty minutes later his dark cross-like shadow floated over the front pasture again, and this time he looped up to land on an old ash tree snag. Finding nothing after a four-minute wait – his head annoyingly obscured by twigs from where I stood – he flew away again to the west.

I saw him several times after that, and even brought back a fresh traffic-killed rabbit I found and left it for him beneath the ash trees. He fed from it each dawn. Afterwards I kept putting bits of meat near the rabbit remains. Then in early December I accidentally startled him while he was feeding on a red-deer carcass, the first calf to fall that winter on the edge of the west wood. That would keep him going a long time.

In early spring I checked the three buzzards' nests I knew in the long woods to the west, to find that two of them had been almost completely blown out and the third showing no signs of being refurbished. This did not surprise me for the young male, still less than a year old, would not be mature enough yet to breed. In any case, he was not turning up in my area any more.

All through the summer that followed I caught very few glimpses of buzzards flying near the cottage. If the young male was still alive clearly he had not yet established a territory nearby. In early June I found the parent buzzard pair had moved to a new territory amid the forests across the loch. I was driving along the narrow little road there when the male came soaring from the light-green foliage of some larch trees over to my right and landed on a telegraph pole. I drove past innocently, eased up on the hill seventy yards away, climbed out slowly and at last got really good photos of a buzzard on a pole. He lifted his tail and ejected a mute, turned his head to give me fine profiles, glared straight down at the ground in search of prey and for once, as I clicked off five good shots, did not fly away.

My lucky day, I thought, and giving in to optimism I started searching among the larches for a nest. I had only wended my way for a few minutes through the tall stately trees when I heard a ringing '*kee-yoo*' call and the female buzzard sailed over the trees, and with wings half closed performed a fair imitation of an eagle's 'jet glide' as she came in to land on a larch tree fifty yards ahead. She stayed for a few seconds as I kept still, then flapped away again. I noted the exact tree and walked forward to investigate. High up near the top was a large new nest. Little white splashes on nearby branches confirmed that it contained a chick or two.

Unfortunately the ground here was flat; there was no ridge on which to put a hide that overlooked the nest, and the trees were too close together to enable me to build a tree hide either, even if I had had the inclination. I was sure the pair would be successful this time, for the nest could not be seen from the road and there was a small river not far away which supported several prey species. Shallow lagoons along the main loch shoreline also contained many frogs, and an area of forest opposite another small loch, which had been clear-felled two years before, now showed a good deal of new vegetation springing up between the stumps and housing large numbers of mice and voles, as well as lizards, snakes, beetles and large insects.

In the autumn that year a pair of buzzards moved into the area near the cottage. I first saw them fly over the west wood on October 16 as I was returning from a trek to photograph stags. The smaller male landed on the top of a pine while the female circled, gained speed and height and then 'buzzed' him with such a fast dive that he had to duck and flirt his wings out. He then took off as she circled back and dived on her, causing her to perform a complete somersault, straightening her wings out at just the right moment after the roll. Were they my nearest pair which had been so rudely evicted by the marten? Perhaps they had decided to move back to their old location. I searched for a nest in the west wood but failed to find one. That they were almost certainly not the old-timers, but probably young adults, maybe the young male from across the loch, who after all had found a mate, was to be confirmed later.

The following spring two foresters were startled when a big buzzard came off a nest right above their heads in the oak woods above the lagoons on the south side of the loch. When I was told this story by Peter Madden, a close friend and himself a forestry keeper with extraordinary powers of observation, who had helped me greatly with golden eagles, we decided to go together and investigate. We located the big buzzard's nest less than half a mile from the larch tree nest my old-timers had occupied the previous year, and this one seemed likely to belong to the same pair. I knew that, like eagles, a buzzard pair will often have several nests in their territory, which in the High-lands can cover about five square miles. I knew also that it was not the pair that Peter and I had observed two years earlier from a tunnel hide on a ridge four miles away – unless that male had found a new mate. Last year the mother bird in that family had vanished from a new nest, leaving the male to feed and rear the fledglings by himself. By the most amazing chance (not dis-covered until some of my films were later developed) I even had photographic evidence of an eagle feeding a female buzzard (which at the time I had taken for a grouse, her distinctive yellow legs only showing clearly on the slide) to the hungry eaglet in its eyrie high in the hills.

There were two week-old chicks in this year's oak-wood nest, and on the same day I also went to check the nest of the brave little male under the ridge. Clearly he had found another mate, for there were two chicks in his old nest too. Within a week we had two good hides looking down on both nests. I had also invested in some costly and very heavy 16mm movie-making equipment. This meant carrying some 53 lbs up the lochside cliff or on to the ridge each time.

At midday on June 6 Peter offered to put me into the long hide above the little male's nest. We had built the hide over a slight hump so it was possible to slide into it without being seen from the nest. As soon as I was set up, Peter took pains to obscure the end of my long movie camera lens, despite the hordes of biting midges. He then left, deliberately showing himself in open areas to delude any flying parent into believing the coast was clear, and hiked back down to his van.

After a few minutes one of the chicks backed up, lifted its grey downy tail stump and squirted faeces well clear of the high sides of the nest. A short time later I heard soft '*ker ker ker*' calls, like a gull's, only more muted. The male buzzard, perched nearby in a tree, kept calling intermittently for an hour before a higher voice answered from the sky as the mother bird swept in and landed on the nest. While she was looking down at the chicks, the male marched like a big brown parrot down a gently sloping branch on the far side of the nest to join her. It was the first time I had seen both adults together on a buzzard's nest, so I photographed them despite the poor light.

Neither bird had brought in any prey. The mother started ripping snippets of flesh from a dead frog, already in the nest, and tendering them delicately to one of the chicks, which behaved quite ruthlessly towards its nest mate, pecking at its head several times and deliberately holding it down with its stubby right wing, as if banging it down with an elbow. There was a desperate look in the black eyes of the smaller chick as it made constant efforts to get up and share in the food. The mother made no effort to bypass the bossy youngster and attend to the weaker chick, and when she finally slipped off the nest on the far side it had still not been fed at all.

After an hour the female returned with a spray of oak leaves in her beak. This she fitted into the side of the nest, as if to freshen it up and make the bowl a little softer. Once she extended her beak slowly towards that of the bigger chick, twisting her head from one side to the other, as if inquiring whether it was feeling all right. The smaller chick lay at the side, head resting on the twigs, ignored by its mother. Then she extended the dark-brown brooding feathers on her belly, stepped forward and sat down on the chicks. As she settled for the night, I

185

stopped taking photos and carefully slid from the back of the hide.

Five days later, after an exhausting night in an eagle hide, I managed to get back to the buzzards again. I laboured with very short steps up the steep terrain like an old man, clothes sticking to my back beneath the pack.

No sooner was the camera fixed on its tripod than the mother buzzard soared in, agilely adjusting the near five-foot span of her wings to avoid the surrounding branches, and looped up on to the nest in the oak-tree fork. She had brought no prey with her. As she strutted about the nest she kept her talons bunched up, as if to ensure that she did not spike or injure her chicks. It was endearing to watch. She appeared to be searching around the nest for any food left by the male. I saw the smaller chick lying motionless over the bottom twigs. It was dead. Well, the ancient law of the wild – only the strongest survive – had asserted itself. The remaining chick was almost twice its size and was sprouting the first brown feathers in its wings and back.

There was no food in the nest, but soon I heard a loud clear '*kee*' call as the male swept in like a flying tawny anchor, a vole in his beak. The mother instantly snatched the vole in her bill, put it between her talons, seemed about to feed the clamouring chick from it, then suddenly stopped. She looked at her mate, now standing with a self-satisfied expression on his broad wedge-shaped face, took two steps towards him and shouldered him right off the nest!

It looked so comical I almost burst out laughing. Her attitude and action were crystal clear. She felt it was *her* place to feed the chick, his to go and get the prey. So he had better go now for some more. Then she tore up the vole and fed the chick. About twenty minutes later I heard the '*kee*' call again, from further away this time. The mother listened, waited, then flew off, returning in a short while with a frog. Clearly she had collected it from the male in a nearby tree and was certainly trying to do all the feeding herself. In the poor light under the thick leaf canopy I took a few photos before the mother left again. I backed out of the hide and hiked down to the truck.

As I reached the open space 300 yards below, I saw her hunting the wooded slopes. When she wanted to hover in the wind, she seemed to click her wings into a half-back and uplifted position, her 'shoulders' high, pinions back, locking herself into the air-space as if settling into a slot. She was as steady and still there as a kestrel, but without having to winnow her wings like the smaller falcon.

On my next visit I was astounded to see the male come in with a small snake . . . no, it was an EEL dangling from his beak. The chick was standing tall, neck drawn back, black eyes huge, as if scared of the horrid-looking thing. Part of the head section had already gone but the fluted body fins were unmistakable. I took two photos before the male buzzard shot off again, still with the eel. Bewildered, the chick looked down into the nest twigs, out of the nest, back into the nest, and then outwards again, with an expression that clearly said, 'What? You didn't leave me anything?' It kept glaring to the south-west, giving soft cheeps. As I watched, the male flew in *with the eel still in his beak*! He dropped it and peered about him, showing the beautiful symmetry of his broad rounded head in the sunlight. I clicked away with the camera until he flew off again.

At first the chick did not seem to know what to make of the eel. Finally it stood on it, ripped bits off and jerked them down its throat, then swallowed the tail section with many convulsive throw-backs and gulping movements of its head and neck. It then flopped down for a sleep.

I wondered just how the buzzard had got that eel. As eels often gorge food quickly, maybe an angler on the river below had beheaded it to retrieve his hook from its gut and left the rest on the bank, where the buzzard had found it. Or had the bird caught the eel in wet grasses when it was trying to wriggle its way round a waterfall? Perhaps the buzzard had seen it lurking in a few inches of water when flying above and had dived down to clutch it before the eel could see him coming. The thought of a buzzard wading through muddy shallows, just waiting like a heron for a passing fish or eel, seemed incredible, to say the least. Yet certainly buzzards took frogs, so why not eels?

Three days later I boated across the loch in bright sunshine to try my luck in the hide overlooking the nearest pair's nest in the oaks above the lagoons. It was a short but steep ascent, almost sheer in places. By the time I had hauled my 60 lb pack up to it my clothes were soaked with perspiration. The two three-week-old chicks were already sprouting most of their brown feathers. They seemed quite happy and amicable together, preened constantly, and one even preened the stubby tail feathers of its sibling. I had never seen that happen before. After three hours the mother landed on the nest with no prey, looked about to see if the male had brought anything, then flew off. Two hours later she returned, still with no food, stayed only briefly and then flew off again. The cheeping chicks looked most disappointed. I noticed that buzzard chicks, unlike bigger eaglets, which stand with their powerful legs wide apart, hold their more spindly legs close together. With their rounded bodies, they look like rootless umbrella pines about to topple over. The adults came over later, calling to one another before settling in trees some distance to the right of the nest. With the light waning at 8.30 pm I left.

Anxious to film these two chicks being fed by their mother before they were old enough to feed themselves, I boated over again late the following morning. As I puttered towards the lagoon I was treated to an extraordinary spectacle. The male buzzard came soaring over a high ridge to the left, performed two small 'golden ball' dives and was pulling out of the second when he must have seen something below. Closing his wings almost completely, he dropped like a stone with talons extended hurtling downwards, and splashed down into about a foot of water in the far lagoon. There was a great squawking and splashing and a female mallard churned across the surface, beating her wings hard on the water, followed by three small ducklings, their little feet paddles flailing away frantically. The buzzard flapped heavily upwards again, his talons empty, shook his wings clear of water like a giant dark tern as the ducks shot into some thick reeds, then beat away over the trees. He had missed that time, but as I had seen the mallard earlier on a nest with eleven eggs, I was sure he had taken a few of the youngsters before.

Of course I could not have filmed the incident, not only because the movie camera was still in my pack but because I needed something steadier than a rocky boat on which to rest the telephoto lens. It is possible to hand-hold a still camera and bang off single shots at a 500th of a second and so freeze the action, eliminating jerkiness and blur due to camera shake. My movie camera is set to expose each frame at the standard rate of a 50th of a second, too long for steady, sharp pictures considerably enlarged through the long-distance lens.

I climbed up into the hide and endured eight backside-numbing hours before there was any further action. With crops a quarter full, the chicks clearly had been fed earlier in the day, and so all I got was some footage of them preening and squirting their wastes out of the nest. I was about to leave, disappointed, when I heard a faint '*kee*' call. I looked through the viewfinder to see the big mother arrive with a nine-inch length of eel, nearly two inches thick, in her beak. As she stood there, I refrained from filming in case the slight whirring sent her away again. She dropped the eel and one chick began pecking at it, having some difficulty pulling off even little bits, while its mother watched with a solicitous air. I started filming and, thank heaven, she did not appear to hear the sound of the camera. She stepped round one chick, grabbed the eel in her talons, tore pieces off and fed them to the chick nearest me.

After it had received ten slivers, the far chick came across the nest and aimed a vicious beak stab at the other's head, which drove it off a little way. The mother now fed the aggressive chick and after it had gulped down thirty-one morsels the first chick seemed to get angry. While its mother was looking away, it grabbed the eel in its beak and heaved it from beneath her feet. Then it had difficulty standing on the thick slippery body, so it just sat down on the eel, on its hocks.

In that position, however, it could not reach down to peck off any flesh. The mother watched carefully, realised the chick's plight and tried to pull the eel back with her beak, but the chick sat tight. She seemed unwilling to disturb it by trying harder to get the eel. After a minute the chick got up again, the mother slipped what remained of the eel away and right on the front of the nest, the view perfect, she fed the chick until it had eaten enough and turned away.

Just before this, however, my last film came to its end. I cursed silently as she fed the far chick again for a good five minutes. The chick nearest me then grabbed the three-inch section that was left, and with many backward jerks (because the eel was now dry) gulped it all down. The far chick watched the eel disappearing down its nest mate's throat with a despairing air! Only then did the mother leave, and with the light fading at 9 pm I left too.

I was now sure that buzzards could catch eels, especially having seen the male splash into the water after the ducklings. Clearly they either dived on them in the shallows or grabbed them as they negotiated waterfalls by wriggling through wet grasses like snakes before re-joining a burn higher up.

I continued to check both buzzards' nests and in late July found all three chicks perched in the trees near their nests, practising their first flights, ready to swell the numbers of these fine birds in the Highland skies.

Meanwhile Mickey Marten was still coming every night for titbits. By now I had taken so many pictures of him that I no longer bothered to keep the camera to hand as I sat at my desk in the study, where I had taken to eating my supper.

One fine evening I left the window open a few inches to let in some fresh air before going to bed. Lying sleepily under the blankets at around dawn, still only half-awake, I saw an animal on the sill. Cautiously Mickey poked his head in, took in the situation at a glance and decided to have a little fun. He hopped on to the desk, then on to my chair, then the floor, where he hared across to the fireplace, and, like a wall-of-death rider, ran round the walls below my bookshelves, leaped on to my feet as I lay in bed, bounced off again, jumped up on to chair then desk, and was out through the window again in a trice. It all happened so fast I had not even moved. Then he stood on the table peering in at me with an impatient look, which seemed to say, 'There! It's time you got up and gave me my grub!' I hauled myself out and spread butter and jam on a slice of bread. As I opened the window wider, he leaped to the ground, but as soon as I threw the bread on to the table he jumped back and was chewing avidly before I had even closed the window again.

So long as he kept up this sort of behaviour, presumably any buzzards that settled in the area could feel safer about their nests than the veterans whose home he had wrecked getting on for three years earlier.

PART FIVE

16 · A Badger in the Kitchen

Bessie did not like having a bath. I lifted her up below the shoulders as she seized my gloved fingers and set her down in the three inches of water in the sink. She must have thought I was trying to drown her because she fought hard, trying to scramble out again with her powerful forefeet and curved claws. I handled her firmly, letting her snap at the gloves, making sure she did not get at my vein-filled wrists, and swabbed her down thoroughly. Then, as she sat on her bottom like a small bear in the sink, I took a clean towel and dried her, dodging her snaps.

I weighed her in a net – nearly 20 lbs. As soon as I put her into the netting run which I had erected beneath the kitchen window, she calmly began nibbling at itches in her rear legs, as if knowing the worst was over. She then pushed the hay about with her nose, ripped into the blue sweater I had put into the den box as a bed, then hauled hay under her with her long whitish claws. I noticed her teeth were brownish yellow and she had grey hairs on her muzzle, so she was not a young animal. Like all badgers, her dress was sober and respectable, matching their behaviour, for they do not go around causing trouble. Her long hairs were buff white-grey near the skin, then black, tipped with white. She had a hoary appearance, like an aged but miniature Kodiak grizzly. As she did not go into the den box, I poked hay into it and then prodded her rear with a finger until she finally

191

crawled in. She seemed to feel secure there and curled up for sleep.

My adventures with Bessie had begun one afternoon in late May while Moobli and I were exploring the two miles of oak and birch woods which clothed the steep slopes of the lochside east of our home for any new buzzards' nests. It was rough terrain with high snagging bracken, a constant obstacle course of sudden dells, gullies, ridges, burn ravines, rockfaces and high sheer cliffs, on one of which a pair of ravens had already fledged three young.

We zigzagged down to the shore, where we found two small badger dung pits along a high trail, the droppings filled with the black wing-cases of dor dung beetles. We went on to check Sett 2. It was a big dry sett, its entrance under a huge slab of overhanging rock. There were no dung pits near it now; a pile of dry white molinia grasses under the rock had been depressed into a definite bed bowl. It seemed as if a smallish badger had been using it for naps between nightly foraging expeditions for meals.

Moobli picked up a scent from the breeze ahead and paused with one front foot lifted like a pointer. I followed his gaze to see a small fox with a white-tipped tail, probably one of Aspen's earlier cubs, looking intently down at the shoreline from a grass-covered ridge of rock. There was a sudden harsh croaking from above as the raven family flew over. The fox heard these alarm calls and without even looking round shot off into the bracken and disappeared. Then I saw two red-breasted merganser males come steaming along the surface of the loch from the east. I spotted some ducklings and a large brownish duck leading them up a brown granite shelf on a land spit further away to the east. As they disappeared over its far side, I thought they would disperse in the thick herbage or else go down again and take to the water.

I quickly changed the telephoto for a standard lens, dashed as quietly as I could over the tussocks, dropped to my stomach and slid to the edge of the shelf. I peered over cautiously. They were all still there, on a lower ledge of rock. Eleven ducklings, brown with yellow stripes, were staring upwards in frozen fear with their little button eyes, all facing east. Their mother, like a giant barge next to them, was also looking up, ready to fly off. I noticed the blue patch on her wing, the smooth head and broad beak, and realised she was a wild mallard with her brood, and nothing to do with the male mergansers. The mallard may be the ancestor of our Khaki Campbell ducks but in the wild it is warier than most other water birds. As this one proved to be.

I took a few photos before she sloshed down into the water and began swimming with hunched wings, flopping about, to appear injured, so as to distract my attention from the ducklings.

Then all the youngsters took off too, panicking, falling over each other and their own big-paddled feet, looking like an amateur fire brigade in a Keystone Cops comedy film trying to turn out in a hurry. They dived or just threw themselves off the three-foot shelf, which to them must have looked like a high diving board to a novice. As they steamed across the loch some of them flailed madly and managed to climb on to their mother's back.

My faint guilt at thus alarming them was assuaged by the fact that the fox had certainly been intent on snaffling a duckling or two and our sudden arrival had prevented that.

We climbed upwards to the end of the wood and began trekking home at a height of some 500 feet, having so far found only two unused buzzards' nests. Suddenly there was a faint crashing through the bracken higher up. As Moobli started forward instinctively, I hissed, 'Don't hurt it', a command he well knew. I wondered if we had come upon the fox again, but there in an open patch I caught sight of a smallish badger humping along. It had been out foraging in full daylight, which seemed odd. To Moobli, wild foxes or badgers were nothing more than potential playmates, but the badger did not know that, and as he romped playfully alongside, catching it up with ease, it snarled '*kak kak*' and slashed sideways with its jaws to make the dog keep his distance. The two bounded along together for a few more yards, then there was silence.

When I caught up it was to find that the badger had vanished into a perfect sett in a cairn of mossy boulders. It had several entrance holes, outside only one of which could be seen three shallow dung pits, all containing much the same size smallish droppings. As I watched, Moobli stood well back from the hole, tongue lolling in a toothy grin, a kind expression in his huge brown eyes, his tail wagging with friendliness. Then I saw the badger's white-striped face appear in the hole's darkness as it looked back at him, not with alarm but with apparent interest. I called Moobli away and we went on home. I had the odd feeling that the badger was living alone in the sett, which seemed strange, for I was sure it was a young female. It was a sett I had not seen before, but it helped to explain the badger pits I had often found in that area when Sett 2 had remained empty.

A few mornings later we found a large area between the larches in the east wood that looked as if it had been worked over by a miniature bulldozer. Every yard or two the grasses had been dug through in deep whorls about three or four inches across and roots ripped apart, typical badger's work. Badgers are fond of earthworms, beetles, grubs, chrysalises, as well as a host of other invertebrates. They also like hazelnuts, beech mast, edible toadstools, acorns and are very fond of the scrumptious underground tubers of pignut flowers. They make deep whorled diggings with the thick claws on their powerful front feet to get at any combination of these foods. Yet there had been no sign of a badger in our woods since the previous winter.

At dusk two evenings later Moobli became agitated inside the house, and whined, wanting to go out. I let him go but hissed him back when it was clear he wanted to dash into the east wood. What had he sensed there – another dog, a human? He kept pleading, so I grabbed my torch and went out with him. He hurried off. I kept up with him, ran to a glade to the south-east and shone the torch. A badger, unaware of Moobli, was rooting about with nose and claws near some old stumps. Moobli ran past it behind some bracken, then circled trying to get a scent against the north-west wind. I cursed silently, wishing I had grabbed my camera and its flash gun along with the torch. The badger froze, crouching its long body close to the ground. Then as it heard Moobli running behind it, beyond the stumps, it headed straight towards me, running slowly, sort of hopping along, straight for the torch light. As it ran past me a mere two yards away I felt sure it was the same badger we had seen on our trek. Had it followed our scent trail home for some reason? I said, 'Hello pal', but it appeared not to hear for it loped on, headed towards the woodshed behind the cottage before turning north through the thick bracken on the north hill.

Moobli now picked up its scent and would have chased after it had I not stopped him. My thought now was to try and make friends with this badger, keep it coming round the house. At least Moobli had not barked, so it might feel the big dog was not too much of an enemy.

On June 11 we went to check the new sett and had a hard task locating it again at the top of the steep woods. It now appeared deserted, with cobwebs over the holes. The same droppings were in the pits and were now turning mouldy. Had the badger found a new home nearer our cottage?

Three days later fresh diggings appeared near the rhododendron bush by our path. This was the time when I started putting out raspberry-jam slices to keep the marten near the cottage, so I also set out some cheese and fruit cake for the badger, for surely *it* would not be interested in the jam. I waited up a fair time but being tired after the trek I went to bed before midnight.

I woke at 3.10 am with a raging thirst, and went to the kitchen for a mug of water. As I looked sleepily out of the window, up trundled the badger and demolished all the raspberry-jam slices! It was indeed the same smallish one we had seen before. I tried to get the camera and flash unit working in the dark but the badger trundled away into the east wood as I reached the window. Hell! I threw another fat slice out of the window, went to obey a call of nature, and returned just in time to see the badger rumble up again. Was it my imagination? In the brief light of the camera flashes there seemed to be something wrong with the creature's neck and ears.

The following night, after a day of dull drizzly weather, I again set out food then went to siphon off some home-brewed beer. I returned to the study to find all the cheese gone. The raspberry slices had great slashes across them as if made by long scrapes of big claws. I immediately set out more cheese and at 10.35 pm was eating my supper when a large dark object moving outside caught my eye. It was the badger again. I took eight flash photos, which it did not appear to notice, as it guzzled the cheese *and* the jam slices. It chewed them like a dog, lifting its head and

195

smacking its lips, more like the raccoon of North America than a dog really. Once it shook itself hard, getting rid of the rain on its blackish grey coat in a cascading spray. The odd thing was that the animal moved so slowly, tottering occasionally as if it was ill. When it had finished the food it trotted, yes trotted, shakily off into the east wood.

For two more nights I fed the badger. Its coat had begun to look dirty, uncared for, unless it was just moulting. Again there seemed to be something wrong with its neck and it still seemed shaky on its feet. Next evening, I returned exhausted but triumphant from a hard trek, having found the new eyrie in which my nearest eagle Atalanta was successfully raising twin eaglets. Tomorrow I would have to dash out to get the necessary Government licences to photograph them and also a batch of new films and supplies to last me a month. Tired as I was I decided to try and catch the badger. I wanted to find out what was wrong with it and nurse it back to health.

I cleaned up the old box-cage live trap which I had used for catching wildcats and Mickey, re-inforced it with double netting and set it outside with a slab of raw mutton for bait.

At 3 am I was woken up by loud scuffles and thumping noises. I dashed out with the torch. There in the trap was the badger. Now I was close to it I was sure by the slimness of the head and smallish size that it was a female. She didn't dart about or snarl, nor even cringe as I approached but just watched me carefully. There was a sore behind her neck and her right ear also seemed torn. Still totally naked, I rushed to the woodshed for an old tea chest, held it to the trap's entrance and lifted its trapdoor. The badger waddled into the darkness of the chest. In the hot still air the midges were at their diabolical worst and quickly assailed my naked body. I got bites in places where I didn't know I had places. I shoved a thick plywood cover between the trap and chest, tipped up the chest, set a rock over the cover, then nailed the cover down. All this time the badger made no sound, and did not struggle.

I snatched two more hours' fitful sleep then, smeared in insect repellent, went to repair the old wildcat enclosure. I re-inforced the hefty wooden door of the main den and wired on a water-bowl. As I picked up the chest I noted with alarm that the bottom was rotting and one of her rear feet, black with long claws, was sticking out of the hole. One assault on that rotten bottom and she would have been free. I carried the tea chest and the badger over to the enclosure. As I tried to shake her out of the chest through the narrow opening at the top of the enclosure I realised the under-side of my left wrist was over the hole; one bite across the veins would inflict great damage. She resisted my attempts to shake her out and bit hard at the rubber end of my hammer when I tried to push her out with it. I would have to find another way of lifting her into the pen.

Putting the tea chest back on the ground and replacing its cover and rock, I went indoors for a thick rope in which I made a non-slip noose. With the help of a fishing-rod tip I managed to manœuvre the noose over the badger's head. I only had to lift her a couple of yards up into the enclosure and I reckoned with her typical strong neck and the thickness of the rope that the operation would cause her only momentary discomfort.

I tightened the rope, then lifted her out gently. She gasped a bit but as she came level and I got my gloved left hand under her backside for more support, I saw to my horror that the 'sore' on the top of her neck was in fact a gaping wound, two inches long, and festooned with maggots. She would not have lasted much longer in the wild. She had either been in a snare, or had been attacked by terriers and had run a long way, or she had been in fights with other badgers. It explained her living alone in the sett, and perhaps why, after getting our scent and somehow sensing we were friendly, she had come close to us. It was odd how many sick wild creatures, including dying red deer in winter, came close to us, as if knowing they would be protected. And now, in the brief seconds in which I was thus lifting her into the pens, she must have felt I was letting her down, was even trying to finish her off. She made odd rasping sighs of resignation, her huge claws dangling from powerful short legs, back and front, like those of a miniature black bear.

Quickly I lowered her to the grass of the pen where she crouched, hiding her head under her body, her neck exposed. The wounds were bad, her ears torn too. I raced indoors for a tube of antibiotic cream and got back to remove all the maggots and smear the entire area thickly with the cream. She lay quiet as if knowing exactly what I was doing. When I had finished she did not move away but looked up at me with a pathetic, submissive expression. Then she began to tremble, no doubt with shock. What could I do but speak to her, knowing the soft loving human voice can calm almost any frightened animal?

'You're going to be all right Bessie,' I murmured, the name coming from nowhere. 'We're going to love and look after you and then you can go free.' Our eyes still held and I told her again and again, silently with my mind, as animals do. I left plenty of good food, filled her water bowl, then boated out to go about my urgent business.

After steering home in rising winds and falling rain, I went to check Bessie. She was not in the den proper but lay curled up in the turf on its roof like a giant squirrel, head tucked into the grasses, below the protective aluminium sheet I had nailed above the den. At least she had shown enough sense to get out of the rain, and she had eaten all the food. I set out more – a slice of bread, with margarine, glucose and jam on it, an egg, cheese, a quarter-pound of pet mince, fruit cake. I put Aureo-mycin, a broad-spectrum antibiotic, in the meat. I also refilled her water bowl. I was glad to note she had not tried to dig her way out.

Westerly gales with torrential rain blew all night and it was cold enough for me to light the study stove. The loch had risen two feet by morning, which meant bailing and hauling out my two boats beyond its swelling waters. Bessie had again eaten all the food and had now found the real den, but getting into it she must have knocked its wooden door down so that it was open to the draughts. She lay curled up into a ball, her head beneath her body. As I gently levered the door back into place with a pole, she looked up briefly, as if to say, 'Oh, not you again. Leave me to sleep will you?' As she lifted up her pointed white and black striped head, the eyes not far from her pink nose, it seemed almost as narrow as an ant-eater's. Then she stuffed it under her body again.

I put out some fruit-bread slices and these disappeared during the day; she would still forage in daylight, despite the rain. At dusk I gave her a slice of honeyed bread, a slice of jam, fruit-bread, cake, a quarter-pound of meat with Aureomycin, cheese, a new egg and filled her bowl with long-life milk. If she did not mend on this rich diet, nothing would save her.

Next day, the rains and gales still continuing, I went to check her first thing. All the food had gone. As she raised her head to look at me, she still appeared weak, and was shivering slightly. She looked so sad. In the afternoon I had another look at her. This time she did not move when I let down the den door. I saw two more maggots on her neck, the antibiotic cream having worn off by then. I was afraid she was dying, that with her bad injuries the cold, rain and gales would prove too much for her. I determined to get her into the cottage, where I could keep her warm and look after her more closely. The bad weather meant I could not get the eagle hide up anyway, so I could devote more time to her.

Wearing two old sports jackets and two pairs of gloves (knowing the badger's terrible bite) I carried the wildcats' best old den box into the enclosure and re-tied the gate. This was a wild badger and would certainly bite when I got hold of her, yet oddly I felt no fear.

I talked softly to Bessie for a while, and she even let me stroke the top of her muzzle. But when I reached in to edge her out gently so I could get the other hand round her, she snapped, upwards, as if naturally protecting her throat. I pulled her out gently with both hands on her whole head, taking care to avoid the rear neck wounds. Then I got my hands round her shoulders. Heck, did she bite those gloves then! I could feel the power of her jaws, but strangely she just took hold of my fingers, didn't bite with full power, as if indicating she had me now and if I hurt her she would bite really hard. I lifted her into the den box and carried her into the house, noticing that she smelled awful, probably mainly from the pus in her wounds.

I quickly made her a netting run beneath the kitchen window, carried in hay for her bedding, then decided to give her a bath and clean her up. I warmed some water, put in Dettol and a dash or two of perfumed deodorant (this would soon wear off, so she would smell normal on final release) and poured it into the stainless-steel sink. After bathing her and drying her with a clean towel, I dressed her wounds with fresh antibiotic cream, and was glad to see they were getting better. I then hauled her out, receiving the hardest bite yet – three times as hard as a fox bite, capable of taking off a finger. Even through the gloves it hurt.

Bessie slept curled up in the den box, obviously feeling secure there. As I peeled vegetables in the evening she woke up, poked her head over the side of the den box casually, on her right side, peered at the food I had set out, then at me. She seemed to decide to wait a bit longer. Eventually she toddled out, sniffing the air, and ate the lot, raw egg and all. She did not appear to hear my movements, the cutlery and plates being set on the steel draining board, and I wondered if she were deaf.

On June 21 the rain was even worse. The loch had risen six feet in three days. I had to bail and haul out the boats once again. Bessie slept most of the day after breakfast and was still fast asleep at eight o'clock in the evening. Her jerking and odd snoring snorts led me to think she might be dying. I stroked her for a while. Her eyes opened and she enjoyed it for half a minute, then her head shot up as if she had just woken. When I bent close I found she had a salty scent, not sickly sweet like the fox, but more like old singed larch cambium. It did not pervade the room as does the scent of foxes. She had left a dropping a good yard away from the den box and it too had little smell.

I set out a huge meal for her – egg, cheese, cake, raspberry slices, bread and butter, apple, a handful of mince and bits of ox liver, plus glucose in the milk. At 8.35 pm she poked her head over the box side, her pink muzzle twitching, and I brought Moobli in and sat him down near me at the sink. As the badger came out and padded over to start eating, he didn't move, just sat there, watching with his great ears forward, whining slightly with interest and concern. Bessie did not appear to hear him. She was certainly far from dying for she tucked into the food with gusto, grabbing the bigger bits in her under-shot jaw, even forcing her pink nose up slightly on the concrete as she took a good hold. She smacked her lips a lot too. Sometimes she paused to look at Moobli with what seemed friendly interest and no trace of fear or ferocity at all.

After eating Bessie trundled back to the den box, sat down with a hefty *flump* sound on her backside, leaned her back against the walls of the box, then nibbled methodically and carefully between the claws on all four feet, keeping the claws clean.

Occasionally she paused, looked about with what appeared to be a smile on her face, her lips parted, and scratched her tummy with one set of claws, again just like a little bear. Then she stood up and scratched her front shoulders with her rear feet like a dog, but much faster.

I was surprised by how quickly she adapted to the kitchen, to our presence. Although a completely wild badger, she would have been easier to tame than any of my foxes. Even so it was my job to release her back to the wild, so I did not try to tame her. She was already so passive, however, that I removed all the fencing so as to give her completely free run of the fourteen-foot-square kitchen.

Bessie improved rapidly, her wounds healing fast. She was full of life, scratching herself, rearing up on to objects to see what was behind them, and she now even took biscuits from my hand. She often slept with her huge paws and claws held tight over her face and eyes, no doubt to make even the curtained light darker. Her position reminded me of a sloth – see nothing, hear nothing, say nothing. When she had eaten she seemed to ponder on life, squatting on her rear and shoving her head between her rear legs as if having a good long think. I was now sure she was totally deaf, although her chewed ears were healing well. I talked more loudly to her until finally I tested by yelling in her ear, 'Hey Bessie!' There was no reaction to the sound, only to the *feel* of my exhaled breath. My earlier notion about calming her down while talking softly had been mere fancy. All badgers are short-sighted but she seemed blinder than most, so she had been surviving mainly on the senses of touch and scent, which of course for a nocturnal animal are almost enough.

I was woken in the early hours by thumps and the sound of empty bottles being knocked over. I dashed into the kitchen with a torch and found Bessie perched on the top of the cooker's Calor-gas bottle like a raccoon. Luckily the gas tap had been turned off. Although she had waddled into my wine bottles and knocked seven over the floor, none were broken. She had recovered so well, her wounds almost healed, that she was beginning to explore her territory. And a fourteen-foot-square kitchen was certainly not big enough for a wild badger that had recovered most of her strength as well as her natural curiosity.

This·view was soon re-inforced when I found that during her nocturnal explorations Bessie had ripped her way through the plastic sides of my wine incubator. Now, despite its Heath Robinson appearance, I was rather proud of this incubator for it was extremely effective. I had made it by nailing together a 5-foot by 3-foot by 2-foot wooden frame. Round the outsides and top and bottom I had tacked thick plastic, and round the plastic, for insulation, an old blanket. Inside the frame I put an ancient Rippingale paraffin heater someone had given me years before. Above the heater's burner I upended half the stout cage the Putney RSPCA had given me to bring Holly owl back to Wildernesse, and on top of the cage I set a one-gallon pan of water. The other half of the cage lay beside the heater and kept the bottoms of two 25-litre wine containers off the floor. Halfway up the frame, well above the heater, I built a shelf of hazel wands covered with plastic, and on this shelf I could dry things. Thus, for the cost of a mere gallon of paraffin (which lasted a week) I could 'cook' 50 litres of wine, have a constant supply of hot water and also dry strips of wild edible fungi or my laundry. In winter the incubator gave out enough heat to keep the chill off the air in the kitchen, useful when looking after the wet and chilled red-deer calves I often found round the cottage.

Luckily as I still had thirty unopened bottles of deliciously dry blackberry wine in stock, the heater had not been on. Clearly, Bessie had clambered in through the front flap then, feeling trapped, had torn her way out through the far side. Judging by the pile of split wood faggots lying over the floor, the thumps had been caused by her burrowing through the box of firewood I kept to fuel the study heater, which I had made from an old 44-gallon oil drum.

Obviously an animal of Bessie's strength was capable of causing a lot of damage. What I was more afraid of, especially if she broke some bottles, was that she might injure herself again. It was time to start the tricky operation of releasing her naturally, and safely, back to the wild. With a titbit of food I manœuvred her back into the den box, closed it up, and carried her through the midges to the wildcat pens.

There I set out more food and water, not milk this time, and went back to bed.

17 · *Wild Badger Nights*

Twelve hours later I floated back over the hills in a kind of ecstatic dream, after one of the finest days ever in an eagle hide. Arriving home to a delighted reception from Moobli, who insisted I threw sticks for him to fetch and exercise his cooped up legs, I went to check Bessie. She had eaten all the food and was lying not in the den, but under the shade of the leaves of the huge hogweeds at the back of the pen. When she saw me she got up and waddled forwards to the water bowl and gave it a big scrape with the claws of her right forefoot, to show me it was empty. Then she looked up at me with a quizzical expression, so comical in its obvious demand for more water, I couldn't help laughing. I quickly re-filled the bowl and put out all her night food too.

Over the next three days Bessie seemed fine in the pen and I often saw her out in the daylight. As I went out with her food on the third evening, however, she must have felt my tread for she dived back into the den through the hole in its wooden door. She was getting wilder, which was really a good thing.

After two more eagle watches I boated out on a supply trip and found two fresh traffic-killed rabbits on the road. I set one aside for the eaglets and gave the other to Moobli after removing its back legs to see if Bessie would eat them. I was not surprised when she ate the lot, bones and all, for I had long

203

since discovered that badgers will eat carrion, especially that of dead deer in winter, and that they will flense the skin off a carcass neatly while eating the meat. It also confirmed my findings in the wild that badgers will chew the rib bones of carcasses right down to the spine, and even bite right through the spine.

It was shortly after this that I received some scientific papers on fox behaviour from Dr Raymond Hewson, the agricultural scientist with the Institute of Terrestrial Ecology at Banchory, Kincardineshire, some of which I reviewed in the earlier fox chapters. Among them was an interesting paper published in the *Journal of Zoology*, London, on the different ways foxes and badgers scavenge on sheep carcasses. Badger tracks had been seen near two ewe carcasses in mid-Argyll from which the flesh had been cleanly stripped from the mandibles. A dung pit had been found at an old carcass where the spine had been bitten through. Two carcasses near the badger setts had been rapidly broken up with the shin bones bitten through, the fleeces pulled off and the limb bones disarticulated and scattered.

In an interesting experiment with captive reared foxes and badgers at the Highland Wildlife Park, Kingussie, Dr Hewson and Dr H. H. Kolb fed a 35-kilogramme ewe carcass to two foxes and a 31-kilogramme ewe carcass to two badgers. The badgers reduced their carcass more effectively, six days ahead of the foxes. As in the wild foxes chewed off an ear and the tail, while badgers bit through the spine just behind the rib cage. The foxes moved the carcass four metres to the corner of their enclosure while the badgers moved theirs thirteen metres. Both discarded the gut; foxes pulled out the stomach, moving it six yards and left it, torn open. The badgers removed the gut more or less intact, to lie alongside the carcass. The foxes chewed the ends of some of the ribs, while the badgers bit four ribs off and left them. (In the wild in winter they would have eaten these too.) The foxes ate one kilogramme of meat a day, while the badgers ate at the rate of 1.2 kilogrammes, though were also fed some vegetables from the 17th day of the 23-day experiment as most of the meat on their carcass was gone. Also interesting was that the foxes pulled out a great deal of wool, several pailfuls being collected from their enclosure, whereas there was none from that of the badgers.

When I got back from a 37-hour watch in the hide on June 29, Bessie was out in the open but again dived into the den as she scented my coming, her short thick grey tail bobbing like that of some monstrous hare. Then she peeped her black and white head out again, watching to see if I put food down, which I did quickly. She had dug a fine deep dung pit a yard from the den and had filled it with big *firm* droppings. I saw too that her neck wound was almost completely healed, apart from the loss of hair.

On July 1 Moobli, who sometimes sat watching the badger with friendly interest, found a fresh scent near the west side of the pen and wanted to track it up the north hill through the thick bracken. Although he did not perform his usual leg-lifting on tufts, I felt it had probably been left by a prowling fox, which would now be far away, and called him back. Then I saw that Bessie had scuffed up a good deal of earth under the pen's gate. Had another badger, maybe a boar, visited her during the night? From time to time I found that badgers had visited a huge cairn of rocks about a quarter-mile up the hill to the north-west. They were undoubtedly from the big permanent sett at 600 feet over half a mile further away, and used the cairn as a day resting place after a night of foraging in our woods.

Because I felt that Bessie was not yet quite fit enough to go free, I went inside the run, blocked up the gate again and gave her fresh hay for bedding. She just looked up as I removed the door. I slowly reached in and began stroking her back before putting down the hay. She just lifted her long head and appeared to enjoy it. As I left she hauled the bedding in with her two front paws and nosed it into comfortable positions, like a dog burying a bone.

Next evening I returned from the eagles to find Bessie standing with her two front feet on the new rock I had used to block the gate, calmly chewing at the fencing. She pushed against it with one paw, as if to find where it gave the most. She got my scent, plodded doggedly into the den, tucked her head between her back legs, rolled over and went to sleep.

In the morning I hastened out in dull and drizzly weather, wondering if she had escaped. But she was in the den and had made no new scuffings near the gate. I put down her breakfast and stood quietly a few yards away. As her head came out, she blinked owlishly and benignly at the chaffinches which were already pecking at the food. Then out she lumbered to eat the nearest piece of jammy bread. The chaffinches scattered only briefly – she made no move to drive them away – and two cocks carried on pecking merely two feet from her head.

With fine weather again next day, we went to check the badger setts in the woods to the east. One was empty and so was the one that Bessie had used. It was certain now she had been living there alone. We then hiked up to the rocky cairn to the north-west, and I was not surprised to find a big badger had used it recently. There was a large dung pit and a dropping about three days old in it but from Moobli's scentings, no badger was in the cairn now. Perhaps a young boar, born to the permanent pair in the high sett to the west a few years earlier, had come to investigate Bessie's scent and had decided she was too old to be interesting. On the other hand Bessie looked a lot younger now than when she had first come to us three weeks earlier with her bad injuries. I had no real idea of her age, of course.

On July 5 both eaglets flew successfully and next day I dismantled all the vegetation from the hide and carried it home. Bessie was now in superb shape and I fed her more meat than usual, so she would be strong when she went free. On July 8 I took what I thought would be my last photos of her in fine balmy weather, fed her well, then opened up the pen completely to make it easy for her to go during the night.

Next morning the pen was empty and Moobli gained strong scents in the north-hill bracken. He wanted to follow Bessie's trail but I called him off. She would have enough problems re-adjusting to the wild without him making her jump out of her skin by his sudden appearance on the first day of her new freedom. Because he was so full of energy, I packed two sheep hearts from the butcher's into my pack and took him on an exhausting trek. On returning I set food out in the pen, but next morning it was still there, apart from the jammy titbits which had been scoffed by the chaffinches. Tired after the exhausting eagle treks, I took the day off, just working quietly on a book at my desk. In the evening, after cutting a quarter-acre of hay with

206

my home-made scythe to help feed deer in winter, I again set food out in the pen.

To my astonishment, after waking up next morning to the dull drizzle that had fallen most of the night, Bessie was back in her den. She had eaten most of the food and was curled up on the hay, her broad paws covering her eyes to help reduce the light. Now what? Had she in her animal way decided she knew full well where her bread was not only buttered but jammed, and to appoint me as her permanent provider? On my small earnings, solely from my books, I was not too keen to keep on feeding a badger that ate almost as much as Moobli. My job had been to nurse her back to health and free her, and I had done that.

I need not have been concerned for the following morning she had gone again, and this time she did not return. I began to worry about whether she was all right and became consumed by curiosity as to where she might have gone. Three days later, as there had been no rain in the interim, I put Moobli's lead in my pocket and let him have his head to try and track her.

In his own way Moobli had become fond of Bessie and he needed no encouragement. He lost the trail often but persevered as we trekked the steep heights northwards. To my faint surprise she was not in the big rocky cairn as the trail led due north for over three-quarters of a mile. Puffing, we were approaching a tangle of boulders below a steep cliff when Moobli became more excited. I slipped on his lead, to hold him back from going too close, and he led me near to a big hole between the rocks. I told him to sit then went forward alone. There was a fresh medium-sized dung pit near the hole and I had no doubt at all that Bessie was inside. Not wanting to interfere with her adjustment back to the wild, we left quickly and made our way home.

I thought that would be the last we would know of Bessie but I was wrong. On July 19 we found many medium-sized scrapes in the east wood, far closer to the cottage than any other wild badger had foraged before, clearly made by Bessie. Nor was that the end either. A year later we found she had indeed met up with a young wild boar which had moved into her new sett.

On long treks for eagles or deer over the years I had found a total of nineteen badger setts. No more than ten of these setts were ever occupied in any one season. A badger family might stay in one sett for two or three years and, perhaps because they had worked the immediate area over well, would then move to another sett, sometimes a mile or more away. Having made the decision to move, they search over a wide area to find a sett vacated by other badgers, or one where a family has died out, and take it over. Or else they dig out a new sett. Often this will take them out of their old territory (which could be as large as a mile square on the open hill but perhaps a third of that size in food-rich woodlands), to establish a new territory. A family of badgers moved out of a sett right on the loch's shore becausé a young stag had died just outside it, and they probably could not stand the smell of its decomposing flesh. I finally found them, at a height of 400 feet to the north-east, in a new sett they had made between a fall of huge gnarled boulders in a birch and oak glade.

I found setts in the earth banks above the loch and amid the natural tunnels under big rock cairns in the woods. Once I located a four-hole sett in a sandbank at forty feet because the half-ton of sand thrown out by the badgers gleamed through the trees like a beacon in the morning sunlight. Some of the sand came in useful when I mixed it with cement for repairing my chimneys. In the high hills I found setts by first looking for a lone tree or stump on a ridge. In these open places badgers prefer to excavate under trees because the roots form effective buttresses for the roofs of their tunnels and bed-chambers.

Badgers seem to be highly sociable animals and, while fights over territory are recorded in literature, I have never heard badgers fighting or found evidence that they did — unless Bessie *had* been injured by others of her kind. Indeed I found evidence that in autumn one badger family would take its cubs, born between early February to mid-April, to visit another family over a mile away. It was as if the parents were introducing the youngsters to each other in a 'match-making' ritual, giving them a chance to get to know each other before possible pairing later. Some young badgers leave their parents in their first late autumn and set up junior setts in a suitable place no more than a hundred yards away, before striking out to look for their own territories in the spring. Other cubs, however, remain with the

above: A male badger emerged from his 600-foot-high sett
after dusk and worked his way down a steep gully to the long
lochside woods to dig for worms and beetles.

above: Bessie did not like having a bath in my sink, but it was essential to get her clean before doctoring her injuries.

below: Bessie curled up for a sleep in her den box. She was so placid I let her have free run of the kitchen.

above: Bessie's wounds healed rapidly and she became so tame she ate freely in front of Moobli and myself.

below: Bessie spent three weeks in the kitchen before I put her in the old wildcat pens to get used to being outdoors again.

above: The following spring I was surprised to see a large boar badger emerge from the direction of Bessie's sett and romp about in the daylight. It was good to know she had found a mate.

below: A fine photograph of a male badger taken by my friend, Geoffrey Kinns.

sow in the main sett throughout the winter, and then the boar will sometimes set up on his own in an unoccupied sett not very far away.

Since finding the first setts years ago, I have thought of trying to photograph badgers outside them. Thinking became a strong desire one late June day when I first saw badgers running about in daylight. I was descending a very steep hill after photographing the highest eyrie I knew in dark forbidding cliffs at a height of 1,600 feet, when suddenly I saw what looked like four giant hedgehogs romping towards me along a deer path between gaps in the short bracken. They were badgers, heading for a jumbled cairn of rocks I had just passed.

I cursed silently for I had just shot off the last two frames of my film on the eagle's nest and had not brought a spare film with me. Frantically, I reeled back to the start, to where I always click off the first two or three frames with the lens cap on, hoping at least one of them had not been exposed to the light while loading.

As I raised the long lens to focus, the two smallest badgers, clearly cubs, gambolled about in a mock fight, rolling over and over, grabbing at each other's necks and throats with open mouths. Then the big boar climbed on top of the female, bucked her several times, holding her round the chest with his thick powerful paws. Evidently she did not feel like coupling right then for she dragged herself onwards and he rode her rodeo style for a few yards before falling off. Then they all vanished into the cairn, where I saw they had their sett.

Keeping downwind, I circled round and climbed a tall flat rock which gave a perfect view of the sett, and the piles of white molinia-grass bedding that had been put out to dry.

After a few minutes both the cubs came out again and began sniffing and digging in the earthy debris above the sett. With their rounded tops and spread-out fur, they looked like toy animals without feet, moving around like animated mops. I groaned again, for never had I known such fine chances to photograph wild badgers. Then, in a trice, one of the cubs lifted its long snout and must have got the scent of my earlier passing for it darted back into the sett, closely followed by the other. I left some camouflage netting draped as a screen between two rocks atop the big flat one, then went back a few days later for another try. Although I waited six hours, bitten by midges, I did not see the badgers again.

All this occurred in the summer of my meeting an extraordinary character who was to become one of my best friends. I had gone to the Natural History Museum in London to get some boyhood birds' eggs re-identified and had been sent up to the floor where Geoffrey Kinns worked as an artist. As this shy, snow-haired bespectacled man, who appeared to have a slight limp, talked to me in a rather quavering voice, I noticed fine pictures of golden eagles above his desk. I was astonished to learn that *he* had taken them, that he had a great passion for Highland wildlife, spent all his holidays in Wester Ross or Skye and had already put in seven seasons tramping the hills to photograph eagles at their eyries.

We had lunch together, and that evening he invited me back to his flat in Kew to see his other wildlife pictures. I soon realised he was one of our finest photographers, and that he had photographed, often in the wild, almost every mammal, bird, reptile and amphibian that exists in the British Isles. His photographs filled many authoritative nature books, and the postcards and posters issued by the Museum were almost all from his pictures. Determined, patient and inventive, he had once photographed a wild pine marten – in the years when they were near to extinction – by rigging up an amazing tripwire device using a wedding ring as a pulley on a branch along which the marten often ran. His pictures of wild badgers were especially superb.

His life had been oddly heroic too. Despite his short-sight, he had been a Battalion Shot in the Hampshire Regiment. Having survived the North African campaign, where he had been called 'Snake Charmer of the Eighth Army', because of his ability to pick up poisonous puff adders and horned asps in his hands, he had endured the push through Europe. Just before the Rhine crossing, his left leg was blown off below the knee by a mine, and his right leg broken in two places. Yet, although he now also suffered from heart trouble, he still enjoyed nothing better than carrying a hefty pack up the Highland hills.

By the end of the evening we were firm friends, and I invited him to stay at Wildernesse. He arrived on May 21 and after boating him home with a huge amount of gear, we had a cup of tea.

Geoff said, 'Erm ... these badgers of yours. Er, should we have a try tonight?'

Geoff had photographed more badgers than I had chaffinches and I was anxious to learn his methods. There was a fresh northerly breeze blowing and I immediately thought of Sett 5, the high one above the lochside at 600 feet to which Moobli had tracked a boar badger from a red-deer carcass in winter. It was a three-hole sett, running along an earth ridge below a small cliff, and I knew it now contained a family. Also, it faced south; by standing below it, that would be the ideal sett for us to work in the north wind. 'Let's go!' I said.

We landed from the boat and weaved our way up to the sett. We moved slowly up the nearly sheer tussocky heathered ground. Despite what he called his 'slight handicap', 55-year-old Geoff was carrying a 45 lb backpack, containing no fewer than four Hasselblad cameras, three hefty tripods, remote-control cables, lenses, batteries, binoculars and other extra-ordinary paraphernalia.

I felt excitement as we neared the sett, the wind blowing ideally into our faces. Swathes of yellow molinia grasses lay along the run where the badgers had set some of their bedding out to dry in the day's hot sun.

Geoff cast an experienced bespectacled eye over the holes of the sett and the smaller dung pits which were being used by a cub or two. He set one electric Hasselblad on a tripod for me over the eastern hole, then set the flash gun separately on a special two-foot-long arm from the lens.

'Only an amateur puts the flash *on* the camera,' he whispered. 'That way you get shine in the animal's eyes.'

Then he set his own camera facing the westerly hole, clever-ly overlooking part of the main run too. As dusk fell and I stood below the run holding the button on my remote-control cable, I could just make out Geoff's shadowy figure and cropped white hair as he struggled up from his pack to fit on his cable.

Suddenly not one but TWO badgers came out of the central hole! Their twin white facial stripes gleamed dimly in the twilight. The bigger of the two, obviously the boar, got on top

211

of the female, put both thick arms round her neck and jigged up
and down very fast, banging his jaws on the back of her head!
With badgers, who like martens enjoy delayed implantation of
the blastocyst, the fertilised eggs from the first successful
mating persist. This means they can copulate from February to
October without further fertilisation occurring, and now I was
rapidly learning that, unlike most mammals, badgers' sexuality
approached that of humans. Was he really mating with the sow
now or just fooling about? I heard a slight sound below – Geoff
was still fitting up his camera and had not seen the badgers.

Trying to warn him they were already out, I hissed. Once,
twice ... four times. No reaction from Geoff. I gave a brief
bird-like whistle. He heard that, looked up, saw the badgers and
to my surprise waved at them.

'Relax,' he whispered. 'We'll get eleven shots tonight.'

I could hardly believe it for the badgers did not see or hear
him. They stayed where they were, irritatingly out of camera
focus, and only went back down the hole when Geoff was set up
and sitting on a rock.

A few minutes passed, then out came a badger again,
trundling over the run towards Geoff. FLASH. He had it. FLASH.
He got another.

I've got the worst hole, I thought.

Then the boar came out of my hole, furtively looking up and
down with jerky head movements, sniffing the air. Further out
he came and FLASH – I had him. He gave a sharp grunt and dived
back down again.

A few minutes later he emerged from the central hole, looked
all around, came out more and looked over the edge of the
run. Then he walked, looking gigantic, as if he weighed at
least 30 lbs, to my end and posed superbly. FLASH. Another
grunt and he made a rapid, noisy but smooth dive down my
hole.

I thought that would be all for a long time, and we would
have to go, but a minute later the badger repeated the same
moves. Then he acted as if, far from being scared, he was having
games with the flash. He kept peeking out, flinching only slightly
as the flash lit up the wild scene, the rocks, earth, new green
bracken shoots, and his head like strikes of quiet lightning. It

was as if he was saying to himself –

'Every time I move forward, like this, that light comes on. Look, I'll do it again!'

I realised I was simply repeating all the same kind of shots, so I stopped. Silence for five minutes, then the female came out of the central hole, gathered a whole armful of dry grasses with a one-arm sweep, did a similar circular sweep with the other arm, then raked the grasses in together so her claws were fairly close. Then holding it all together, half-carrying the bundle, she retreated backwards down into the hole again. She seemed unconcerned at the flashes.

Hoping she would gather bedding from outside *my* hole, I waited. She did not appear, but a cub came out and gave me a fine broadside view, then a full frontal with head and chest elevated. Then it trundled towards Geoff. FLASH. He got it too.

As we negotiated the steep dark slopes down to the boat, we congratulated ourselves on a fine night's badgering. What also surprised me was that we did get precisely eleven shots! After this great experience with Geoff it was obvious to me that I needed better equipment.

18 · In Touch with Old Friends

I hiked alone back up to Sett 5 on a cold evening early in March. A bitter north-east breeze was curling into the central hole and would have carried my scent if I had stood in front of it. I set up well to the west of the western hole and the dung pits near it. Hell, it was cold sitting there in gloves, balaclava helmet and scarf, as well as my camouflage jacket and two sweaters!

I was just thinking I was out of luck when my eyes made out twin stripes moving about in the dim light. The boar was out scenting the air, as badgers always do just before and immediately after leaving an entrance hole, his head moving up and down like one of those toy dogs one sees in the rear windows of cars. I photographed him digging a pit, squatting over it, turning sideways, then heading down an almost sheer slope before he galloped off to his favourite foraging area near the Long Wood. Unfortunately, I had obscured a red dot on the 'sync' button of my new camera with camouflage paint, and none of the photos came out.

Eleven evenings later I trudged back to try again. Because the breeze was blowing directly from the north, I set up overlooking the central hole. I was taking a chance, with the tripod and camera only seven feet from the hole, and feared the badgers would see me and either not emerge or dodge out of one of the holes I could not cover. I waited, cooling down rapidly, and was suddenly enveloped in whirling snow. I groaned, knowing that, if reasonably well fed, badgers (like foxes) will not venture out into the first snowfall, as if hoping it will be gone next day.

Then I had an idea. I had also brought with me my old camera and its little flash gun, intending to take a few hand-held shots if a badger stepped out of the focal range of the tripod camera. I sneaked over and set it up on a rock overlooking the westerly hole and pits, attaching it to a long air release cable. In this way I could operate both cameras from one position. I would not be able to see a badger going down to the dung-pit area because of the earthy ridge between, but I could guess the right moment if I saw it heading that way.

To my delight the ruse worked, and I got pictures on both cameras. The boar came out of the central hole, had a good stretch after scenting the air, then plodded towards me. After the third flash, he turned and headed for the pits. I timed it and pressed the air bulb, later finding I had captured the whole of him from above as he worked his way round a big rock. Well, that would be enough badger photography for a while.

I discovered that the boar was living alone in Sett 5. Perhaps his mate had died. But what had become of Bessie? Occasionally I visited the new sett which Bessie had made under the steep cliff to the north, where she still seemed to be living. I also found evidence that she still came to our woods to dig for pignut bulbs, beetles and worms.

One November night, rain teeming down, Bessie turned up at the cottage. I was keeping an eye open for Mickey the marten, who was still coming regularly for his food on the big grass-topped bird-table complex, when suddenly there was a loud thump, and Bessie's head and neck, her ears still short, appeared above my window-sill as she stood on the old box-cage live trap which now lay rotting below the table. As I watched, her head turned sideways, her jaws opened, and she seized a chunk of bread and raspberry jam that had fallen there. She must have scented the food. I quickly dropped a whole jammy slice on to the box-cage, knowing that she could not get up on to Mickey's table. Within minutes she was back. She jumped right on to the trap with another loud thump, grabbed the slice in her jaws and ran off with it.

That winter she came to two deer carcasses in the dark, flensing the skin off neatly and eating even large bones. In harsh weather I put food out for her.

On a sunny day early next May I set off northwards on my longest eagle trek and checked Bessie's sett on the way. Next to her pits were much bigger ones containing really large black droppings. I wondered if the unattached boar from Sett 5, over a mile away, had found her. After the laborious return hike, I sat down for a rest about a quarter-mile south-west of Bessie's sett, binoculars out to see if I could spot any foxes.

I had not been there long before I saw a movement high up to my left. It was a large boar badger trotting along, his body looking supple and streamlined, almost snake-like. He slowed down, padding this way and that, sniffing tussocks and working his way along the banks of a small burn. I struggled to get the camera from my pack and fit on the telephoto lens. I just managed a few distant photos before he vanished behind a tufty ridge to the south-east.

Dashing down as quietly as I could, I caught him up. I was not surprised to see him out in daylight, for although badgers are normally crepuscular or nocturnal creatures, they will often forage during the daytime too in wild areas where they are undisturbed by man. He was heading south-west, so I cut west and then south, coming closer to him as he urinated and set his rear-gland scent on two more tufts. I took two more photos as he looked towards me. Knowing the badger's poor sight, I reckoned at that distance he could not see me. Then he vanished again as my film ran out.

After I put in a new film I saw him again, now heading up towards me. He came within thirty yards and paused, heard the click of the shutter, saw me and turned and hurried back up the way he had come. He began to gallop, and disappeared behind a ridge above the burn. New energy coming from somewhere after the hellish hard trek, I scrambled up after him and spotted him again 200 yards higher as he crossed a gap between rocks and hurried into Bessie's sett! What exciting moments! I knew better than to go close to the sett again for that might make them desert it.

When I checked Sett 5 a day later, expecting it now to be

empty, I was taken aback to find it occupied by a badger family. That boar must have found a new mate and Bessie's was a new fellow, possibly a son from Sett 5 in earlier years. I was sure they had just met recently and therefore had no cubs. I hoped they would now stay together and breed.

Many times during that early spring Crowdy, the youngest owl, came making her loud '*whick*' calls in the trees around the cottage. I went out to hoot back to her, hoping that if I stayed still she would land on my shoulder, but she never did. She always replied and came nearer, once to within twenty feet, where I could just make out her cowl-headed form on an oak branch. She looked to be in fine shape, but did not appear to have a mate for I did not hear more than the one owl calling in the woods that season. Where, I wondered, were Holly and Wallie? Was either still alive?

A few days later I found out. I had started photographing rare black-throated divers at their nest on an island three miles from my home. It is a really wild place where small oaks, birches and thickets of rowan and ash have sprung up between the tangled white skeletons of huge fallen pines, last remnants of the Caledonian Forest which once covered much of the Highlands. As I wended my way through the thickets, clambering over the great fallen trunks, a huge dark broad-winged owl shot out of a hollow snag just above my head, flew to a branch twenty yards away and turned to look back at me. It was Holly all right, the same dark-barred plumage, wide duchess head and thick strong body. She looked old now, and a bit tatty. When I called her name she turned her head again, and then flew out of sight. I looked in the tree-hollow but there was no nest or sign of eggs there. Her breeding days were probably over.

On my next visit to the island I decided to go and check the dens in the two large rock cairns which Cedric and Aspen had used for breeding. I was sure both foxes were dead now, for I had neither seen them nor found their signs anywhere near our woods for the past two years. Both dens were empty, but as I zigzagged down the steep slopes back to the boat, which I had beached near a small wood of pines and silver firs covering the peninsula opposite the divers' island, I saw another large rocky cairn to my right. I walked round it and found fox scats and wool and hair from sheep and deer carrion scattered in front of the large rocks. A new fox family had taken over the territory, probably one of Aspen's cubs, now an adult. If so, it was interesting they had ignored the old dens of their parents and had made a new one.

Before boating to the island I wandered round the peninsula wood, where trees sprang out of shallow earth on huge rock mounds and escarpments. I trod quietly over a bronze carpet of pine needles and climbed over a dead tree trunk. Suddenly, the top foot of a slim pine stump seven yards ahead sprouted wings and flew off! It was another owl, and as I saw the bright colours and the short blunt wings, I felt sure it was Wallie. It flew in a half-circle of about twenty yards and landed on a short branch about fifty feet up a tall pine. Then it shuffled on its furred legs until close to the trunk and tried to imitate a piece of loose bark.

I swung the pack from my shoulder, took out my camera, fitted on the long lens and walked closer. As I came within range the owl turned to look at me, turned away, then looked back again. I balanced the lens against a trunk and looked through the viewfinder. Yes, it was Wallie. The same squat chunky shape, the same fat little face, though he was bigger now. He regarded me with sleepy eyes, seeming not at all perturbed, and even yawned when I said one of the old phrases.

'Good old Wallie Wallie. Good old Wallie Wallie.'

I took three photos before my film ran out. I walked back to the pack, put in a new film, and then returned to him. No completely wild owl would have stood for that, stayed there as I walked about, taking a few more pictures. I found dark owl pellets, mostly filled with mouse and vole fur, under many of the trees. As the peninsula wood was only fifty yards across the water from the island, it was clear that, even if Holly could no longer breed, the pair were still together. It warmed my heart to know that. They had probably moved through the lochside woods to inhabit a new territory three miles away after being scared by Mickey Marten, who I was sure had taken one of their eggs, so many years ago it seemed. Or maybe they had just handed the cottage territory over to Crowdy for she, at least, did not seem to be inhibited by the presence of the marten.

Mickey was still coming every night for his titbits. I noticed that sometimes he would just stop chewing, as if thinking hard, then turn and bound off the table, carrying the morsel away. Or he would eat a few, gather two or three more in his jaws, then race off with them into the depths of the huge rhododendron bush by the path. After a minute or two, he would be back to demolish the rest.

Imagine my shock, therefore, as I sat at my desk one evening in mid-May, when my eye caught the familiar gleam of his creamy-orange throat patch in the lamplight and I looked out to see *two martens* on the grassy table top! The newcomer, a smaller and thinner marten, was at the far end, crouched down as if clinging to the grasses for dear life. And as it saw my head move, it sort of treacled over the surface and vanished again, clearly terrified.

At last, four years after I had first found traces of him in our east wood, Mickey had a mate.

When she darted off the table, he ran to the edge, peered with his pointed face over into the dark, looked back at me and then at his new mate, grabbed some bread in his jaws and leaped off himself, presumably to give it to her and assure her there was nothing to be afraid of.

Nevertheless, Michelle, for so I called her, did not appear again over the next few evenings. I hoped she might be lying up in a den, preparing herself for the birth of kits. Yet that seemed impossible, for she was too thin to be heavily pregnant, and if the two had only recently met they would probably mate now and produce kits next year. I was quite sure that the new marten was not another male, for Mickey would never allow a marten of his own sex so close to him on the table.

After that Mickey would eat a little and then run off with food in his mouth. On May 23 Michelle arrived for the first time on her own. I kept perfectly still, watching her out of the corner of my eye, as she crept, belly low, in nervous fits and starts, round the table, gobbling the food down as fast as she could. Slowly she grew less shy, usually coming to the table on her own, as if taking turns with her mate, though she only came at night. Her throat patch was slightly different from Mickey's for she had two dark spots amid the creamy orange on the left side of her chest.

219

The summer weeks passed; then late one August night I heard an odd growling on the bird table. I looked out by the light of the lamp to see Michelle sneak up to Mickey as he scoffed and put her muzzle near to his, whereupon he made a brief '*chrroom*' growl, dropped the piece he was chewing so she could have it, and went in search of another. They repeated this procedure several times, Mickey briefly antagonistic before dropping each bit, as if such fierce little carnivores did not find it easy to maintain the pair bond where food was concerned.

Mickey's growing tameness took on the air of an absurd fantasy, for he ran about the place in full daylight like a little pet dog. One hot afternoon I saw him come bouncing up the path from the rhododendron bush, pause below my bramble bushes, then rear up like a miniature bear and slowly pluck a blackberry with his teeth before chewing it up. Then he ran up the slanting logs and on to the grassy table top. Finding no food there, he came to my window and reared up, scrabbling loudly on the pane with his front claws of both feet.

I gave the usual calls and whistle and saw him prick up his wide buff-tipped ears as he moved back on to the table, where he waited with a look of expectation on his face. I hurried to the kitchen for buttered bread and jam. Then, quietly and slowly, so as not to frighten him, I held it out through the slightly open window.

He looked at the slice, and up at me, then at the slice again. As my heart pounded with excitement, he hopped forward, his perky ferocious face coming nearer and nearer, and with great delicacy and gentleness he took the bread out of my hand with his mouth. It was for me an incredibly touching moment.

For the next few nights both martens came separately and collected three or four pieces in their mouths before racing away with them. Mickey usually gulped down a few first, showing that the martens' world has strong macho overtones. Surely, they must be taking food to kits, I thought. The books told me that young martens run with their parents from mid-July onwards. Well, the books have been wrong before. I found only one rowan-berry 'offering' in the woods during the weeks up to September 1. Clearly, now that Mickey had secured a mate there was no need for him to deposit 'gifts'. By

In early summer during the fourth season Mickey the pine
marten still seemed to be living alone. I hoped he would find a
mate. His graceful movements and attitudes were endearing to
watch.

Mickey became as tame as a litle pet dog and often ran about the
area in full daylight. He came regularly to the bird table at
night. Four summers after first finding Mickey, I looked out to
see two martens on the bird-table complex. At first his mate,
Michelle, was extremely shy.

By the autumn, Mickey was actually coming through the study window to take food from my hand, while Michelle eagerly awaited her turn. Behind them, out of reach of the flash light, was their first surviving youngster.

September 5 Michelle was as tame as Mickey. She too would arrive in full daylight, bouncing up from beneath the bramble bushes, rearing up on her haunches on the table to look for him, or pausing to scratch a midge out of her ear with a rear foot.

At dusk the following day I photographed both martens on the table together. I had lined up a row of jammy squares inside the window and held one up, waving it. Mickey hopped nearer, but seemed reluctant to take so small a morsel from my hand, so I dropped it. Twice more I repeated the offer and he ate it as soon as I let go. I held out the fourth piece, refusing to drop it. Up he came and took it from my hand, then another, and another. Michelle watched all this before hesitantly she too approached and took her turn delicately accepting the food. Both were careful not to touch my fingers with their teeth, yet each piece was taken with a firm grip and the head was turned away before chewing. What a moving experience this was, to have two wild martens taking such tiny scraps right out of my hand.

I took to setting their titbits on a blackboard inside the slightly open window, and next evening both martens came across the threshold to help themselves time and again as I sat at my desk a mere two feet away. The martens were getting through four loaves of jammed slices a week by this time.

As I lined up their food on the windy evening of September 8, I looked out to see FOUR martens on the table! I turned to work my camera, but by the time it flashed they had gone again. Later both Mickey and Michelle returned to take food but I saw no more of the other two.

Two days later I left a trail of scraps up to and all over my desk before going to bed. At four in the morning I was woken up by a pounding noise. All the food on the desk had gone and one of the martens (it was too dark to see which) was pounding on the blackboard with its feet, as if asking for some more. I lurched sleepily to the kitchen for extra supplies which I set out before getting back into bed. As I listened to the news on the BBC World Service, the two adults came back and quarrelled over the food with brief '*chrroom*' growls. I began to fear that the third and fourth martens had been figments of my imagination. Perhaps they had been no more than the thick tails of the regular two adults flapping over their heads in the wind as they had darted about in the dark.

My spirits soared again on the following evening when I clearly saw by the brief light of my camera flash a *third* marten with the other two, perched at the far end of the table. There was no doubt about it now: Mickey and Michelle had at least one youngster, and it was only slightly smaller than its mother. Returning at dusk from a supply trip two days later, I made all the usual calls and whistles as I set out the food. Within five minutes, all three martens arrived. At first the kit took pieces only from the table, but as it watched its parents eating from my hands, it too ventured to copy them, and in a few days became almost as tame.

Mickey usually arrived first, jumping on to the ringstone boulder and scenting the air as he waited for his family to catch up. Having taken food from my hand, the kit on one occasion ran down the sloping logs and leaped on Mickey's back, where it began to make mating movements as its father crouched on the ringstone. Though Mickey tolerated this behaviour, he kept his tail held firmly down. Soon all three martens were coming in through the window regularly, crowding in over each other's backs and making occasional '*chrroom*' growls as each grabbed its morsel and slithered back past the others to eat it on the table.

As I see the cheeky elfin faces of these, our rarest major mammals, so wild yet so trusting, take the food from my fingers, I think how privileged I have been over these recent years. For I am convinced that if the human race is to survive on this planet then we must lose the idea that we are separate from the rest of the natural world, infinitely superior to other creatures, predestined to dominate and survive because of our highly developed intellect and inventive genius. As we destroy the life-giving rain forests, shower our acid rains, extend the deserts, pile up nuclear arsenals, increase our careless industrial management and greed for consuming material goods, it is becoming clear that even we may not survive the hostile environments we are creating. I fimly believe that the solution lies in extending the spiritual love of which we are capable beyond that of merely human for human to encompass all living things.